THE BIG HOLE

THE BIG HOLE

LYN HARDEN

Palmetto Publishing Group, LLC
Charleston, SC

For information regarding special discounts or for bulk purchases, please contact Palmetto Publishing Group at Info@PalmettoPublishingGroup.com.

ISBN-13: 978-1-944313-26-5
ISBN-10: 1-944313-26-5

Dedication

For my friends at Palmetto Publishing Group; you were all so helpful and patient. Thank you for every amazing thing you did for me and for believing in my story.

For all of you who believed I could do this, for all of my test readers, and for all of the "boots in the butt" who wouldn't let me quit.

For Ashley Cheney, who steered me toward Palmetto Publishing Group when I was just about to give up looking for a publisher.

For Paul and Brenda Harden, who drove me all over my childhood home of Savannah, Georgia, and shared long, nostalgic conversations with me to help refresh my memories.

For Cindy Miles; thank you for your encouragement and help, and for not letting me give up. Who could've known where all the whispering and storytelling in bed at night when we were little would lead someday?

For Ann Harden; thanks for all the memories. I wish you were still here to pop the top on an RC, tear open a Snickers, and read this book.

And for my "Huckleberry"; Mandy Kea, I could never have done this without you.

PROLOGUE

"Well, who'd-a-thought?"

Who indeed? Who would have ever imagined that the roar of a bull-dozer snarling to life could have brought on such a torrential rush of memories, and from so long ago? And that voice! To hear again in my mind the sound of that rich, melodic voice, unheard for almost forty years, yet just as clear as fresh air and as sweet as warm honey, exactly as I remember.

Remember. That's not something I've done over the past four decades or so. Not that I couldn't, but some things are better left to molder away and die. Some things are better left pushed down and forgotten. Some things are better left buried.

Besides, I've had too many other things to worry about in my life, too many other responsibilities, all of which seem to multiply with each passing year. Adulthood beckoned and childhood faded to a dis-tant memory, becoming almost like a dream, or perhaps a nightmare, much of it having been embellished or altered by my growing imagi-nation and intellect. Most of my childhood memories were surely not real. Surely not! And no one would expect me to remember every petty little thing that occurred during my childhood, especially as the years pass and my life becomes more and more cluttered with a myriad of occurrences and responsibilities.

As a child, I excelled academically and eventually attended one of the finest private schools in Savannah, Georgia, after which I won a scholarship to the University of Georgia in Athens, where I majored in American history. I was rushed by every sorority on campus and thought carefully before choosing to join Alpha Omicron Pi ("AO Perfects!"). I was also a member of the Blue Key Honor Society; I maintained a 4.0 GPA all four years. Additionally, I served as a "game day hostess" when our football team played between the hedges ("Go, Dawgs!") and will always be a proud citizen of the Bulldawg Nation.

Upon returning to Savannah, I began working with the Historic Savannah Foundation, where I remain to this day, striving to save historical sites and renovate and protect important downtown locations. I also work closely with the Savannah Area Chamber of Commerce and the Telfair Museum to raise public awareness of the importance of immortalizing our Southern heritage and salvaging the remnants of our fair city's history. I am also an avid supporter of the Girl Scouts of America which was founded by our very own Juliette Gordon Low and I donate a great deal of time, energy and money to every local charity that exists.

On a more personal note, I managed to court and marry one of the most eligible and successful businessmen in the state, a building contractor who shares my love for our hometown and who proudly and tirelessly works by my side on every project I undertake. Most of the renovations I help oversee downtown are contracted out to his company, and together we bring beauty and charm back to our beloved Savannah.

Yes, I've had an awful lot on my plate during the span of my life but, then again, there has been an awful lot to forget. There are things in the past that are best left there, buried and forgotten, things that lurk in the dark recesses, pushed down and hidden . . . until today, when that damned bulldozer roared to life and brought it all bubbling to the surface.

Strange how something so life-altering could be filtered by the passage of time until it fades to near nothingness, as though it had never happened at all. How odd that someone who was such a constant part of life back then could, in the blink of an eye, be gone. Strange. Odd. Perfect words for describing that time in my life, way back, forty years ago. Back to that summer when I was eleven. Before the unthinkable happened.

Strange and odd.

CHAPTER 1

Savannah, Georgia, 1975. I was eleven years old and lived with my parents in a small brick house on Old Montgomery Road near Hermann Hesse Elementary School. Snuggled in behind the trees out back of Cresthill Baptist Church and just downwind from Crumrine's Farm, it really wasn't much of a house, not much more than a cottage really, but it was home and I loved it there. . . except for maybe first thing in the morning on school days.

"Good morning, Glory!" Every weekday morning began the same way: my mother practically pirouetted like a ballerina en pointe, trilling in her most operatic voice her favorite play on words as she danced her way across my bedroom to open the handsewn drapes. I grimaced, squeezing my eyes more tightly closed. My name was NOT Glory and, in my opinion, a day that started with any kind of opera was by no means a good one. After her initial burst of sunbeams and unicorns, my mother flitted out to the kitchen to check on breakfast. I groaned and nestled myself further beneath the homemade quilts. I knew I had maybe five more minutes before the trilling and flitting turned dark and I wanted to take advantage of every second.

"Rachel Anne Holland! You get up outta that bed right now, young lady! Don't you make me come in there, ya hear?"

I groaned again, dragged myself out of my cozy, warm bed, and staggered into the kitchen while my mother continued her tirade. "You know these grits'll stand up if you don't get at 'em while they're hot! If I'm willin' to slave over a hot stove before sunup every mornin', the least you can do is get to it while it's still pipin'!"

I sighed as I picked up my spoon and dug in. The breakfast menu varied only slightly each school day: grits or oatmeal, two pieces of cinnamon toast (the one saving grace!), and the inevitable glass of Tang. (In 1969, while watching man walk on the moon for the very first time, I made the mistake of declaring my intention of being the first woman in space. My over-the-top supportive mother had served me Tang, the breakfast drink of American astronauts, nearly every single blessed day of my life since.) Another sigh escaped me as I pushed my glass to the side and picked up a piece of cold cinnamon toast.

I knew I should be more appreciative of the efforts my mother took to make sure her only child was given every possible opportunity to make something of herself. I was also aware that my family on my father's side had very prestigious roots that would someday allow me to be accepted into proper Southern society. I wasn't too excited by the prospect but my mother felt otherwise, and she would not be thwarted. No effort or expense would be spared to guarantee my family's reentry into Savannah's upper echelon. By the time I was in kindergarten, I knew our family history by heart and already felt the great weight of responsibility. My path had been preordained, and I could not deviate from it.

I come from a long and illustrious line of Savannahians that can be traced back past the War Between the States to before there were plantations and slave trade, all the way back to the city's founding fathers. My ancestors were members of the British colony of Georgia, and our family name can be traced back to the original twenty-one trustees. If something of historical significance was happening in olde Savannah, you could be sure the Holland family was in the mix. By 1975, however, the name was about all we had left . . . but it was a good, solid name and we were proud of it.

One particular Friday morning two weeks before school let out for the summer, after many warnings of "elbows off the table, Miss Priss" and "back straight and ankles crossed," along with a multitude of other mealtime instructions from my mother, I finished my toast and swigged the last of my Tang (judging from the look on my mother's face, swigging was yet another unacceptable practice when at table) before grabbing my book bag and heading out the door. I had no way of knowing that this day would usher in an era that would change my life forever.

I was a "big" sixth-grader at Hermann Hesse Elementary School and was a member of the School Patrol, which was actually nothing more than a glorified group of tattletales. A School Patrol member could best be described as a cross between a kiddy cop and a member of the German Gestapo. Basically, I got to wear a florescent-orange harness with a badge pinned to it and order other kids to stop running in the halls and to spit out their gum. I had the power to write tickets that sent the more serious offenders to the principal's office and on rare occasions I even got to sail in and break up fights. (My mother would have had a cow if she'd known about *that* aspect of my job!) I was also expected to be on duty a half hour before the first bell. That really wasn't a problem for me, though, since I lived right across the road from the schoolyard and could see the buildings from our driveway.

On this particular morning, however, it wasn't the school that held my attention; it was the moving truck that was backed into the driveway of a house directly across the playing fields, on the other side of Whitfield Avenue. A new family moving in was big news; everyone in my class would be chattering away about the new arrivals and the possibility of new kids in the neighborhood. Most of the other girls would be hoping for a new girl to jump rope and play hopscotch with, but I was a tomboy and immediately set my heart on a new boy. Our class's kickball team could use another outfielder! I kept my eyes on the yard where the truck was parked as I strolled toward the school, but there were no kids in sight. I hitched my book bag higher up on my shoulders and picked up my pace. If there were any new kids, I would know soon enough.

"Hey, knucklehead!" That was the only warning I got before someone thumped the back of my head. "Whatcha frownin' for?" I turned toward the voice and looked into the laughing, sea-green eyes of my first cousin. Robert E. Lee DeLoach, a.k.a. Bo, was the son of my mother's sister, and I envied him the fact that he wasn't a Holland and could therefore speak or behave in any manner he pleased. The fact that he was a boy made it even worse; back then, boys could go anywhere and do just about anything they liked while girls were expected to stay close to their mamas. I sighed at the unfairness of it before answering.

"Morning, Bo. I'm not frowning. I'm just wondering if the new family moving in across the way has any kids." I nodded toward the moving truck as Bo squinted in that direction. "We sure could use another player on the kickball team."

"Ohhh!" Bo spit onto the red dirt road, something else I was never allowed to do. "I ain't even noticed! Yup, a new feller'd be nice alright . . . although two would be better. Then we could get rid o' the only girl on our team!" He ducked the punch I threw at him and we both laughed. Bo liked to tease about how embarrassing it was to be on the only team with a girl on it, but I knew he didn't mean it. I was one of the best kickball players in the school, and Bo was glad we were in the same class so we could play on the same team. We continued to tease and jostle each other as we walked toward the school.

"Well, if it ain't the kissin' cousins!" The Strickland brothers had joined us. Bubba was in our class while Tully and Aubrey were in the fifth and fourth grades, respectively. While Bo and I were often referred to as "kissin' cousins," the Strickland boys were known as the Stairsteps. It was funny how Southerners were always coming up with cute little nicknames for everything.

"Anybody know if the new folks over yonder got any kids?" Bubba voiced the question that seemed to be on everyone's mind.

"Naw," Bo replied, spitting into the dirt again. "So far it don't look like they do. Be nice if they had a boy, though." The two younger Stairsteps bobbed their heads in agreement.

"Yeah, a sixth-grade boy," agreed Bubba. He looked at his watch and frowned. "Say! Y'all better get a move on if y'all don't wanna be late!"

Bo and I glanced at our own watches and took off running. Like me, Bo was a member of the School Patrol. Neither one of us wanted to lose that privilege due to tardiness. Lord knows, it had practically taken an act of Congress to get my mother to let me do it! If my badge got taken away, I'd never hear the end of it. Bo pulled ahead slightly, but I was right on his heels as we crossed the grass and flew down the breezeway that led to the school office. In no time at all we were checked in and headed to our assigned posts, Bo in the back by the lunchroom and me out front by the entrance to the upper-school classrooms. I sucked in a breath as I approached the area; there was already a fight in progress. It looked like it was going to be one of those days.

I gritted my teeth, smiled, and threw myself into the fray.

CHAPTER 2

The ring of screaming, cheering children grew as word of the fight spread. I had planted myself firmly between the two squabbling boys, both of whom were much bigger than me, and had each of them by their shirtfronts, but that did little to slow the rain of punches that continued to land on and around me. When one punch landed squarely on my jaw, I realized I might be in trouble. If only Bo had been assigned to this area with me! My eyes began to water and for a split second I felt fear trying to rise inside of me. I struggled to hold the furious boys apart while blinking back tears, but I could tell it was a losing battle. I was running out of steam.

Then, like sweet music to my ears, I heard a raging roar as an avenging angel flew out of the crowd and touched down gracefully beside me. He always seemed to appear at just the right moment, and no one had ever questioned his authority or challenged his right to tell them what to do. In no time flat, the fight was over and the crowd had dispersed. I bent over and put my hands on my knees, sucking wind and trying to regain my composure.

"You alright, Rae? It looked for a minute there like that one was about to get the best of you!"

At the sound of his voice, I tilted my head back and looked up into the concerned, glacier-blue eyes of my avenging angel. Scott Bashlor had been my best friend for as long as I could remember, and this wasn't the first time he had pulled my taters out of the fire. That was okay, though; I had been his saving grace just as many times. That's what best friends did, right? They looked out for each other and helped out when needed.

I straightened up and nodded.

Scott took my chin in his hand and leaned in close to look at my jaw. "Uh-oh, looks like you're gonna have yourself a goose egg. Your mama's not going to be happy when she sees that!" He shook his head and grimaced. Yup, best friends knew things alright.

I frowned slightly at the sensation of butterflies that suddenly fluttered through my stomach. Maybe I had taken a punch there and hadn't realized it. I took another deep breath as Scott let go of my chin and stepped back. That was weird, too, the way I suddenly wished he had stayed where he was. Now, why would I care where he stood? My ruminations were interrupted by the appearance of yet another heroic avenger.

"Aw, Great Gawd Awlmighty! Is it over?" Bo skidded to a stop beside us and looked around wildly, his green eyes blazing. "Man-oh-man alive, I miss out on all the good stuff!" He glanced first at Scott, then at me. "Oh, sweet Carolina, Rachel! Did you get punched?" He grimaced. "Yo' mama's gon' give birth to livestock!" Yeah, cousins: nobody knew you better.

I shook my head and sighed. Fridays were always the hardest day for the School Patrol, and today had started out as a doozey. The sound of police whistles and adult voices floated down the sidewalk toward us.

"Oh, look." Bo's voice dripped with sarcasm. "Here come the teachers! We're saved!"

We laughed as we headed off to class.

***

The rest of the school day passed without incident until recess. As sixth-graders, we had a great schedule. The little kids took recess earlier, so ours was the last period before school let out. That meant we got to play, then go home! We gathered at the kickball field, ready for action.

"Aw yeah, y'all!" Bo loved taunting the other team. "It's 'bout to be woodshed time, right here, right now! Oughta call it kick BUTT 'stead o' kickball!" We all laughed and took our positions: Big Bubba Strickland covered third base, Scott had shortstop, Bo was all over second base, and I stood ready at first. The rest of the team was rounded out by five boys who all lived down the road a piece at the Bethesda Home for Boys.

As always, we were a force to be reckoned with and it wasn't even close as we entered the top of the fifth inning. (Recess wasn't long enough to play nine innings like in baseball, so the fifth was the last.) The first two kickers were easy outs, and the next kicker up would be the final out of the game if all went well. The boy gave the ball a good, solid kick as it crossed the plate then came tearing toward first base, where I stood ready, one foot on the bag. His only mistake was kicking the ball to Bo. My cousin, who played every game like it was the World Series, scooped up the ball on one bounce and fired it to first. There must have been more pepper on it than usual because the unthinkable happened: it smoked past my waiting fingers and hit me square in the side of the face. I still caught it as it bounced back into my hands, and the runner was out by a mile, but holy mackerel, did I get my bell rung!

"Lawd in heaven on high!" Bo had already gotten over to me. "Another smack to the face—that's twice in one day! You gon' look like that there elephant feller we was readin' about in science class. Cheese an' rice!"

"You really shouldn't say 'cheese an' rice,' Bo," Scott chided as he jogged over to check on me. "That's just one step away from taking the Lord's name in vain. It's like putting training wheels on a curse word." We all went to the same church, but Scott took it a lot more seriously than Bo did.

My cousin rolled his eyes and spit on the ground. "Whatever you say, GODfrey. I'm more concerned with havin' to listen to Rache's mama holler an' squall when we get to the house. Aunt Syl's gon' throw a hissy fit when she sees the size o' that bruise!" He looked more closely at me. "Say!" Bo's eyes lit up. "Now ya don't have to tell her about breakin' up that fight this mornin'! The ball jus' hit you smack dab in the same spot!"

What an excellent idea! I smiled and nodded as I touched my twice-hit jaw, which had already begun to turn an interesting shade of purple. I massaged it, felt the fresh swelling and grinned. Yup, an excellent idea indeed!

Shaking his head, Scott grinned crookedly at me and dropped a wink in my direction. Butterfly wings tickled my tummy again as we laughed and headed back toward the classroom.

I glanced across Whitfield Avenue and saw that the moving truck we'd seen that morning was gone. The new family must be all moved in. Before I could look away, movement in one of the windows caught my attention and I found myself looking into two enormous, dark-brown eyes. There was a new kid after all, but she wasn't a boy. I stopped and looked back at her for a moment before lifting my hand in a tentative wave. Her eyes widened and she seemed to gasp; then the curtains closed and she was gone. How odd, I thought.

Bo's clear, shrill whistle reached my ears and I hurried to catch up. Within minutes, I had forgotten about the strange little girl at the window.

Then the bell was ringing and we were free at last.

CHAPTER 3

"Rachel Anne Holland! What on earth have you done?" My mother had begun her tirade as soon as Bo and I walked through the door. He lived a little farther down Old Montgomery Road than I did but could never seem to make it home without stopping at our house for a snack. Apparently school took too much out of him to pull that off. He sauntered toward the kitchen as I stopped to face my demons.

"I just cannot seem to make you understand how important it is to behave with at least some modicum of decorum! A proper young lady does not allow herself to be drawn into a situation that could result in THIS!" My mother frowned as she gestured toward my bruised face before crossing her arms and looking me up and down, searching for more evidence of impropriety. "How on earth could you have let something like this happen?"

I caught sight of Bo watching me over my mother's shoulder. He was standing in the kitchen doorway, trying not to laugh at my predicament as he took a huge bite out of a peach.

"I'm sorry, Mama," I crooned. "Bo hit me in the face with a ball at recess." I shot him a big toothy grin as my mother spun on him and prepared to release the Kraken.

Choking and sputtering, Bo paled and suddenly lost all interest in the peach. "B-b-but I didn't . . . w-we were . . . she just . . ."

Wow! Bo DeLoach was speechless! When had *that* ever happened? I decided to save his bacon. "No, Mama!" I rushed to stop her before she could get worked up. "It was an accident! Bo wasn't trying to hit me."

"Nuh-uh! No, ma'am," Bo sputtered. "Aunt Syl, I'd never hit Rachel, not ever! Ya gotta know that!" He swallowed hard as my mother, one eyebrow cocked, carefully appraised him. She snorted, turned and stalked away.

"I might just stomp her into the mud, though," he muttered under his breath as he glared at me. Bo seemed to remember the peach in his hand and took a minute to lick the juice from his fingers before taking an angry bite.

I put my hand over my mouth to stifle a giggle, then sat down at the kitchen table and pulled the books out of my book bag. I liked to get my homework over and done with as soon as I got home on Fridays so I'd have the whole weekend free. Bo was more of a last-thing-on-Sunday-night kind of guy. He could never understand how I could come in from school and go right back to studying without taking a break.

He watched me for a few seconds, shook his head, and shot me one last evil glare before heading for the door. I could tell he really wanted to peg me with the peach pit he was holding, but he didn't dare do it in case my mother was looking. I heard the screen door slam and his Converse sneakers slap across the front porch. He was whistling before he reached the road. I smiled to myself. Good ol' Bo. It just wasn't in him to stay mad for long. Besides, he'd have done the same thing to me in a heartbeat. That's what it was to be "kissin' cousins." I opened my social studies book and began to read.

***

Later that night, I was lying in bed, thinking about the events of the day. My mother's morning and afternoon tirades flitted through my mind and I smiled in the darkness. It was kind of funny when you thought about how differently she spoke when she was just plain mad ("redneck mad," my father called it) as opposed to being righteously angry and grammatically correct when schooling me on the finer points of being a lady. It was almost like listening to two different people. I doubt she even realized she did it. I shook my head in the dark; then my eyebrows came together in a small frown at the memory of butterfly wings in my stomach when Scott had been near me. That was something I'd have to think more about when I was a little less tired. Kind of nice though, I thought, having him lean in and touch my face, though I couldn't for the life of me understand why. My eyelids slid closed and I started to drift off. The last thing I saw in my mind was two enormous, dark-brown eyes staring into mine. Strange new girl, I thought. Really weird.

Sleep took me.

CHAPTER 4

Saturday was, in my opinion, the best day of the week and I liked to get an early start. Most kids, I knew, were either still in bed or propped up in front of their TVs watching Hanna-Barbera cartoons. I was sure Bo was still sprawled in bed at his house, snoring and drooling on his pillow. It would be at least two more hours before his feet hit the floor.

Scott was an entirely different story; he liked to kick the rooster off the fence! I knew he would already be up and headed off to mow grass and pick up pinecones for some of the older ladies from our church. Afterward, he would probably jump on his bike and pedal down to the Bethesda Home for Boys to visit and invite some of them to church. He had read a verse somewhere in the Bible about caring for widows and orphans and had taken it to heart. Scott called Saturday his "ministering day."

Saturday morning was also grocery-shopping day, and my mother had set out early with Bo's mother, coupons in hand, to buy groceries for the upcoming week. That meant breakfast was catch-as-catch-can, which was fine with me. I poured myself a bowl of cereal and a glass of chocolate milk and sat down at the kitchen table. (No Tang on Saturdays; thank the saints and angels!) I read the cereal box as I munched and wondered when they had exchanged the toy surprise inside for the puzzle on the back of the box.

"Hey, pumpkin! How's my girl?" My father shot me a smile as he came in from outside. Miles Holland was a good, hard-working man, handsome and well built. It was from him I had inherited my dark blond hair and sturdy frame, although my hazel eyes came from my mother. It was also from him that I had inherited the Holland name and the chance to join the upper echelon of society. I could never hold that against him, though. He was just about the best husband and father you could ever hope to meet and I felt lucky and proud to be his daughter.

"Morning, Daddy!" I couldn't help but smile back at him. My father had one of those smiles you just couldn't resist. My mother called it "infectious."

He placed a finger under my chin and tilted my head back. "Let's have a look at that jaw." My father had been a whole lot less upset than my mother when he'd seen my bruised face the night before. "Well, look at that!" His face lit up. "It looks a lot better today. That'll make your mama happy!" Our eyes met in a conspiratorial way and we both chuckled.

Daddy felt a little bad about how hard Mama pushed when it came to me taking what she considered to be my rightful place in Savannah's high society, but he had to agree when she insisted that I deserved to be given every possible opportunity to succeed in life. His smile grew as he grabbed a bowl and spoon and joined me at the table. "Please pass the cereal, your majesty," he implored with a slight bow. I choked and sputtered, and we broke into fresh laughter. Saturday mornings were definitely my favorite time of the best day of the week.

After breakfast, I grabbed one of the books from my summer reading list and set out to find a quiet place to read. We still had a couple of weeks of school left before it let out for the summer, but I loved to read and wanted to get a jump on the assignment. (Bo would have called this further evidence that I was certifiably bonkers.) I usually enjoyed sitting with a book on one of the many docks that jutted out over the Vernon River, but I knew that this close to summer, the waterways would be filled with roaring motorboats pulling water skis and inner tubes, and I hoped to find a more peaceful place to relax with my book.

I walked across the playing fields by Hesse Elementary School, waving absently to Nudgie Harden, who was shooting baskets on the outdoor court next to the upper school building. Nudgie, pronounced "New-gee," was a fifteen-year-old ninth-grader who attended Calvary Baptist Day School downtown. I really didn't know her all that well, but in the South we all wave to one another in passing, friends and strangers alike. She sank one from the top of the key before waving back. Nice shot, I thought, and it probably explained why she had won the Jr. Varsity MVP Award that year. I would be attending Calvary myself next September, and I wondered if she would still acknowledge me then. Probably not. She would be a sophomore by then while I'd be a lowly seventh-grader. As it was, the only reason we knew each other at all was because we attended the same church and our fathers both worked for the Savannah Electric and Power Company.

I reached Whitfield Avenue, stopped to look both ways before crossing, then started down Beckman Avenue. The Hardens lived down this road, right on the river, but my destination was only half that distance. Beckman Avenue was a narrow dirt road that was barely wide enough to allow two cars to pass. It was bordered on the left by a row of older brick homes set on large lots while a pine and oak forest lay on the right. Where the row of houses ended, the road doglegged to the left and traversed another three hundred yards or so before dead-ending at the Vernon River. The Hardens, the Godwins, the Tuckers, and the Sikeses all owned riverfront property down there. The first three of these families attended my church and allowed me to use their docks whenever I wanted to swim or go crabbing; but the Sikeses, who lived in a rundown, rusty-tin-roofed shanty at the edge of the marsh, were bad news and everyone knew to steer clear of them— not that I was worried about that today. My destination was where the road doglegged to the left. I stopped when I reached the spot and looked up.

It was huge.

CHAPTER 5

This was, I'd be willing to bet, the most massive live oak within at least a five-mile radius. I'd been all over these and the adjoining woods, and no other tree even came close. Last year, Bo, Scott, and I had joined hands and tried to encircle the trunk. It had not been possible. That alone would have made this tree a legend in our minds, but that wasn't even the best thing about it. Every kid in the surrounding neighborhoods of Grace Drive, Halcyon Bluff, and even across Whitfield Avenue down Kings Way knew this tree and had spent time playing in it, but no matter how many of them climbed it at a time, there was always room for more. It was a Magic Tree; we all knew that. The first branches were a good eight to ten feet off the ground and they spread up and out from there; they were so thick you could walk up and down any of them without having to hold on to anything or even hold out your arms for balance. This was the kind of tree that called to children the way Sirens called to sailors in Greek mythology. It practically begged to be climbed, and the Spanish moss hanging in thick sheets from every branch waved and beckoned in the wind, adding allure to the invitation.

This was my destination. I had learned long ago that I could relax in the boughs of this majestic tree and, hidden by the Spanish moss, read undetected and undisturbed for hours at a time. Trees were, in my opinion, wonderful things, and I knew I wasn't the only one in the neighborhood who thought so. Lots of kids I knew had a favorite tree they practically lived in. Our pastor, J. Cohen Arms, loved to tell the story of how he could have sworn he'd heard angels singing once while driving around the neighborhood years before. He had stopped his car and gotten out to investigate. It turned out to be Nudgie Harden, eight years old and happy as a clam, sitting thirty feet up in a hickory tree, singing hymns and swaying in the breeze. This wasn't a hickory tree and I didn't sing, but I could definitely relate. Trees are awesome!

I walked over to the base and looked up. This was the only place you could stand and actually see up into the branches, and I was happy to find that no one was already up there. At some point in the past, Paul Harden, Nudgie's older brother, had nailed short lengths of two-by-fours to the trunk, creating a makeshift ladder so it was no problem reaching the lower branches. I tucked my book into the waistband of my shorts and started up. I had the usual fleeting thought that there was no telling how much longer these old rungs were going to hold weight, but I brushed aside that fear and continued up. At the last rung, I scrambled onto the large branch to my right, stood upright, and carefully walked out to where I knew some of the smaller, leafier branches intertwined, forming a natural hammock. Pausing to admire the view of the river (yup—full of motorboats), I lowered myself into the gently swaying seat and pulled out my book. An audible sigh escaped my lips as I began to read.

***

I hadn't worn my watch, so I had no idea how long I'd been reading, but I was interrupted by the sound of twigs snapping somewhere below me. Someone was approaching the base of the tree, but rather than coming down the road as I had done, this person had elected to approach from the back side, which meant winding around smaller trees and scrabbling through scrub brush and stickers. I grimaced. Someone was going to have some stinging scratches and bug bites to deal with later, not to mention the beggar lice that would have to be pulled off of his or her pant legs.

I watched the spot where I thought the interloper would emerge, and within seconds, the top of a small head came into view. I frowned slightly, not recognizing the tousled mane of thick, wavy dark hair. Whoever it was, they'd obviously never seen this tree. Like every other first-time visitor, they gasped upon reaching the trunk, then stepped back and gaped in wonder as their gaze traveled up and up and up. There was another gasp as our eyes locked and I found myself looking into the same enormous, dark-brown eyes I'd seen through the window the day before. It was the strange little girl whose family had just moved into the neighborhood. She'd looked fearful then, but that was nothing compared to the look that froze on her face when she saw me staring down at her now. This look was one of sheer terror, and I thought for a minute she might cry out. Stepping backward, she started to retreat into the woods.

"Wait!" I practically screamed at her. She stopped abruptly, but appeared ready to bolt at a moment's notice. I swallowed before continuing, making an effort to sound more pleasant. "Please! Don't go away. I'd like to meet you!" She seemed to relax slightly. "I'm Rachel, Rachel Holland, and I live across the schoolyard from you." She seemed torn, so I continued quickly, hoping to keep her there. "What's your name?"

The diminutive girl dropped her eyes from mine and glanced around fearfully. Seeing that we were alone must have emboldened her because she stepped out of the bushes and looked back up at me. "I'm Della, Della Rooney," she answered shyly, and the sweet, melodic strains of her voice caught me completely by surprise. Rich and warm, her words seemed to enfold me in a gentle embrace. How could such full, dulcet sounds come from such a tiny body? I couldn't help but smile down at her and, visibly relaxed, she smiled back. Her thick, dark hair and large, brown eyes brought to mind a beautiful gypsy princess dancing gracefully around a campfire to the lilting sound of a violin and the ring of a tambourine, and her dimpled cheeks made her that much more adorable. Add to this her small stature and the rich timbre of her voice and I was certain there was no one like her among the cornbread-fed yokels I was accustomed to seeing around the neighborhood. I decided I wanted to know her better.

"Would you like to climb up? We could chat and get to know one another."

Frowning slightly, Della shook her head. "I've never climbed a tree," she said. "And from where I'm standing, it looks like it's got to be about a mile up to where you are! I don't see how I'd ever be able get up there."

I couldn't help but smile again when she spoke. That voice was just too much! "It's nowhere near that far," I said, laughing. "More like eight feet, give or take. As for how, if you come around to the other side, you'll see there's a ladder built right into the trunk." I gestured in that direction.

Still frowning, Della circled the base of the tree. Reaching the rungs, she stared at them as though they couldn't possibly exist.

"Well, who'd-a-thought?" Her voice was filled with wonder, and I found myself delighted by her surprise. "Why, it looks like something out of a Tarzan movie!" She laughed joyfully, and I had to join in.

"Well, then come on up, Cheetah! Omgawa!" I had no idea what that meant, but in the movies Tarzan was always saying it to the animals when he wanted them to move. Della must have seen the same movies because she giggled and reached for the rungs.

"Okay," she said. "I guess I could try."

I would never have believed that watching someone climb a tree could be so nerve-wracking, but when that tiny girl started up the side of that green behemoth, I felt like chewing my fingernails to the quick! The higher Della climbed, the tinier she seemed to become. I was nearly trembling by the time she reached the top, but it was nothing compared to how she was shaking. When she reached the last rung, Della crawled out onto the first big branch, lay down on her stomach, and wrapped her thin arms and legs as far around that branch as she could reach. She clung there as though her life depended on it. Perhaps it did.

"Oh, no! No-no-no-no-no," she moaned. "This was a very bad idea. Very bad. I need down! I need down *now*! Please! Please-please-please-please-please!" Della's eyes were screwed shut as she continued to mumble and I knew if I didn't do something fast, falling could become a very real possibility for her and, at her size, that would be a very bad thing. Oh, why hadn't I realized how truly small she was? I was so stupid!

"Della! Della, it's okay! You're alright," I soothed. "Look at me, Della. Look at me! Keep your eyes on me!" I put down my book, stood up and approached carefully, trying to shake the branch as little as possible. "You're going to be alright, Della!" I knelt down next to her head and grasped the back of her shirt as tightly as I could. "You are not going to fall. I won't let you fall! I promise, Della—I will not let you fall! Now . . . look at me!"

Della Rooney clung to the branch even harder, squeezed her eyes more tightly shut, and shook her head vehemently. It seemed this was just too much to ask of her.

I grimaced. How was I going to help her if I couldn't get her to listen to me? I tried again. "Della," I crooned. "Della, I really need you to do as I say. If you don't, you'll never get down." I switched to my School Patrol voice, "Look at me, Della . . . NOW!"

I held my breath as she grew still, seeming to think. Then, very slowly, she tipped her head back and stared up at me. Her expression of sheer terror and the tears in her eyes nearly broke my heart. I swallowed and forced a smile. "Hey!" I made my voice sound light and cheerful, as though nothing were amiss anywhere in the world. "There you are! Why so scared, silly? It's just a dumb ol' tree. You're fine! Everything is just fine." I forced a laugh, hoping to ease the tension; it sounded more like a shriek. "All you have to do is keep your eyes on me and you'll be okay. Now, stand up."

By the look that crossed her face, you would've thought I'd told her to leap into a raging inferno. "No, please," she begged. "I can't! It's too high!"

I laughed again, though it didn't seem to be helping. "Sure you can," I insisted. Then I had an idea. "Della Rooney! Are you telling me that you think I would let my newest friend fall out of a tree?" I held my breath and crossed my metaphorical fingers.

She tipped her head back and looked at me again. "Your newest friend?" An expression of doubt crossed her face. "Am I really your friend?" Then I saw what looked like wonder and hope flash in her eyes, and she actually smiled at me . . . a little.

Yes! It was working! "Well, sure," I answered. "Do you think I'd invite just any ol' body to climb up here and sit with me? We're definitely friends now."

Della turned that over in her mind for a few seconds then she smiled in determination. "Okay! I'm standing up now." She gave me a quick look. "Just please don't let go of me!"

"I won't," I promised. "I won't let go and I won't let you fall." I felt a lump form in my throat as I watched Della rise to her feet.

That was a feeling I will never forget: to know that someone had

23

placed absolute faith and trust in me. It was a first and I felt like I'd just reached some sort of threshold, some turning point of maturity.

Della Rooney grasped my outstretched hand and stood to her full height. I held tightly to her hand; nothing in heaven or on earth could have made me let go. Down deep inside, I felt that I had crossed a line I couldn't turn back from. She looked up at me and I knew, without a shadow of a doubt, that I had become her rock.

I swallowed again and looked into her eyes. "Now," I said softly, "come with me." I led her along the bough, back to the leafy branches I'd been reclining on. Her eyes never left mine. "Okay," I continued, stepping aside and carefully turning her around. "Now, sit." She didn't even hesitate. She lowered herself into the natural hammock, which cradled her as though it had been made for her, and I let out the huge breath I hadn't known I was holding.

"Well, who'd-a-thought?" Della took a moment to look around. "You can see everything from up here. Oh! Is that the river?" She had craned around and was staring off in the direction of the water. "Look at all the boats!" She seemed to have already recovered from the terror that had gripped her only moments before. "I've never been this close to a river before!" The warmth of her laughter was like fire in winter.

I smiled at her, then felt my mouth drop open as I realized what she'd just said. "No way!" I couldn't believe it. "Are you telling me you've never been on the water?" It was unimaginable. "You've never been swimming or crabbing? You've never been out in a boat?" It was incomprehensible.

"Nope!" Amazingly, Della was actually swinging her legs, causing the branches to sway. It didn't seem to faze her at all. "We've never lived on the coast before. We just moved here from Nevada, and my family really doesn't get out and go anywhere. I'm pretty shy, too, so mostly I've always just stayed in the house." She dipped her chin slightly. "I guess that's why I'm so nervous and kind of scared of everything.

And I'm not really supposed to wander too far from home. Even now, my mama thinks I'm just out in the yard somewhere." Della frowned. "She'd be really upset if she knew how far away I am. And if she saw me way up in this tree. . ." Her words trailed off, but they sure explained a lot. I, however, was still stuck on her previous statement.

"Well, Della Rooney," I loved the way her name just rolled off the tongue. "We can't let you go through life never having experienced the water!" I grinned at her. "You and I are going to spend the summer introducing you to the Vernon River and seeing to it that you two become better acquainted." I laughed, a genuine one this time. "You're about to spend the next three months swimming, crabbing, and discovering the joys of waterskiing and tubing. Prepare to be thrilled!"

Della's eyes were shining and she opened her mouth to speak.

"Ay-oh-ay, whadda we got ovuh heah?" We both snapped our heads in the direction the voice had come from. Standing below, looking back up at us, were two very large, very mean-looking boys, neither of whom I'd ever seen. They appeared to be a couple of years older than me, which would put them at around thirteen. I didn't like the look of them and glanced over at Della. Her lips were pressed tightly together in a thin line and she had gone completely white. The branches where she perched had gone from gently swaying to violently shaking and I knew she was quaking with fear. I looked back down at the boys. Their grins were just plain evil.

"We hadn't planned on havin' to share dis tree wid anybody else," the bigger of the two sneered. Every true Southerner knew a Yankee when they heard one, and these boys were definitely from up north. "So," he crowed, "yuz have got to go!"

They started up the ladder.

CHAPTER 6

Things were not looking good for the home team, and I would've given anything if some of the cornbread-fed yokels I'd just compared to Della had shown up right about then to help us, but no such luck. It was still morning and no normal school-aged child would be out from in front of the Saturday morning cartoons until they ended at noon. I knew we were on our own. One glance at Della had me amend that thought: I, as in "me, myself, and I," was on MY own. If we were going to get out of this, it looked as if it would be totally up to me. I turned to face the ascending boys, planting myself firmly between them and my new friend.

The first one to reach the bough on which I stood was the bigger boy and he leered at us as he stepped out onto the branch. "Well, look at what we got ovuh heah!" He glanced at the slightly smaller boy, who was just straightening up behind him. "Ay, Tony! Whadda ya know, huh? Looks like we got us a coupla birds up in dis tree!" It came out "boyds" and I would've laughed had the situation not been so serious. The larger boy's leer widened. "Whaddaya t'ink we oughta do wid 'em?"

The younger boy, Tony, peered around the bigger boy. "I dunno, Vinnie," he answered. "Whadda YOU t'ink we oughta do wid 'em?" Tony was obviously Vinnie's toady.

Vinnie scratched his head, then snapped his fingers. "I got it!" His eyes took on a frightening gleam. "I t'ink we oughta find out if dese little birds can fly! Oh!" The guttural sound made me jump. He took a step toward us, followed closely by Tony.

I didn't like the direction things had taken, but I'd be damned if I was going to let a couple of Yankee boys knock me out of a tree in my own Southern state! They had obviously never dealt with a true, red-blooded, Deep-South-born-and-bred female. There were lessons these two needed to learn, and I was just the Georgia peach to teach them . . . I hoped!

"Cheep-cheep-cheep!" Vinnie chirped absurdly at us as he approached. "Come on, little birds. Let's see if yuz can fly."

"Yeah," echoed Tony the toady. "Let's see if yuz can fly."

They were fast approaching the midpoint on the branch between the trunk and where I stood and I still had no idea how I was going to stop them. Behind me, Della had begun to whimper and I knew that had I been able to look at her, I would see those enormous dark eyes squeezed tightly shut. My heart ached for her and, feeling a sudden overwhelming wave of protectiveness and resolve, I clenched my fists and prepared to do whatever it took to protect her. These boys might throw me out of this tree, but by gum, I was taking both of them with me! Della Rooney would have no flying lesson today! I gritted my teeth and steeled myself for battle.

WHAP!

A basketball came out of nowhere and slammed into Vinnie's chest. It must have had some fire behind it because he had to pinwheel his arms like crazy to keep from sailing backward out of the tree. Behind him, Tony squawked like a "boyd" and dropped to his knees. We all looked toward where the ball had come from.

"Howdy, boys!" Nudgie Harden was smiling up at us. "Welcome to Georgia!" Her expression turned cold. "Now you boys weren't about to try and throw these two little girls out of this tree, were you?" Her eyes were ice.

Both boys started talking at once. Vinnie was sweating profusely, but whether from his close call with the basketball or from getting caught bullying us, there was no way to know. He slapped Tony in the chest to silence him, then began to speak. "Ay-oh-ay, we wasn't doin' nuthin' o' da sort," Vinnie protested. Next to him, Tony echoed the sentiment. Vinnie swallowed before continuing. "Not for nuthin', it was just a goof!"

Nudgie nodded. "Right . . . just a goof. Yeah, I can see that now." She walked over and retrieved her basketball from the bushes where it had come to rest. Returning to the base of the tree, she took a moment before speaking again. You could have heard a pin drop. "I'll tell you what, boys." Nudgie shifted the ball to her right hand, as though preparing to throw it again. "Why don't y'all move to another branch so my two friends here can climb down? Then I believe we can put this entire . . . um . . . *episode* behind us."

Vinnie and Tony scrambled to obey.

"Now," Nudgie continued, "Rachel, why don't you grab hold of your little friend there and help her over to the ladder." She must have seen Della blanch because she rushed on. "If you'll get her to the ladder and start her down, I'll catch hold of her and make sure she makes it okay. What's your name, kid?"

Della's lips were still pinched closed, so I answered for her. "This is Della Rooney. She just moved into the neighborhood yesterday and this is the first time she's ever climbed a tree."

Nudgie smiled warmly. "Well, Della Rooney," she said gently, "you couldn't have picked a better tree to climb for your first time. See, this is a Magic Tree! Everyone around here knows that, right, Rachel?" I bobbed my head in agreement. "Do you know why, Della?" Nudgie gazed deeply into Della's eyes. Looking back, Della shook her head. "Because," Nudgie answered, "no one has ever fallen out of this tree. It's like the tree holds on to you and keeps you safe! Come on, try climbing down. You'll see; you can feel the magic!" Nudgie smiled and Della smiled back.

Then, to my amazement, Della stood, traversed the bough and reached for the rungs. I lunged for my book, stuffed it down the back of my pants then grabbed Della by the shirt collar to steady her as Nudgie reached up, ready to catch her if she slipped. In no time at all, Della and I were on the ground and were ducked behind Nudgie.

She turned back to the two boys, still in the tree. I found myself hoping its magic didn't work on Yankees. She gave them one last frown then turned to leave.

"Oh!" Something seemed to occur to Nudgie. She turned back to the boys. "You know," she said, "you really aren't as high up as you think. It's just sort of an optical illusion when you're up there. You're not even as high up as the roof of a single-story house. In fact," she went on, "a lot of us kids jump out of this tree, you know, for fun."

Vinnie and Tony looked skeptical, so she spoke on. "The secret is to gather this gray stuff that's hanging all over the tree. You gather up as much of it as you can and pile it up real thick right under the branch you're standing on. It's soft and spongy, and it cushions your landing when you jump." You could practically see the lightbulb come on over Vinnie's head. "It's just like jumping onto a mattress! A lot of us kids like to pretend we're paratroopers landing behind enemy lines. It's so much fun! Really!" Nudgie smiled. "All of us have done it, and no one's ever gotten hurt. You should try it . . . unless you're scared."

Vinnie and Tony looked at each other then broke into identical grins. They whooped and hollered as they started pulling the Spanish moss out of the tree.

29

I had a sudden thought. "Uh, Nudgie," I began. "You know that moss is full of—"

Nudgie interrupted me. "No, fellas! Y'all gonna need a whole bunch more than that! There ya go," she exclaimed as Vinnie and Tony grabbed as much moss as their arms could hold. "Keep pullin', fellas. Y'all want to have a nice, big, soft bed to land on. And be sure to grab more to add to the pile every now and then so your bed stays nice and plump for ya."

"But, Nudgie," I tried again, "that moss has—"

Nudgie cleared her throat, tucked the basketball under one arm, and took me by the elbow. She turned to leave, pulling me with her. Della was glued to my side.

We crossed Beckman Avenue and entered the woods, taking a path that would eventually come out down the road from the Harden house. Behind us in the distance we could hear the two Yankee boys laughing and shouting to each other as they prepared to jump out of the Magic Tree and into the huge pile of Spanish moss they'd gathered. Speaking quietly, I finally voiced the thought that had occurred to me back at the base of the tree. "Nudgie," I said. "You know that Spanish moss is slap full of red bugs. Those two Yankee boys are gonna get eaten alive!"

"Really?" Nudgie kept her eyes on the path as she spoke. "You don't say!" We continued deeper into the woods as Nudgie began to sing "The South's Gonna Do It Again." She laughed and smiled saucily. "Yes siree," she said. "I sure do like me some Charlie Daniels!" She started whistling "Dixie."

It was my turn to have a lightbulb go on and I let loose a huge belly laugh as I realized what Nudgie had done. I turned to tell her how cool I thought she was, but the sound of Della's sharp intake of breath stopped me cold. We had come to a clearing at the center of the woods and Della was reacting to what lay at our feet.

We had reached the Big Hole.

CHAPTER 7

Della's eyes were like saucers as she stared down into the Big Hole's depths. You could tell from the look on her face that she was trying to process what she was seeing but it just wasn't happening. Nudgie and I looked at each other and laughed. This place could be hard to wrap your head around.

"Well, Della," Nudgie finally said, "if you just moved here yesterday and climbed your first tree today, I guess you've never heard of the Big Hole." Della, mouth agape, shook her head. "Okay, then," Nudgie continued, "let me tell you the story of how it came to be."

I'd never heard the history of the Big Hole myself, so I was just as interested as Della. We all sat down on the edge with our legs dangling over the side and Nudgie began the story:

Many years back, before all the houses were built and there were only the woods and the river, the land belonged to an old man by the name of Beckman. At some point, he'd decided to sell off parcels to bankroll a house for himself. He sold the parcels to the Godwins, the Tuckers, and the Hardens, among others, while reserving a large parcel in the woods to build on himself and a second waterfront parcel strictly for recreational purposes. But when he started planning his new home, he realized he would rather build right on the water rather than back in the woods. Unfortunately, he hadn't allowed himself enough right-of-way to provide access for the large machinery and truckloads of building supplies he would need. So Mr. Beckman went to Wimpy Harden (Nudgie's father), whose parcel was not on the water, and asked if they could rework their property lines. After reaching an agreement, Mr. Beckman had the access he needed to build on the water and Wimpy Harden had riverfront property. Once all the legal paperwork was signed, all Mr. Beckman had to do was bring in fill dirt for the foundation of his house to ensure it would never sink or flood. So he brought in a fleet of bulldozers and dump trucks to dig up the dirt from the center of the woods and deposit it on his lot. Load after load was removed and dumped by the river, and when all was said and done, Mr. Beckman had his buildable lot and the woods had a deep, gaping, red-clay hollow at the center.

The Big Hole was born.

***

It was a good story, and I was glad to finally know how this wonderful place had come to exist. All the kids had opinions about how it had gotten there; many believed it had been dug to help fight fires. If a big one ever raged through the woods and got out of control, firefighters could parachute safely into the Big Hole and fight it from the inside out. There were many other, less likely stories that circulated every year or so. Anything this remarkable was bound to become a legend at some point, and if the Magic Oak Tree was well known, then the Big Hole was infamous! You could ask any kid in the area and they'd tell you it was absolutely THE most popular place to play. In fact, you could go anywhere on this side of Savannah and mention it to any kid and they'd know exactly what you were talking about.

Bo and I had been thrilled beyond measure when our mothers had decided we were old enough to play there. (My mother, of course, had taken longer to convince than Bo's, and at first I wasn't permitted to go there without him.) We'd heard the older kids talk about it all our lives and we were chomping at the bit to see it for ourselves. Believe me, it was worth the wait.

It wasn't called the Big Hole for nothing! I know a child's perspective can be skewed, but I swear you could've dropped a small house in there and not been able to see any part of it until you were right up on the edge, looking over the side. Fifteen years of children running and sliding up and down had made the clay sides as slick as a whistle and all the bicycles constantly riding through it had created actual riding trails. And steep? I remember riding my own bicycle at breakneck speed out of the woods and down into the Big Hole and still not being able to achieve enough momentum to get up the far side. For a while, Bo and I rode our bikes there every day after school and it took weeks before I developed enough leg strength to make it all the way down, across, and up the other side. The first time I made it, Bo and I both let loose rebel yells and danced all along the edge. Once I'd mastered this, I was able to join the other kids in stunt riding. The Big Hole was elliptical in shape, like a bathtub, with small scrub trees growing inside on either end. There were eventually entrance ramps formed by all the bicycles that rode through it—shallower ones at both ends and one wide, deep one straight across the center. Lately, the kids had begun crisscrossing from corner to corner, too, so the trails were getting really interesting. If you could hover over the Big Hole, the way it was cut would probably make it look sort of like an elongated pizza.

We all experienced an awful lot of fun and excitement there, but the biggest adrenaline rush was when we'd put someone on a bike at the top of every ramp, count to three, then all go at once. The trick was to miss each other and the small trees, not wipe out, and make it up and out on the other side. God must have assigned a special team of angels to watch over and protect all of us kids who did this because even though we fell frequently while trying not to crash, I can't remember a single time any of us actually smashed into each other.

As for the kids who didn't have bikes, it was fun to sit on flattened cardboard boxes and slide down or just run the trails on foot. The trick there was to keep your feet; the sides were slippery and steep, and you got to going so fast it was nearly impossible not to fall and, of course, there were all the kids on bicycles trying not to run into you as they rocketed through. There were also the "diggers," kids who would excavate huge holes in the sides that were large enough to back into and hide in. Sometimes girls would bring their dolls, dig out shallower holes and play "caveman Barbie." The things you could do and the fun you could have at the Big Hole were unlimited. It was little redneck Disneyland!

Della and I sat resting for a few more minutes with Nudgie after she finished her story; then the three of us stood and continued along the path through the woods. I decided I'd have to bring Della back to the Big Hole sometime so she could actually experience it for herself. Right now I just wanted to get her home. I knew she must be exhausted after all she'd been through and, from what she had told me earlier, her mother hadn't even known she'd left. Della's absence had to have been noticed by now; I hoped her mother wasn't as prone to having a cow as mine was. At the very least, the poor woman was probably worried sick and maybe even scouring the surrounding neighborhood looking for her missing daughter. I hoped Della wasn't in too much trouble.

We stepped out of the woods and onto Beckman Avenue. The way the road cut through the woods could be confusing; after it doglegged at the Magic Oak Tree, it continued down toward the Vernon River, but halfway there it also cut sharply to the right, where it eventually ended at a bend in the river. If you were to keep going straight instead of cutting to the right, you'd end up down by the Godwins', the Tuckers', and the Sikes's, but following the road to the right brought you to the home of Fred Morgan, a cantankerous but lovable old man who originally hailed from Clyo, Georgia, and who loved fishing and coon hunting. He and his wife had lived down there for many years and also had a dock out on the river, which he allowed me to use whenever I liked. The Hardens' house sat on the corner where the two roads diverged. I thought Nudgie would say goodbye at her driveway, but she had other plans.

"I think I'll walk with y'all a little farther," she said. "If I'm not mistaken, I saw a moving truck at the house directly across the schoolyard from yours yesterday, didn't I, Rachel?" I nodded. "Okay, then. That means that's your house, Della. Am I right?" It was Della's turn to nod. "Those boys are probably still at the tree," Nudgie continued, "so I think y'all should cut across Robinson's Field and go down the little road that comes out across from the church. That'll put both of y'all right by your houses." She noticed my frown. "Is that not alright?" She looked confused.

I shook my head. "No, I'm sure it's a good idea to stay as far away from those boys as possible, but . . ." I paused before continuing. "I don't know where Robinson's Field is!"

Nudgie looked dumbfounded for a moment before bursting into laughter. "Come on," she said, walking toward a row of mailboxes across the road from her house. There was a line of trees behind them and a small dirt path to their left, which led under a natural arch formed by the trees and vines. Four steps brought us through and out the other side. Nudgie stopped and gestured toward the large overgrown lot that lay to our left. "This," she said, "is Robinson's Field."

"Oh!" I smiled in understanding. "All us kids nowadays call it the Round and Round because we like to race our bicycles and mini-bikes around it."

Nudgie smiled back at me. "I don't know who owns it now, but when I was little it was owned by the Robinson family and they built a real baseball diamond here. It had team benches and a scoreboard and everything! Then, when the city built Meridian Park, everybody started playing ball there, so Robinson's Field just went to weeds." She frowned. "A lot of things sure have changed since then." She sighed and shook her head, then looked back at us. "I'm gonna let y'all go on by yourselves, but I'll stay here for a few minutes, just in case. I don't think they will, but if those boys do see y'all and try to start more trouble, you just holler and I'll come running." She looked back at the cars parked behind her house. "My brother, Paul, and his wife, Brenda, are here now, too, so if I need to I'll call them to come with me. Those Yankee boys definitely wouldn't want that!" She chuckled at the thought, then waved goodbye.

I gave her a smile and Della and I stepped out from under the trees, into the sunlight. Farther off to the left, we could hear the boys still whooping and laughing as they played in the tree. It wouldn't be long before they'd begin to wonder what was making them itch so badly. By tonight they'd be miserable! I looked down at Della; she was frowning in the direction of the tree. I took her hand and when she looked up at me, I squeezed it and gave her a smile. She smiled and squeezed back.

We started across Robinson's Field.

CHAPTER 8

On the other side of Robinson's Field lay a narrow, rutted dirt road barely wide enough for one car; I suspected it must have started out as a walking path since it didn't even have a name, as far as I knew. It ran straight as an arrow through a small wooded area and ended at Whitfield Avenue, directly across from Cresthill Baptist Church. Nudgie had been correct: At the end of this road, an immediate left turn would take us to Della's house, while crossing Whitfield Avenue and circling behind the church would bring us in sight of mine. When we reached the end of the road, Della and I both turned left. I hoped her mother wouldn't be as upset about her having been gone for so long if she brought me home with her. Hopefully, knowing her daughter had made a new friend would make her feel more forgiving.

"I'm sorry about what happened at the tree," I said. "I've never seen those boys before in my life. If I'd known they would be there or that you'd be so scared, I never would've asked you to climb up there with me." I still felt horrible just thinking about it.

Della sighed. "It's alright, Rachel." That voice again! I hoped I never got used to hearing it. "There's no way you could've known what was going to happen. I'm just sorry I was such a baby about it. I wish I could've been as brave as you were." She frowned, her eyes on the ground. "It's too bad, really; it would've been nice to have you as a friend. I'm going to miss getting to do all those fun things you told me about—you know, all the river stuff." I looked over and noticed that her eyes had welled up.

"Hey!" I pulled her to a stop. "What makes you think we aren't still going to do all those things?"

Della looked up at me in disbelief. "You mean we still can? You don't think I'm too much of a baby to bother with?" Hope touched her eyes.

"Are you kidding me?" I smiled at her. "Not only am I still going to introduce you to the joys of living near a river, I'm already making plans to take you back to the Big Hole sometime so you can see how much fun it is when it's full of kids and bicycles. You're not going to believe how great it is!"

Della squealed and jumped up and down. I smiled and shook my head; she was just the cutest little thing. A thought occurred to me.

"Tell me something, Della; how old are you, exactly?" I was hoping she wasn't so young that her mother wouldn't let her hang out with me.

Della grinned mischievously, her eyes gleaming. "Well," she answered, "I bet I'm a whole bunch older than you think I am." She paused, tilted her head to the side and cut her eyes at me. "I'll be twelve years old at the end of July."

If I'd been chewing gum, I would've choked on it! "Holy cow, Della!" I nearly shouted at her. "You're older than I am! I don't turn twelve until the first week of August!"

She practically danced with delight, knowing she'd had me fooled. I still couldn't believe it; she was just so tiny! I'd had her pegged for seven, possibly eight years old. It was unbelievable!

"My parents are both really small too, so I guess that's where I get it," she explained as we continued toward her house. "I actually think you and my mama are about the same size, except she's a little thinner than you."

I tried to process the idea that someone's mother was my size, but I just couldn't picture it. I shrugged my shoulders; it didn't matter whether I could picture it or not. We had arrived at Della's house, so I'd be seeing it for myself in a moment. We followed a paved walk that led up to the front porch. When we reached the front door, Della turned the knob, pushed it open and waved me in.

"Mama, I'm home." Della closed the door behind us. "Guess what! I made a new friend!"

From the back of the house came the sharp bang of a door slamming open followed by the sound of feet hurrying up the hall toward us. Within seconds, the tiniest woman I'd ever seen had blown past me and grabbed Della in a bone-crunching hug.

"Where have you been, girl?" The woman was almost in tears. "I looked everywhere for you! I thought for sure something bad had happened."

"Mama, please!" Della disentangled herself from her mother's arms and shot me an embarrassed look. "Don't you see I brought home a new friend for you to meet?"

Della's mother turned an appraising eye on me. I spent the next few seconds trying not to squirm under her intense scrutiny. I had the distinct impression she was wondering if I had any ulterior motives for wanting to be friends with her daughter. Her suspicions made me a little uncomfortable and I struggled not to fidget.

Della seemed unaware of my discomfort. She smiled widely as she made the introductions.

"Mama, this is my new friend, Rachel Holland. She lives directly across from us on the other side of the schoolyard, but I met her in the woods just out back of the house." Della was smart, making it sound like we actually hadn't been that far away when we met. "Rachel's been showing me some of the fun things to do around the neighborhood, and I even met a few of the other kids from around here." She was brilliant. "Rachel, this is my mama."

Collecting myself, I stood up straight, lifted my chin and made direct eye contact with Della's mother as I offered her my hand. "How do you do, Mrs. Rooney?" I smiled and greeted her respectfully, as I'd been taught. "It's so very nice to meet you. I'm sorry if you were worried. We were having such a good time talking and getting to know each other, we lost track of the time." My mother would have been so proud.

For a split second Mrs. Rooney appeared to be weighing her options. She apparently decided in favor of trust because she returned my smile and took my proffered hand. Beside me, I heard Della exhale softly with relief. I knew exactly how she felt.

Mrs. Rooney invited me in, apologizing that the house was in such shambles; there was still so much unpacking to do! Mentally thanking my mother for teaching me proper etiquette, I said all the right things to put Della's mother at ease. I could tell she appreciated it and had begun to like me. I decided to push my luck a little.

"Mrs. Rooney," I asked, "would it be alright if Della came back out to play awhile longer, now that she's checked in with you? I really didn't get to show her as much of the neighborhood as I wanted to, and there are several more kids I'd like her to meet."

Mrs. Rooney frowned and appeared to be on the verge of refusing my request, but Della beat her to the punch. "Oh, please, Mama!" she pleaded. "Please let me go. I want to meet more of the kids around here. Then I'll at least know a few of them when I start school Monday. It's going to be so hard going to a place where I don't know anyone. If I meet at least a few of the kids, maybe it won't be so bad." I could tell the fearfulness in her voice wasn't an act; she really was nervous about starting school.

And who could blame her? Poor Della! I couldn't even imagine what it would feel like to start at a new school with only two weeks left in the year. That would be awful! I suddenly felt very glad that we had run into each other and I vowed to make sure she met not just some kids, but THE kids. I knew if I got her hooked up with Bo, Scott, and the Stairsteps, the next two weeks would be easy as pie for her. As my mother had always told me, it's all in who you know. I decided our first stop after we left would be my cousin Bo's house. He'd get a kick out of how tiny she was and what a deep, melodic voice she had, and she'd . . . well, just like everyone else who'd ever met my cousin, she'd be naturally drawn to him. He was too much of a sweetheart and a clown not to like. Then, if Scott took her under his wing, no one would dare treat her any way but nice. He was such a natural-born leader, whatever he said would go; that's the way it had always been. And the Strickland brothers would be the icing on the cake! Bubba was too big for anyone to want to start an argument with. Throw in Tully and Aubrey and that was just too many Strickland boys to mess with.

Come Monday morning, Della Rooney would start school with the best group of friends she could ever have hoped to make.

CHAPTER 9

I'd been right to bring Della over to meet my cousin first, although it didn't seem that way initially. We could hear the television blaring as we climbed the front steps. Family doesn't knock, so we walked right in.

Bo was standing in the middle of the living room in his underwear, staring at the TV and scratching his butt. His honey-blond hair was sticking up all over his head and there was a dried milk mustache on his upper lip. He broke wind. Della slapped her hands over her mouth to stifle a giggle and I just shook my head. Okay, maybe it was time to rethink the "family doesn't knock" rule. I cleared my throat.

"Oh! Hey, Rache—" Bo started. Then he spotted Della standing behind me. "Aw, good Gawd in heaven, Rachel!" He started slapping himself all over, trying to cover everything at once. "Gimme a break, man!" He scurried down the hall, his hands covering his backside. "Cheese an' rice!" His bedroom door slammed.

Della and I held it together for a split second, but as soon as our eyes met, the laughter exploded up out of us. I sputtered and doubled over while Della squealed and giggled through her fingers, trying not to laugh out loud. She finally gave up and just let it go. Her laughter was rich and infectious and got me going even harder. I felt tears squirting out of my eyes as I held my belly and tried not to fall to the floor. Della was doubled over next to me, whooping and gasping for air, and I knew poor ol' Bo would be able to hear us, but there was nothing we could do about it. It was just one of those moments. I wondered how long he would hide in his room before he collected himself enough to come back out. Still gasping for air, I put my hand on Della's back and guided her to the sofa.

"I guess maybe it'll take my cousin a few minutes to get dressed," I told her. "We might as well relax and watch a little TV."

It took more than a few minutes, but Bo, red-faced and unable to make eye contact, finally made his appearance. His hair was damp and freshly combed, the milk mustache was gone, and he had pulled on cut-off jeans and a tee shirt. His blush deepened as I rose and pulled Della up from the sofa to make introductions. When they shook hands, Della displayed enough decorum to smile up at him without giggling. Bo still couldn't make eye contact.

"Um, yeah!" He fiddled with his earlobe and looked everywhere but at us. "So . . . what've y'all been up to so far today?" He was making a valiant effort to put his earlier indiscretions behind him and pretend Della hadn't seen him in his all-untogether. I told him about the two Yankee boys at the Magic Oak Tree. His eyes blazed with green fire when I got to the part about us nearly being pushed out of the tree. He was literally hopping mad by the time I finished.

"Are you kiddin' me, Rache?" Bo was hot! "Yankees? In OUR tree? Thinkin' they was gon' throw MY cousin out of it? Are they still there?" He was fired up and ready to wage part two of the Civil War right then and there, but I stopped him.

43

"It's okay, Bo." I spoke soothingly. "They got theirs." I told him what Nudgie Harden had done to them with the moss and the red bugs. That brought a twinkle to his eyes.

"Aw, man!" He whooped and slapped his thigh. "Them ol' boys ain't gon' know what hit 'em . . . or rather, what BIT 'em!" He chuckled with evil delight.

Next I told him about Della having to start school on Monday with no friends and only two weeks left in the school year. "I was thinking of calling up the Stricklands and seeing if Scott was back from Bethesda yet," I said. "I want to take her down to one of the docks. Do you know this girl has never seen a river or been swimming or out in a boat or anything?"

Bo's reaction was classic: He gaped at her, shook his head in disbelief, then ran to the kitchen to use the phone. Within minutes he was back and had a solution to all of Della's problems.

"Okay, y'all!" He was already talking before he entered the room. "Here's how it's gon' go: The Stricklands are gon' meet us at Morgan's dock in about an hour. Scott just got home so he's gon' grab a quick sammich, then gas up his motorboat an' put air in the inner tube. He'll pick us up at the end o' the dock as fast as he can get there. We're gon' spend the day tubin' right there off Bird Island." Bo looked down at Della. "While we're waitin' for Scott, I suggest we teach this little munchkin how to swim because, from the sound o' things, I bet she don't know how." He grinned. "An' don't you even worry, Della; I'm a good lifeguard. I'll save ya if ya sink." He gave her a wink and it was her turn to blush.

I smiled and shook my head. Good ol' Bo. He really was the best. "Alrighty then." I looked at Della. "Let's go back to your house and get your swimsuit."

I sent up a silent prayer that Della's mother would let her go.

CHAPTER 10

It felt like it was all about to go south when we arrived back at Della's house and told her mother what all we had planned. But between Della's pleading and Bo just being Bo, everything was back on track in no time at all. In fact, not only did Mrs. Rooney give Della her permission to go, but the next thing we knew, we were seated around their kitchen table having BLTs, Wise potato chips and fresh-squeezed lemonade. ("fresh-squozen," Della called it) There was even extra of everything wrapped up and packed in a big basket for us to take for later, along with a gallon jug of lemonade! Bo was ecstatic about that, and was definitely developing a "Mama crush" on Mrs. Rooney. The way she kept doting on him, offering him more sandwiches and refilling his glass, it was pretty obvious she had fallen for his charms as well. My cousin was impossible not to love.

We were running late by the time Bo finally had his fill of BLTs and we were able to head out to Morgan's dock. We walked briskly straight down Beckman Avenue, past the Magic Oak Tree (the Yankee boys were gone by then, which was a good thing for them considering the look in Bo's eyes as we approached), cut through the woods past the Big Hole, which was just starting to fill up with kids, and came out just up the road from the Morgans' house. We headed down that way, turned left at the end of the road, and hurried along the sandy path to where we could see the Stairsteps waiting by the dock. When he saw us coming, Bubba made a big show of looking at his watch. Yes, we were late, but all was forgiven when Bo, after introducing Della, made an equally big show of displaying all the food Della's mother had sent for us to share.

The dock was long and narrow and snaked over marsh grass and oyster beds until it reached the open river. At high tide, there would be water below, but the tide was just coming in, so everything from the mud up was visible. I half expected Della to have another bad bout of fear, but she stepped out onto the dock between Bo and me and started walking. The only indication that she might've been a little fearful was the tension I could see in her shoulders. It occurred to me that she was bound and determined to show me that she wasn't the scaredy-cat little baby she felt she'd been earlier in the tree. I knew it was taking a Herculean effort on her part, and I was proud of her. We reached the end of the dock in no time flat.

The expression on Della's face was priceless when she got her first look at the Vernon River and I wished I'd had a camera. It was warm and sunny and the few wispy clouds in the sky looked like white cotton candy. There was a light breeze that blew tiny peaks up on the surface of the water, and the sunlight sparkled and glinted off of them, while across the river a small family of porpoises spouted and frolicked. It was the perfect day for someone to see their first river and Della was mesmerized. She stood on the end of the dock and just stared and stared while the rest of us tramped down the ramp to the floating dock. It took her a moment, but she finally snapped out of it and looked down to where we were waiting. She eyed the ramp uneasily and I thought we were about to have a problem, but she swallowed hard, took a deep breath and slowly started down. She smiled when she made it, and I was amazed thinking about how many firsts this tiny girl had experienced today and how much fear she had overcome. Once again, I felt proud of her.

"Well, who'd-a-thought?" That seemed to be her catch phrase whenever she was caught by surprise. "This part of the dock isn't built the same way as the rest of it; this part just floats up and down on top of the water. That is so smart!" She smiled at the boys and they all blushed as they smiled back. Yup, that voice! You couldn't help yourself; you just had to love her when she spoke.

Regaining his composure, Bo walked over and handed her the life vest he had retrieved from Mr. Morgan's fishing shack at the top of the ramp. She turned it around in her hands, then looked up at him quizzically. He quickly explained what it was and told her to put it on.

She held it out from herself and gave it a funny look. "Uh, Bo?" she asked. "How exactly do I do that?"

He took back the vest. "Here," he said, "lemme help ya."

Oh, this was going to be priceless! Smirking, I crossed my arms and watched. Bubba stepped up beside me; he had a big grin on his face, too. Obviously he, like me, knew what was coming.

The type of vest that Bo had handed her was made for younger children, but it was the only one we had that would fit Della. This particular vest had to be put on like you'd put on a jacket. Then you had to reach down to the top of your thighs, hook the zipper together and get it zipped from crotch to chin. Next there were three separate straps connected in the back that wrapped all the way around and hooked together over the zipper: one at the lower belly, one just below the ribs, and one across the chest. Finally, you had to reach down and under and pull a final strap forward between your legs and attach it securely to a ring located just below your belly. Normally this was no problem, but Bo had just offered to do all of it for Della, and it would be interesting to see how far he could actually get. He didn't even make it past the zipper.

"Um . . . I . . . uh . . . I can't . . . uh. . . ." Bo's face was scarlet. He took a step back, still stammering. There was sweat popping out on his forehead and he seemed to be at a real impasse.

I grinned over at Bubba, who seemed to be enjoying my cousin's predicament a little too much. I shook my head and stepped over to Della. "Never mind, Bo." I grinned at him. "I've got this. Why don't you boys go ahead and get cooled off?"

Bo shot me a grateful look, kicked off his old sneakers, and stepped to the edge of the dock.

"NUTCRACKER!" Bo screamed and leaped off the edge. He hit the water in a most undignified position, but when he came up sputtering, he was back to his old self. The Stricklands were right behind him, and within seconds the water was full of slippery, screaming boys.

"What did he just say?" Della's eyes were huge.

I shook my head. "Bo just said exactly what you think he said," I answered.

Della shook her head. "And why didn't he help me put on this vest like he said he . . . OH!" I had reached between her legs to retrieve the strap. "I see!" She giggled and blushed. "I guess it's better that you help me, huh, Rachel?" We smiled at each other.

"Okay," I said when I was done. "The vest is on. You are now *The Unsinkable Molly Brown!*"

Della grinned up at me. "Oh, I love that movie!" she said.

Hmm . . . Tarzan at the Magic Oak Tree, Molly Brown at the river. It seemed Della had an affinity for the same kind of movies I did. That might be something else we could do this summer. Right now, it was time for a swimming lesson.

Della had walked to the edge of the dock and was watching the boys splash and horse around. Bo noticed her standing there and swam over to the ladder. "Over here, Della," he called up to her. "You can ease in right here . . . unless ya wanna jus' jump." He noticed the alarm that crossed her face. "Okay," he conceded, "the ladder it is. Come on over an' sit at the top of it with your feet on the rungs." She did as she was told. "Now." Bo looked her in the eyes. "I promise you, I will not let ya sink. I already told ya that once today, remember?" Della nodded. "You couldn't, anyway, because this here vest won't let ya." Bo appraised her quickly, and then smiled. "Okay," he said, "ease on in!"

It had gone dead silent as we all held our breaths, waiting to see what Della would do. Most kids took a little coaxing and some you just had to push in, but I didn't know of a single one of us who would've had the heart to do that to Della. I just hoped her newfound courage would extend this far.

Della slid down to sit on the top rung. Bo put a hand through one of the straps on her vest and gave her a reassuring nod. Della glanced back at me, gave Bo one last look, and slid into the water. She squealed once, very softly, and gasped, but that was it. She bobbed like a cork as we all clapped and cheered for her.

Della's smile was huge and radiant as Bo pulled her away from the dock and began showing her how to kick and stroke. "Hey! Look at this, y'all," he crowed. "She's a natural."

I started to make an Esther Williams comparison, but I decided we'd had enough movie references for one day. Instead, I took two big steps and leaped off the dock. I hit the water right beside Della and came up sputtering. It was the end of May, but the water was still a little chilly. I looked over at Della; her face was so full of delight I couldn't help but laugh out loud.

"Okay, y'all," I called to the boys. "Let's hurry up and get this girl comfortable in the water. Our river chariot shall be arriving post haste."

Bo screwed up his face in confusion. "What the heck did you jus'
. . . . Oh!" He finally got it. "You mean Scott! Yeah, we need to get
her ready if she's gon' go tubin'. Come on, Della. Get back up on the
dock. You need to practice jumpin' in an' climbin' out. Scott's boat
don't have a ladder."

By the time Scott arrived, Della was as comfortable in the water
as the rest of us, although she still wore the vest. The Vernon River
usually resembled split pea soup and visibility was never good, so
we all came to a silent agreement that Della should keep the vest on
until we were positive she didn't need it anymore. I, for one, didn't
want to have to explain to Mrs. Rooney how we'd lost her daughter
in the river.

***

Scott's family lived in a big house on Burnsed Island, right on Moon
River. (Yup, THAT Moon River.) His father's contracting company
did well enough to allow Scott a few luxuries. They had a nice, big
dock with a covered gazebo and a screened-in, outdoor kitchen built
right onto the end of it, and a floating dock attached to one side with
several different kinds of boats moored to it. Just a few steps across the
yard, a brick and concrete patio surrounded an inground swimming
pool and a basketball court.

When I thought about it, I was amazed that they could have so
much and still be so down-to-earth. Scott just considered himself
"highly favored." That's why he never seemed to mind including his
friends in his good fortune. He said God wouldn't have blessed him
with so much if He hadn't wanted Scott to share. That was just who
Scott was, and none of us took for granted how lucky we were to have
him as a friend. He also just happened to be a bunch of fun to have
around and I, for one, couldn't wait for him to arrive.

Because of how sound travels across the marshes, we could hear him long before we could see him, so we'd already scrambled up onto the dock by the time he roared around the bend. He was in his bright-red-and-white ski boat, the one with the walkthrough windshield and extra seating in the bow. Bo must've told him how many of us there were. Despite his youth, Scott was an experienced river pilot. His father had spent a great deal of time teaching him. He cut the motor just short of the dock and let the boat's momentum carry it up to where we waited. He tossed a line to Bo to tie off, then joined us on the dock.

"What a day!" he exclaimed. "This was a great idea, Bo!" Scott took off the aviator sunglasses he was wearing and smiled at us. (More butterflies! What was wrong with me?)

His smile deepened when he turned to Della. "Well, hello there." Scott extended his hand in greeting. "You must be Della. My name's Scott Bashlor. It's really great to meet you." Della, seemingly in awe, looked up at him for a moment before finally taking his hand. She appeared unable to speak. "I hear this'll be your first time in a boat. I hope you enjoy it." He smiled warmly down at her, obviously trying to put her at ease. She blushed, swallowed hard, and nodded. Scott chuckled, let go of her hand, and turned back to the rest of us. "Well, what are we waiting for?" He stepped back into the boat. "Let's go tubing!"

Bubba untied us from the dock, and Bo made sure to grab the basket of food and the lemonade as we scrambled into the boat and found seats. The boys all sat in the main section near the stern so they could help with the tube and towline, and maybe get a chance to drive the boat. I took Della with me. I loved sitting in the bow, and I wanted to show her what it was like. She was smiling and her eyes shone with excitement as Scott started the engine and eased us away from the dock. Once we were clear, he pushed the throttle all the way forward and we were off, cutting through the water like a hot knife through butter. As always, the bow rose high above the waves. That was my favorite part, and I whooped and hollered at the thrill. Beside me, Della squealed and laughed.

Scott motored up and down the river several times to let Della get used to the speed and the way the boat cut sharply when it turned. He finally throttled down and turned to help the others with the tow-line and inner tube. We floated peacefully midway between Morgan's dock and Bird Island. I reclined on the seat cushions and took a deep, contented breath through my nose. There was nothing like the briny smell of the river. It had been a part of my life since I was born, and it smelled like home. Next to me, Della stayed seated as she took in her surroundings. She still had a huge smile plastered across her face. I couldn't blame her for that. This was paradise on earth!

Finally the boys had everything ready. It was decided that Bo would go first since he was the one who had offered to teach Della how to do everything. He brought her back to the stern of the boat and showed her the tube and towline, explaining how to lie on the tube and hold on to the rope. She paid close attention so she'd be ready when it was her turn. Bo positioned her in one of the backward-facing seats so she could see everything; then he tossed out the tube and jumped in after it. When Bo had swum far enough away to be safe, Scott nudged the boat slowly forward, just far enough to pay out the line while Bubba fed it out by hand to keep it from getting tangled.

"Okay," Bo called up to Della. "Let's go over it again: first I just scooch myself up onto the tube an' grab the rope. I put my belly in the hole, then spread my legs out for balance, like this." He demonstrated and asked if she understood. Della nodded her head, her brow furrowed in concentration. "Once I'm ready, I jus' wave one o' my arms, then grab the rope again real quick. Bubba's our spotter, so he'll let Scott know to stop if I go flyin' off."

"What do you mean 'if'?" Scott called back to him. We all laughed, but Della looked confused.

Bo saw her face and explained. "The challenge is to stay on for as long as possible, but half the fun is flyin' off. My job is to stay on for as long as I can, but Scott's job is to see how quick he can sling me off. It's like playin' Crack the Whip, only with a boat an' a' inner tube!" Della smiled in understanding. "Okay, GODfrey, let's do this big, bad thang! Yeehaw," he screamed.

Bo was pretty good on a tube, but Scott took it easier on him than usual at first so Della wouldn't get too scared watching. Eventually, though, Scott had the boat up to top speed and the inevitable happened: Bo went flying sideways off the tube, skidding over the surface of the water, flailing and somersaulting from one unbecoming position to another before finally sinking below the surface. Bubba had signaled Scott as soon as Bo went flying, and the boat had already circled around by the time he went under. We watched him bob to the surface as Scott slowly pulled the boat up nearby.

Bo swam over and hauled himself up and over the side, yelling from the adrenaline rush. We all joined in on the celebration and congratulated him on his tubing prowess. Grinning, he stood and gave a mock bow, then turned to Della. We were instantly silent. "Okay, squirt," Bo teased, "you're up next!" Della nodded solemnly.

Scott broke in, "But don't worry. "I'll go a whole lot slower and easier on you than I did on Bo. We won't do anything crazy until you're ready."

"Yeah," Bubba added, "an' if ya do slide off, I'll tell Scott right away an' we'll be back around to pick ya up, quick as lightnin'." It was funny how quickly they'd all taken on the mantle of overprotective big brothers.

I had to put in my two cents: "Just remember everything Bo showed you and you'll be fine."

"Oh, yeah," Bo added, "I forgot to tell ya: If ya want Scott to go faster, jus' point your finger up in the air an' make a circle with it, like this." He demonstrated. "That's our signal for more speed. Got it?"

Looking more like she was headed to the gallows rather than about to have the time of her life, Della nodded, took a deep, quivering breath, and jumped over the side. Bo had let out the towline and had the tube in position for her. He coached her up onto it and got her hands into place. When she looked as comfortable as she was going to get, he asked if she was ready. She gave him a very shaky thumbs-up and Bo returned it with a grin. "Atta girl," he called to her. Then to Scott, "Okay, let's go!"

I think every single one of us held our breaths when Scott eased the throttle forward, and every eye stayed glued to our newest friend. We needn't have worried, though; Scott drove the boat so slowly I think I could've gone faster if I'd gotten out and swum. He towed her at a snail's pace up and down the stretch of river in front of Morgan's dock. I shook my head at one point, thinking she looked more like alligator bait in a Louisiana bayou than someone tubing behind a speedboat. Bo finally called to her, asking if she was ready for more speed and she nodded in affirmation; Scott inched the throttle forward.

Della's eyes, shining with excitement, grew to moon-size. I expected her to squeal and beg Scott to slow down, but she kept signaling to go faster. Soon she was skimming over the water at nearly full speed. She was doing very well, but we were getting near the point in the river where Scott would have to turn the boat around and go the other way—her first time turning at this speed. He swept wide to starboard before banking gently to port, being as careful as he could, and we all cheered when Della held on all the way through the turn. Scott added a gentle slalom pattern and she still held fast. It wasn't until Scott banked to port again that she finally lost her grip. It had been a long ride, and I think her little arms must have given out. She skipped across the surface on her fanny, tumbled end over end a couple of times, then came to rest bobbing in the water.

Her smile was radiant, and we all cheered and pounded on the gunwale as Scott brought the boat around and slowly pulled up next to her. Bo was so excited and proud that he hit the water next to her before the boat had even stopped. He wrapped one arm around her as he fist-pumped the air with his free hand and let loose a shrill rebel yell. Beside him in the water, Della cut loose with a rebel yell of her own, probably the first one of her life. She started to scramble into the boat, but Bubba got to her first. He reached over the side, grabbed her by the top of the vest, and hauled her straight up out of the water and into a huge bear hug.

"Ya done good, girl," Bubba crowed, nearly crushing her. "Ya done real good!" The two younger Stairsteps, cheering and clapping, echoed his sentiment.

Della was beaming when Bubba set her back down and I grabbed her in a bear hug of my own. By the time I let go, Bo had gotten back in the boat. He grabbed her and danced in a circle with her, both of them laughing and stumbling over all our bare feet.

When Bo finally turned her loose, I realized Scott was stepping up to offer his own embrace. I felt the blood drain from my face and a strange clenching sensation in my chest that I'd never experienced before. I felt a sudden flash of resentment toward Della and had to force myself to continue smiling. Okay, I thought, this is getting to be too weird. I don't know what's going on, but it has to stop. I took a deep, cleansing breath, trying to shake off the negative vibes.

Scott gave Della one quick, proper squeeze ("squozen," I heard her say in my head) and let her go. She was still beaming as she turned back to me and grabbed me in another hug. "Oh, Rachel," she whispered. "This has been the best day of my whole life! Thank you, thank you, thank you!" I hugged her back, feeling the resentment drain away. She was just too sweet and lovable to be mad at. I couldn't figure out for the life of me why I'd felt that way anyway.

We spent the next three hours roaring up and down that stretch of river, taking turns on the tube, and I have to admit: I'd never enjoyed it as much as I did that day. Bo made sure we stopped long enough to polish off the sandwiches and lemonade Mrs. Rooney had packed for us. No child anywhere truly believes the old wives' tale about waiting one hour after eating before going back into the water, so we went right back to tubing as soon as the food was gone. By the time we were done for the day, the sun was just beginning to dip toward the horizon, and everyone was ready to head home.

Scott pulled up to Morgan's dock and let us out. We all thanked him profusely and said our goodbyes. He smiled and told us to not be late for Sunday school the next morning, then reminded Bo and me to invite Della and her parents. Then he pushed the throttle forward and roared away from the dock, his light-blond hair red in the setting sun and his aviator sunglasses sitting perfectly on his sunburned nose. He turned and waved as the boat roared around the bend; then he was gone. We could hear his boat in the distance as he barreled toward the channel that would take him to Moon River.

Bo picked up the lunch basket, I grabbed the empty gallon jug, and we all headed back up the dock toward home. No one spoke; we were all too tired and content.

It had been a perfect day.

CHAPTER 11

Sunday morning dawned clear and warm and, as always, I was awakened by the mouthwatering aromas of coffee brewing and bacon frying. Sundays were the day we were able to enjoy breakfast together as a family, and my mother always went all out: eggs, bacon, sausage, grits, toast, REAL orange juice (hang the Tang!), and coffee. This year, I'd been permitted to start having a little coffee on Sundays—more sugar and milk than coffee really, but it made me feel grown-up and I was proud to be old enough to have it.

As always, I sat and enjoyed my breakfast while sharing the Sunday funnies with my father. We both got a big kick out of *Li'l Abner* and *Beetle Bailey*, and I never missed reading *Prince Valiant* . . . and Daddy never missed teasing me about liking someone who cut his hair that way! My mother let us tease and didn't correct me even once. Sunday mornings were a wonderful time at our house.

After breakfast, I headed back to my room to get ready for church. My mother had laid out my clothes on the bed, and I grimaced at how girlie my dress looked. I shrugged and started getting ready. In the mirror over my dresser, I noticed how red my face and shoulders were from my day on the river, which reminded me of what a great time we'd had. The memory brought a smile to my face and made up for my having to wear such a frilly dress. It only took a few minutes to get ready, brush my teeth and hair, and grab my Bible. I returned to the kitchen to wait for my parents.

Bo and I had done as Scott suggested and invited the Rooneys to church when we dropped Della off the day before. My parents and I were meeting them in the schoolyard so we could walk to church together.

It took twenty more minutes before my parents were finally ready to go, my mother in a frilly dress of her own and my father looking dapper in a gray suit, matching shirt, and burgundy tie. They made a beautiful couple, and I couldn't help but feel proud of them. Daddy smiled at me, letting me know that he had his own reasons for being proud. We headed out the door and started across the schoolyard to the place we'd arranged to meet the Rooneys.

We'd just arrived at the designated place when the Rooneys emerged and started across Whitfield Avenue toward us. Della was beaming and waved enthusiastically. She was so happy to be able to spend more time with her new friends, and her parents were looking forward to meeting mine. I guess they were excited to make new friends, too.

Since I'd already met the Rooneys, I took it upon myself to make the introductions, and I could tell that I did my mama proud. She gave me a quick smile and a nod before shaking hands with the Rooneys and saying all the right things. We started over to the church, the women pairing up to chat about women's things and the men striding along beside them, talking about fishing and the weather. Della and I followed behind. She was wearing a pretty floral dress and was just as sunburned as I was. We laughed about how everyone at church would be able to tell which group of kids had been out on the river the day before if the boys were as red as we were. Della said she was glad to be recognized as part of that group.

My family had been going to Cresthill Baptist Church since before I was born. It sat on the corner where Old Montgomery Road intersected with Whitfield Avenue and was kitty-corner to our house, so it only took a minute to walk there.

Once we arrived, my parents escorted the Rooneys to the men's and women's classrooms, which were located on the first floor just off the fellowship hall, while Della and I went upstairs to the preteen classroom. Della, feeling a little shy, was quiet when we first walked in, but she perked right up when she saw that Scott and the Stricklands were already there. They were as sunburned as I'd suspected they'd be. Scott's burn would turn to bronze—it always did—but the Stricklands were all strawberry blonds with pale skin and freckles. There was no tan in any of their futures.

Once we arrived in the classroom, I introduced Della to the teacher, then led the way to where Scott and the Stairsteps were waiting. The boys greeted us like it was old home week, and when the teacher indicated it was time to begin, we all sat together in metal folding chairs. Bubba was asked to pray; then we opened our Bibles to the day's scripture passage.

We were just about to start the lesson when the door banged open and Bo came barreling in like a freight train. In his rush, he sent the door crashing into the wall, slammed it closed behind him, and knocked over a couple of folding chairs. He snatched them up, noisily set them right, and flopped into the empty chair next to Scott.

"Cheese an' rice," he said under his breath. Scott shot him a look and Bo ducked his head. I stifled a giggle; my cousin sure knew how to make an entrance. Next to me, Della was leaning out and grinning at him. Bo, his head still down, looked at her sideways and dropped her a wink. The Sunday school teacher cleared his throat, gave Bo a stern look, then continued with the lesson.

The rest of the class passed without incident, and before we knew it, the bell had rung. Scott prayed us out and we all headed for the sanctuary. My parents were already there, settled into their usual pew, fourth from the front on the left, along with the Rooneys and Bo's parents. The Stricklands and Bashlors were in the pew behind them. Us kids crowded into the pew in front of my parents; we were old enough now to be allowed to sit by ourselves but weren't permitted to be too far away in case one or another of us needed to be reminded to be quiet and behave. Scott, of course, never needed a reminder, while Bo couldn't seem to make it through church without at least two or three.

The hour passed quickly and Brother Arms got us out right at noon. He always kept a close watch on the time as he preached because many of the ladies had roasts or chickens in the oven at home and they'd give him holy you-know-where if he preached over and made them burn their Sunday dinners. None of our families had to worry about that today, though; all the parents had decided it would be nice to take the Rooneys out to dinner after church, so we were going to Williams Seafood Restaurant.

Williams Seafood was practically a Savannah institution. Located on Hwy 80 out past Thunderbolt on the way to Tybee Island, it was one of the most popular restaurants in town. On Sundays, the line to get in would stretch all the way out into the parking lot! We knew we had to get there fast to beat the crowd, so after church, we wasted no time getting on the road. My parents and the Rooneys walked quickly over to our house to pick up our car while the Bashlors took Della and me with them. Within moments we had formed a convoy and were on our way.

As always, the line was long but the food was good. Williams served its food cafeteria-style while waiters and waitresses hurried from table to table seeing to the customers' needs and refilling glasses of sweet tea.

My father had asked for two large tables, one for the adults and one for the kids. It was nice having our own table and we all felt like little grown-ups sitting there with no one telling us to sit up and keep our elbows off the table. We were all on our best behavior, and even Bo made it through the meal without getting into too much trouble—although he did knock over his tea and spill the salt.

After the meal, Mr. Bashlor surreptitiously picked up the check and we all loaded back up for the long trip home. Sunday night classes started at six and church was at seven, so we always rested for a couple of hours during the afternoon. Mr. Bashlor dropped Della and me off in front of her house, and we spent a few minutes arranging to meet for church that evening. She wasn't sure if her parents would go again that night, but she said she would. She wanted to spend the evening with her new friends before starting school the next day.

"I'm still a little nervous about going," she told me, "but not nearly as much as I was before I met you and the boys." She smiled at me. "My mama says she will always love you for what you did for me this weekend."

I blushed and wondered how I was supposed to take that. It made me feel both pleased and uncomfortable. I decided I'd just take it in stride and be glad the Rooneys liked me. That meant it would be easy for Della and me to be friends.

***

The evening services at church were uneventful and passed quickly. All of us kids gathered together afterward to plan on where to meet up with Della the next morning. Bo told her that he and I were required to be there early because we were members of the School Patrol. She had no idea what that was, so he explained it to her. We could tell by the sparkle in her eyes that she was impressed, and Bo practically strutted with pride as he talked. I hated raining on his parade, but I interrupted with the suggestion that we meet at the office when the bell rang since that was where Della had to be. I told the boys that I hoped since she'd already made friends with us, the principal would put her in our class. Della's face fell at that; the thought hadn't crossed her mind that she might end up in a different classroom than the rest of us. We were quick to tell her that we'd all make a point of being there when she signed in so we could tell them we wanted her with us. She smiled, but her skin had gone pale beneath the sunburn. She looked nervous and worried, and I knew she wasn't going to sleep well that night.

We parted ways then, each of us hoping for the best and wondering what the morning would bring. I watched as Della crossed Whitfield Avenue and made her way to her front door; then I turned and headed for home.

I looked back once when I was halfway across the schoolyard; Della was still standing on her front porch, staring down at her feet.

CHAPTER 12

With only two weeks left of school, emotional levels were on the rise, and the excitement and desire for it to be over and done with had the troublemakers in high gear. Fights seemed to break out over the littlest things, and Bo and I were frazzled and aflutter by the time the bell rang that Monday morning. We both had to take a few deep breaths before hurrying to the office to meet up with Scott and the Stricklands. They were already there when we arrived, as were Della and Mrs. Rooney, who smiled and thanked us for coming in to add impetus to her request for Della to be put into our class. We assured her it was no problem at all, that we were all happy to be there.

I glanced at Della; she looked a little green around the gills. I stepped over to her and gave her hand a squeeze ("squozen!"). She smiled wanly up at me, grateful for the support, but I could tell it hadn't really made her feel any better.

She needn't have worried. When Mrs. Rooney asked if it would be possible to place Della in our class, the principal smiled and said it would be no problem at all, especially since we were so close to the end of the year. Mrs. Rooney had paperwork to fill out, but we were allowed to take Della to class with us. We were even given a late pass so we wouldn't get in trouble for being tardy.

Once we left the building, we all whooped and hollered and slapped high fives all around. Della looked like she'd just missed being hit by a train, but she happily joined in the celebration. Moments later we trooped into the classroom, handed the teacher our late pass, and introduced her to Della. She, in turn, introduced Della to the class, then we all grabbed desks. Scott was able to get a couple of the kids to change seats so we could all sit together. Everything had gone beautifully and we all breathed huge sighs of relief once we sat down. Della was officially one of the gang!

Last period found us out at the ball field warming up for kickball. Our team was undefeated, and we were not about to lose a game this close to the end of the school year, so we were *pumped*. Bo, in particular, was one huge ball of high-speed energy and couldn't seem to keep still . . . or quiet!

"Awlright! Here we go! Here we go! Here we go!" He paced in the dugout like a caged animal at the zoo. Our team had first ups and Bubba led off. "Okay, Big B," Bo hollered. "Go to school, now! Go to school! Nothin' to it but to do it!" He clapped his hands loudly.

Bubba waited for the pitcher to roll the ball, then put every ounce of his weight behind the kick. The ball sailed out into centerfield; Bubba made it clear to third base and Bo about came unglued. "Baaaaahahahaha! Attaway, Big B! Attaway! Yeah!" Bo had climbed up the dugout fence and was shaking it like a madman.

I was up next, and Bo went wild all over again when I stepped up to the plate. "Aw, yeah, man! Y'all better back up! This here's my cousin, 'bout to cream all y'all's corn, right here, right now! Aw, yeah!" Somebody in the field yelled, "Easy out," and Bo looked like he was ready to murder whoever had said it. "Come on, Rache!" Bo was really geared up. "Show 'em how it's done, baby! Show 'em how it's done! Big stick, girl! Big ol' stick!"

I took a second to look over at Della, who was watching from the bleachers with the rest of the class. She was staring at Bo like he'd lost his last marble! I sputtered and didn't see the pitcher roll me the ball.

"Strike one!" the catcher shouted.

That sent Bo over the edge. "Holy saints an' glory, Rachel! What in the Sam Hill are ya doin' up there? Getcher head in the game, girl! Getcher head in the game! Cheese an' rice!" He pulled his hair and left it standing straight up, then made a colossal effort to compose himself. Sitting on the dugout bench behind him, Scott was grinning crookedly and shaking his head. "That's okay, cuz," Bo shouted to me "Shake it off, now! Shake it off! We got this! Gon' take 'em to the woodshed. Cut a switch, girl! Cut a switch!"

I heard Della's musical laughter floating over from the bleachers, but I resisted the urge to look at her this time. The pitcher rolled the ball and I gave it a good, solid boot. It soared up over the pitcher's head and dropped behind second base; I made it to first and Bubba scored.

In the dugout, Bo lost his mind! "Aaaaah! Aw, Lawd! Aw, my sweet Lawd! Aaaaah-Hahahahahahaha! Yeah, baby! Yeah!" Bo was screaming. He turned toward the players in the field to taunt them some more: "'Easy out,' my sweet Georgia—"

"Bo." Scott spoke quietly, but Bo heard and turned to face him. "You're up, Bo."

"Oh, yeah!" Bo scurried out of the dugout, high-fiving Bubba as they passed each other, and positioned himself behind the plate, shuffling from one foot to the other from the adrenaline. The pitcher rolled the ball and Bo sent it so high and so far, I wondered if it would ever come down.

Standing on first base, I watched to make sure it was uncatchable, then tore around the bases as fast as I could, but Bo was breathing down my neck and urging me on by the time I rounded third. We crossed the plate almost simultaneously. In the bleachers, Della had jumped to her feet and was hollering her head off. Bo picked me up around my waist and ran around in circles with me, screaming in my ear and shouting all kinds of nearly inappropriate things. He finally put me down when he noticed Scott standing quietly behind the plate, ready to take his turn.

The pitcher rolled the ball before Bo had a chance to get worked up again and Scott, displaying perfect form and athleticism, sent the ball every bit as far as Bo had. He sped gracefully around the bases amid cheers and applause and crossed the plate. Bo went nuts in the dugout, and Della joined in from the bleachers. Only four kickers had been up so far, and we had all made it home. This was going to be a massacre!

And so it went. At the end of five innings, the score was twenty-three to five, and the celebration was great. We had four more games this week, then the season would be over. Since the last week of school would be all parties, field day, and the final day's awards ceremony, we had high hopes of leaving school with a perfect record. It looked good for the home team. Bo was nearly uncontrollable and had us all laughing at his antics as we walked back to the classroom. He had a hard time reining himself in as we filed through the door, but he wasn't about to get detention this close to the end of the year, so he clenched his fists, gulped in several deep breaths, and forced himself to calm down.

"How did we do, Scott?" Our teacher smiled as we walked to our desks. While Scott gave her a recap, Bo bounced in his seat as he listened; it was apparent he was giving it all he had to stay calm and not interrupt. When Scott finished recounting our victory, the teacher applauded and congratulated us. It was only a few minutes until school let out, so we were permitted to talk quietly among ourselves until the bell rang. Talking "quietly" was not something Bo excelled at, but he gave it his best try, and the teacher was tolerant. It had turned out to be a great day for all of us.

***

The next two weeks flew by. That first week, our kickball team did, indeed, go undefeated. (Bo made quite a spectacle of himself when the last game ended.) The next week, between Scott, Bubba, and Bo, our class won almost every sixth-grade first-place medal on field day. I took a couple of second- and third-place medals in track and field, and Della surprised everyone by winning first-place medals for Most Consecutive Sit-Ups and the Flexed Arm Hang. Apparently, weighing so little had given her a huge advantage in those two events.

The final Friday was awards day, and Bo and I each received a Certificate of Merit for being on the School Patrol. I also received an Outstanding Achievement Award for having made the honor roll every grading period as well as the Student of the Year Award! It was also a party day, so all we did was play games, eat junk food, and watch movies. When the last bell finally rang, the exit doors practically exploded outward with excited, sugar-high kids. Our gang, led by a screaming, leaping Bo, was the first to exit the building.

Bo and I headed to my house to show my mother all of our awards and, of course, to get Bo a snack, though how he could be hungry after all the sweets he'd consumed at school was beyond me. We happily gave my mother a rundown of the day, and she immediately set my awards up on the fireplace mantle for everyone to admire. That made me blush, but in a good way. Bo got his snack then hurried out the door. He had his own awards to show off.

Summer had officially begun.

CHAPTER 13

After school the day before, we'd all agreed to meet up at Morgan's dock for another day on the water. Scott was picking us up at ten. Bo was particularly excited because Scott had phoned him the night before to say that we'd be boating near his house on Moon River because his parents wanted to have us all over for lunch. That always meant a backyard barbecue with lots of food and gallons of sweet tea and lemonade. It also meant a whole lot more excitement out on the water.

As the song states, Moon River really is "wider than a mile" in some places and very near the ocean. Consequently, it can be much choppier and more unpredictable than the more serene Vernon River. I'd never seen it when it wasn't moving fast and covered in white caps. Boating or tubing on it often seemed violent, and the ride was always wild. The boys loved it for just that reason, but I felt a little concerned for Della. She had done amazingly well her first time out, but this would be a whole new ball game. We would all be wearing life vests and taking safety measures we hadn't bothered with the last time, but

I decided to speak privately with the boys about keeping a particularly close eye on Della, and I knew Scott would take extra steps to make sure she wasn't thrown about too violently. You could be a little lackadaisical on the Vernon River. Moon River was much less forgiving; it took no prisoners.

Always punctual, Scott arrived at Morgan's dock right on time Saturday morning, and we wasted no time getting underway. Once again, Della and I sat in the bow, and this time Tully and Aubrey joined us. The bigger boys had gotten to know Della pretty well at school and thought the world of her, and the two younger boys felt left out. They were so cute with their strawberry-blond curls, cornflower-blue eyes, and freckles, and it was funny to watch them trying so hard to be chivalrous. I was older than them and had always been just one of the boys, but Della was so tiny she looked younger than them and she was much less a tomboy than me, so most of their genteelness was intended for her.

Scott navigated the waterways quite well, and it wasn't long before we'd left the placid green waters of the Vernon River behind and were cutting through the darker, choppier waters of Moon River. A brisk breeze was blowing, and the white caps made the ride a little rougher than I'd hoped it would be. I saw that the two younger Stairsteps were keeping Della busy, so I took the opportunity to slip back to where Bo was sitting. I had a quick word with him about the water conditions and returned to my place in the bow. As I took my seat, I saw him whispering in Scott's ear and Scott, looking serious, nodded in agreement. Our eyes met and he dipped his chin once, acknowledging my concerns and letting me know that he understood and would take things in hand. I glanced back at Della, who was still deep in conversation with the younger Stricklands. She hadn't noticed when I'd slipped away, nor had she noticed the difference in the water. I hoped it wouldn't be too intimidating for her when she did.

We stopped by Scott's house to let his parents know we'd arrived and to pick up the tubing rig. Scott and Bo also grabbed water skis. This was something new we'd tried to learn the summer before. Scott's father had taken him out for solo lessons, so Scott had gotten pretty good at it, and Bo had started to show some prowess as well. I had only been able to stand up a few times and Bubba, maybe once. The younger boys hadn't managed it at all. I wondered if Della would want to try.

As we pulled away, Mrs. Bashlor came and sat in a lounge chair on the end of their dock so she could keep an eye on us and be available if we needed her, while Mr. Bashlor busied himself firing up the charcoal grill in the outdoor kitchen. I could see several lines tied up and running from the edge of the dock into the water and realized they'd dropped some crab traps. My mouth watered at the thought of fresh crabs for lunch. I'd have to make sure Della got a look at how the traps worked, and maybe even have her pull up a couple of them. That would be another "first" for her.

Just like before, Bo would be the first one in the water. That just always seemed to be for the best; he'd be able to work off most of his nervous energy so he wouldn't be bouncing all over the boat, and the rest of us would be able to gauge the water conditions by how much he got thrown around. It was a win-win situation. In no time at all, my cousin was straddling the inner tube and signaling for speed. Scott was happy to comply.

It was hard going for Bo. The water was so rough that the tube bounced and bucked like a bronco, and Bo was thrown violently around. He only managed to stay on for a minute before the tube reared up, sailed sideways, and sent him tumbling wildly, head over heels. Scott whipped around quickly as Bubba held up a red flag, which was used to indicate to other boaters that a skier or tuber was down. With the surface so rough, it could be difficult to see someone in the water. We couldn't afford to forgo this safety measure like we had on the Vernon River. As I said, Moon River took no prisoners.

When Scott pulled up to him, Bo scrambled into the boat and collapsed in one of the seats, breathing hard and holding his belly. "Sweet Georgia Brown," he exclaimed, still gasping for breath. "That's some rough goin' out there today!" I shot a look at Della and saw that she'd finally noticed the water conditions. Bo saw where I was looking and turned to her. "I think maybe we should go a little easier when it's Della's turn, Scott, like less speed an' no cuttin' corners. An' maybe hold off on the slalomin' til she gets the hang o' the rougher water," he said.

Scott nodded in agreement. "This is definitely different from what you experienced a couple of weeks ago, sweet pea," he said to her. ("Sweet pea"? I caught my breath.) "You'll need to be really careful and not let yourself get tired out. This river tends to take a lot out of you. Even treading water can be exhausting." He looked at her pointedly.

Della nodded, looking fearful. "Maybe I'll wait and watch how you guys do it before I try," she said. "Then you can all give me some pointers." She didn't want to be left out no matter how scary the river looked, but she wasn't going to be foolish, either.

Bubba handed the red flag to Bo, who had recovered from his ride, and clambered over the side, sending up an enormous splash when he hit the water. I prepped the line and Bo tossed the tube astern. Bubba's larger bulk made it more difficult for him to mount the tube, but he finally got into position and signaled for speed. He didn't stay on any longer than Bo had, and when he flew off, he sent up such a large wall of spray and foam that we lost sight of him for a second or two.

Bubba finally came to a stop and Bo waved the red flag so enthusiastically he almost pitched over the side when Scott cut the boat back to pick up Bubba. As we pulled up next to their brother, I motioned to the two younger boys, inviting them to take their turns, but they appeared to be quite content to wait. So I stepped to the stern and got ready to go.

"Oh, Rachel, please be careful," Della called from the bow. I gave her a smile and tried to look more confident than I felt. Bo helped Bubba hoist himself back up over the side, and I dropped into the water from the stern.

It was choppier than I'd thought it would be, and I moved up and down with the swells as the whitecaps smacked my face and washed over my head. I swam a few strokes away to give Bo room to toss in the tube and prepare to feed out the line. I couldn't see Bubba, but I could hear him wheezing and pulling in air as he lay recovering in the bottom of the boat. Bo dropped the tube into the water and I pulled myself onto it as Scott moved the boat slowly forward. It was already bucking like a rodeo bull; this was going to be interesting, to say the least. I grasped the towline, pointed to the sky, and signaled for speed.

It was over before I knew what was happening. First, the tube bounced high into the air, then slammed down hard, knocking the wind out of me. Before I could attempt to catch my breath, the tube went airborne again, flipped over, and crashed down on top of me, tearing my hands loose and forcing me far beneath the water. The last thing I heard before I went under was Della's scream followed by an alarmed bellow from Bo.

I was extremely disoriented and struggled to tell up from down as I choked and swallowed large mouthfuls of salt water. By the time my life vest finally forced me back up out of the depths, I had really begun to panic. Unfortunately, when the vest brought me to the surface, I was upside down. I could feel my feet waving in the air; I knew a sweet, fresh breath was only inches away, but I couldn't get myself turned right-side-up to save my life! I could feel myself beginning to black out when I became conscious of the roar of an approaching boat, and I believe it was the wake from that boat that finally turned me upright.

As my head broke the surface and I gagged and coughed and tried to draw a clean breath, something hit the water on either side of me.

The next thing I knew, I was looking up into Bubba's frightened eyes as he reached down from the boat, ready to haul me aboard. I became aware of warm bodies on either side of me and arms locked around my waist, propelling me toward Bubba's waiting hands. I looked to my left, and there was Bo holding me in a death grip so tight I couldn't turn to see who was on my right.

Then I heard his voice in my ear: "It's alright, Rae," Scott spoke gently. "We've got you. You're okay, honey."

"Honey"? Wow! Suddenly, I was more than okay. I felt a goofy smile split my lips at the same time Bubba caught hold of my hands. He pulled me up with such strength, I nearly flew over his shoulder. Instead, I slammed down hard into the bottom of the boat, where I lay floundering and flopping like a fish, the smile still glued to my face as I continued to cough and choke. My head was swimming and I wondered if I would faint.

Bo hauled himself up over the side and landed practically on top of me. Scott was right behind him. "Aw, cheese an' rice, Scott! Lookit her face!" Bo exclaimed. "She's done gone round the bend, man!" He grabbed my shoulders and shook me violently. "Rachel! You look like the devil. Snap out of it, Rachel!" I could hear the panic in his voice as he shook me again. I was woozy, but I still felt the smile plastered across my face.

Scott appeared next to Bo and got me away from him. He pulled me into his lap and rested my head gently in the crook of his arm. He peered down at me intensely, his blue eyes full of concern. "Just take slow, even breaths, Rae," he crooned as I continued to gasp for air. "You're going to be alright. Just breathe." I did as he said and felt my senses come back to me.

Bo was seated beside Scott, breathing hard, his brow furrowed with worry. Bubba was on his other side, and when I looked back at Scott, I saw Della peeking at me over his shoulder. She looked worse than I felt! I could hear the two younger boys in the background babbling to each other and begging to know whether or not I was dead; that made me giggle.

"Scott? Scott!" I could hear Mrs. Bashlor's voice float across the water. "Is Rachel alright?"

"Scott!" It was Mr. Bashlor. "Son, do I need to get into another boat and come out there?"

Scott rose up onto his knees and waved. "No, sir," he called back to his father. "Rachel's alright. She just got the wind knocked out of her."

"Well," Mrs. Bashlor sounded worried, "it's pretty rough out there right now. I think maybe you kids ought to come in and rest for awhile—maybe let us check Rachel out for ourselves."

"Yes, ma'am," Scott called back.

Within seconds we were pulling up to the dock. Mr. Bashlor was next to me before the boat had even stopped. I smiled to let him know I was fine, but he picked me up in his arms like a baby and carried me over to where his wife was anxiously waiting. He set me down in a lounge chair; she tucked a large, dry towel around me, and they both clucked and worried over me for several minutes. Della stayed beside me the entire time.

"Really," I assured them, "I'm alright. I just needed to catch my breath." I looked over at Della. She still seemed rattled. I smiled at her. "You," I told her, "are one lucky little duck! It looks like you dodged the bullet this go-round; it's way too rough out there to do any more tubing right now."

She looked back at me with serious, round eyes. "That's fine by me."

Over at the dock, Scott was quickly tying up and securing the boat while the rest of the boys milled around, talking and wondering how such a thing could have happened so quickly.

Bo was practically spinning in circles, he was so anxious. He finally turned to us and voiced the question that was foremost on his mind: "So is she gon' live or what?"

***

Since the river was too rough to be out on, we had to find other things to do, but that was never a problem at Scott's house. The Bashlors believed they'd been blessed with such abundance so they could share it and use it to enrich the lives of others. There were always kids all over their house playing pool, ping-pong, board games, and the like. But this was an outdoors kind of day, so it wasn't long before the boys had gathered on the basketball court behind the house. I could see it was going to be three against two, with the Stricklands teamed up against Scott and Bo. I shook my head; my money was on my best friend and my cousin. The Stairsteps were in for a butt-whooping! I usually would've been in the thick of the competition, but I was still feeling a little puny, as my mother would have said, so I decided to take it easy. I joined Mrs. Bashlor and Della on the dock. We were going to teach Della to crab.

"There are different ways to crab, Della," Mrs. Bashlor explained, "but this is the fastest and easiest." She hauled up one of the traps. There were two crabs inside, so she dumped them out into a large cooler. "Here's how the trap works. We bait it with chicken necks, which we tie to the middle of the trap. Next, we lower the whole thing down on these strings, which are attached to the sides of the trap. See how it's shaped like a box when we pull the strings taut? When the trap gets to the bottom and the lines go slack, the sides of the trap fall open and lie flat. The crabs smell the bait and crawl over and begin feeding. Every so often, we pull the traps up by the strings, which close the sides up. This traps the crabs inside. Once we have the trap up on the dock, if there are any inside, we dump them into the cooler. We check to make sure we still have bait, then we drop the trap back in the water. It's as easy as pie!"

Della seemed fascinated with the entire process and was thrilled when she pulled up her first trap and there were crabs in it. "Well, who'd-a-thought?" she exclaimed, squealing and dancing in place. She was terribly excited to have caught her own lunch, but she couldn't bring herself to open the trap to shake the crabs out. I understood how she felt; crabs were pretty scary-looking if you weren't used to them, and they sure could give you a pinch!

***

As I'd predicted, the basketball game was a bloodbath. Scott and Bo were several baskets ahead when the game ended. Out on the dock, Mr. Bashlor was just pulling the meat and corn off the grill, and Mrs. Bashlor had just placed the crabs into a large cauldron of boiling water seasoned with salt and Old Bay. The crabs cooked quickly, and we were all seated around the picnic table in no time at all.

Scott, the perfect host, made sure we all had our choice of sweet tea or lemonade. Within minutes, we'd been served heaping plates of grilled steak, chicken, corn on the cob, and hot French bread, while the boiled crabs were piled up in the center of the table within easy reach of everyone. My mouth watered at the sight, and Bo looked like he was about to float away in ecstasy. The Strickland brothers were just as excited, and Della sat bouncing in her seat. Scott and his parents, having finished serving the food, sat down to join us. We bowed our heads and Mr. Bashlor said grace. When he was done, we dug in.

I had invited Della to sit between Bo and me so we could show her how to crack crab and pull the meat out, but Bo was like a human vacuum cleaner and Della just stared at him in amazement for a few moments. The spectacle of my cousin putting away food could be mind-boggling. I nudged Della with my elbow to get her attention and told her to watch how I did it. Compared to Bo, I moved in slow motion and she'd be able to learn more easily. Within minutes, she was munching away, her eyes closed in bliss.

Scott was watching her, looking amused. "So, what do you think, peanut?" He smiled at her when she opened her eyes and looked over at him. She knew the question was aimed at her; who else would he call "peanut"?

"Oh, Scott! I've never tasted anything as delicious as this!" Her eyes were shining and her smile was huge. She turned to his parents. "Thank you so much for having me over and teaching me how to do this."

Mr. Bashlor laughed and assured her it was their pleasure while Mrs. Bashlor told her she was welcome there anytime. You could see how much it meant to Della to be part of a group of friends who cared about her and enjoyed having her around. I was thrilled by her joy and, of course, that voice still got me every time. I reached over and "squozed" her little hand. She turned her radiant smile toward me, and I had never felt so loved and appreciated. Life could not have been better!

It was too bad it wouldn't last.

CHAPTER 14

If this was my summer of freedom, it was also my summer of unrest. Knowing how much was about to be expected of me and how much my mother was depending on me to restore the family name and our position in society was unsettling, at best. Every day, no matter what I was doing, I found my mind wandering back to this one certainty: I had a responsibility and I could not fail. I had known my entire life that this was coming, but I'd always had some time before I had to worry about it. Now I was out of time, and everything I would ever be or have or achieve over the course of my life depended upon everything I did from this moment forward. It was a daunting realization, and I could feel myself about to buckle under the weight of it. Perhaps I did buckle to some extent; that summer, for the first time in my life, I found that I could not sleep.

Each day I would spend time enjoying myself, my family, and friends, having fun and living life to the fullest. Each night I would go to bed utterly exhausted only to lie there staring into the darkness and listening to the sounds of the night while my thoughts spun faster and faster. It was an unsettling situation; I couldn't stop it, I was powerless to change it, and I was unable to escape its control over me.

What does an eleven-year-old girl do all night when sleep won't come? What task does she set her mind to when it won't be still? Where does she go, what does she do to pass the hours of restlessness?

When I first realized how futile it was to try to sleep at night, I would get up and go into the living room. My mother always went to bed at ten. ("It's ten o'clock: Do you know where your children are?"—as all the TV channels droned each night.) Daddy stayed up to watch the news and weather at eleven and was in bed as soon as the newscast ended. I'd wait until midnight, then go out and turn the TV back on. There was no cable or satellite TV in our area in those days, and all four of the local stations would shut down by two in the morning, so my viewing choices were extremely limited. I'd watch whatever was on and then read encyclopedias, *National Geographic,* and *Reader's Digest* until just before sunup. I'd finally fall into bed about an hour before my mother awoke.

This worked for a week or so, until my mother had a restless night herself and caught me out of bed reading at four in the morning. She was not pleased and let me know in no uncertain terms that I was not to be out in the living room in the middle of the night. I tried to tell her that I had insomnia, but she believed I'd sleep if I stayed in bed. I didn't contradict her. Children were much more compliant and agreeable in those days. Besides, how was I supposed to explain what was going on when I didn't quite understand it myself?

I would have to find a different way to spend my sleepless nights.

***

At the end of Beckman Avenue, down on the left past the Hardens, lived the Godwin family. They were one of the original property owners from back when Mr. Beckman first started selling off parcels of land. They had a beautiful lot and a fantastic dock, which they had invited me to take advantage of whenever I liked . . . but I wasn't very comfortable using it. I, like many other people in the neighborhood, was afraid of Owen Godwin.

Owen was the Godwins' only child. As a young man, he had gone off to fight in the Korean War. I'd heard that he was a handsome, bright, outgoing young man who had always shown a great deal of promise. He was proud to fight for his country and cut quite a figure in his uniform, so much so that all the girls who had known him waited breathlessly for his return. But war, as they say, is hell, and courage and patriotism only go so far. When he finally came home, Owen wasn't Owen anymore. He never spoke to anyone, he was unable to drive a car, and the smallest difficulty would either render him nearly comatose or reduce him to screaming fits of rage. Very soon everyone realized it was better to just avoid any kind of contact with him. That seemed to suit Owen just fine; he never seemed to want any social interaction anyway, and he'd always go out of his way to avoid other people. All he ever wanted to do was walk.

Day in and day out, from morning until night, you could find him walking through the neighborhoods. He seemed to stay out of the woods and off the docks, but he was constantly kicking up dust as he wandered the dirt roads. Us kids were accustomed to seeing him, but we tried to steer clear of him; he was just too scary and strange.

That first summer night after my mother had forbidden me to sit up in the living room reading all night, I found myself instead sitting outside in the front porch swing and wondering what I was going to do to pass the long, dark hours if I wasn't able to read. There was only a sliver of a moon—"God's thumbnail," I'd heard it called—and I had no door open and no light on where I sat. I felt pretty much invisible there in the darkness of the porch, so when Owen Godwin walked by,

I was certain he couldn't see me. I watched him pause in his ramblings, glance around, look up at the moon, and take a deep breath of the hot, humid air before going about his business.

I waited several seconds, then left the porch to go stand where he had stood. I glanced around as he had, then tilted my head back and looked into the sky. There was a large pine tree growing there by the side of the road, and when I gazed upward through the silver-green pine needles, I could see the moon where it sat nestled among the stars. In the past, I'd never taken the time to do that, and I found a comforting kind of peace in it. I closed my eyes as Owen had done and inhaled deeply through my nose. The explosion of fragrances was astounding, like nothing I'd ever experienced. The very air itself seemed alive with the perfume of every flower and blossoming tree in the South. I believed I could even smell the briny green water of the river. The tide must be in, I thought; the aroma was different when the water receded and there was nothing left but mud. I looked back to the moon in wonder and inhaled again. The world seemed so alien, so much more tranquil and silent, more untouched. I began to think that maybe Owen Godwin wasn't so strange after all. Maybe he'd just come to know things that no one else did. With this notion came an epiphany, a certain insight into who Owen Godwin had become, and why. Suddenly, I understood his nocturnal wanderings and felt an odd compulsion of my own.

I turned and walked into the darkness.

"The difference was like night and day." I'd heard that expression all my life, but until that moment, I'd never fully understood the significance, the complexities of the statement. I had grown up in this neighborhood, walked these roads, crossed these fields. I knew them like they were a part of me. In many ways, they were.

But in the dark, long after midnight had passed, I felt as though

I were traveling unexplored territory, walking where no one else had ever been. Nothing was the same: colors were altered, stained by the darkness and tinged silver by the moonlight, and everything seemed to glitter slightly from the twinkling of the stars. And there were shadows. I'd never thought a shadow could exist as part of the night. Yet there they were, only much thicker and oilier than their daytime counterparts.

I was also a stranger to the sounds of the night. I'd always thought that darkness bred silence, but I was wrong. The night was alive with the sounds of birds and animals, and even the trees! Did they groan and squeak that way in the daylight? I swear I could hear them growing and thriving. They almost sounded as though they were trying to uproot themselves and walk with me. The velvet darkness gave rise to a symphony of sounds that didn't exist in the light.

I was mesmerized, enthralled, and completely captivated; I had fallen hopelessly in love with the night.

CHAPTER 15

"Okay, Rache, spill it! What's been up with you lately?" Bo's right eyebrow cocked up as he squinted at me.

We were at my house, sitting in the front porch swing, eating fried baloney sandwiches and waiting for Scott to call and tell us what time to meet him at the river. School had only been out for three weeks or so, and I had only just begun my midnight ramblings, but it would seem my sleeplessness was already beginning to show.

"I don't know what you mean," I said with mock innocence.

"Sure ya do!" He spit over the rail and eyeballed me more closely. "You're too dadgum quiet all the time an' ya don't laugh like ya use to, not to mention ya got some pretty dark circles growin' there under your eyes. Truth be told, ya ain't been right since ya took that tumble on the inner tube the last time we went out." Bo leaned in and looked at me even more closely, making me squirm. "You ain't gone slug nutty on me, have ya?"

I laughed then, but more for his benefit than because I felt like it. I should've realized he would pick up on things that nobody else noticed.

We were almost like twins, we were so close; "twin cousins," they call it in the South. Born only one week apart, we'd shared playpens and cribs. We looked alike and thought alike, so nothing I ever did would go completely unnoticed.

I shook my head and sighed. "I haven't been sleeping very well, Bo," I tried to explain. "There's just so much going on in my head right now. I have a lot on my plate."

Bo snorted. "Ya ask me, ya got way too much on your plate!" He spit again. "My mama always said you was gon' bust a nut by the time ya got to high school if Aunt Syl kept pushin' ya the way she does." He dropped an arm over my shoulder and gave me a squeeze. "I always kinda thought so, too. I mean, cheese an' rice! How much is one kid supposed to take?"

I was floored! I'd had no idea I'd been the subject of that sort of conversation at my cousin's house, or that he felt the way he did. Bo was just so laid-back and easygoing, it had never occurred to me that he ever thought that deeply about anything. Touched, I half-crumpled against him with relief. I felt I'd discovered an ally.

Bo gave me another squeeze. "Ya know," he whispered, "if ya ever need to get away from things for awhile, you can always come over to our house. When you're there, you can jus' be a kid." I felt myself start to tear up.

Inside, the phone began to ring. I sent Bo in to answer it while I composed myself.

He was back in no time. "Hot dawg!" Bo's eyes were gleaming. "Scott says Moon River is almost as smooth as glass today. He thinks we oughta be able to ski!" He looked at me sideways. "Ya think you're up for that?"

I grinned at him. "I don't know, Bo," I answered. "You think you're up for having a girl show you how it's supposed to be done?"

"Man-oh-man alive!" Bo practically crowed. "Look out, y'all; she's back!" He leaped off the porch and headed off across the yard. "Come on! Let's stop by an' pick up the little one. I wanna get down to the dock!"

I hurried to catch up as we headed across to Della's.

***

Scott had been right; Moon River was about as placid as I'd ever seen it. The Stairsteps had met us at Mr. Morgan's dock and were now hunkered down in the middle of the boat, arguing over who got to ski first. The younger two hadn't been able to even get into the water the last time we'd gone out because it had been so rough. They both felt they were owed a turn. Bubba argued that we should just start over from the top of the list. Bo agreed with Bubba, but probably because that meant he got to go first. Scott listened to the debate for a few minutes before giving his own opinion, which, of course, ended the argument. He was Scott, after all.

"I'm thinking maybe I should go first today," Scott said. "The rest of you tubed on the Vernon River the first day we went, but I haven't gotten to get into the water at all yet, and all of you should take some turns driving the boat. That way, by the time we're done, everyone will have gotten to be in the river in one way or another. Besides, Della didn't get to go in last time either, and she may want to try skiing once she sees how it's done. Ladies first, right, fellas?"

No one could argue with that, so Scott stepped off the stern into the water. Bo dropped the slalom ski in behind him, and Bubba took the wheel and slowly pulled forward as Bo paid out the line. Scott slipped his feet into the ski, took hold of the tow bar, and signaled he was ready. Bubba pushed the throttle as far forward as it would go, and Scott came up out of the water clean as a whistle. We all clapped and cheered as he began to gently slalom back and forth behind the boat. I shook my head in amazement. Scott was just one of those people who seemed naturally able to do anything once he set his mind to it. It had always been that way.

Bubba took us up and down the river several times before Scott signaled his intention to stop. Bubba throttled down and Scott released the tow bar, gently slowing down until he calmly sank beneath the surface. Tully held up the red flag and Bubba came around to pick up Scott. When we pulled up beside him, he continued to tread water instead of climbing aboard.

"Alright, I think it might be the peanut's turn." Scott smiled up at Della, who had been watching from the bow. "Did you see what I did?" She nodded, so he went on. "I used one ski because I've had more practice, but we should start you with two until you get used to balancing. So if you jump in, I'll help you get the skis on your feet and give you some pointers."

Della made her way to the stern and jumped into the water. Scott swam over to her as Bo dropped in the second ski. Bubba eased the boat forward as Bo fed out the line. Behind us, Scott had swum up behind Della and had his arms around her, keeping her in position while explaining what she needed to do and helping her as she struggled to get her feet into the skis. I felt the same resentment I always experienced when Scott was near Della, but I was beginning to understand why I felt that way. I blushed, then hoped Bo wouldn't notice. He would be sure to ask outright what was wrong with me. My cousin had no social filter whatsoever.

In the water, Scott had finally managed to get Della's feet into the skis, and she was struggling to keep them pointed skyward. He swam quickly to the boat and pulled himself up and over the side. "Okay, peanut," he called back to her. "Hold on tight to that tow bar. When we take off, lean back and let the speed of the boat pull you up." He gave her a smile. "Are you ready?" She gave him a quick thumbs-up, then grasped the tow bar in her white-knuckled fists. "Let's go!"

Bubba pushed the throttle forward and we all held our breath.

It wasn't even close. The line pulled taut and Della pitched forward, smacking face-first into the water. Aubrey, who had the flag this time, let out a yell and started snapping the flag in the air like he was swatting mosquitoes. Bubba throttled back down the same time Bo hit the water off the stern. He reached Della just as she bobbed to the surface. We waited breathlessly for his report. That was the hardest tumble she'd taken yet.

Unbelievably, she came up laughing. "Oh, wow," she yelled, her rich voice expressing her excitement. "I have got to try that again! Woohoo!" We were all smiling and shaking our heads. She turned to Bo. "Is that okay, or is it someone else's turn?"

Bo gave her a quick hug. "What turn?" He laughed. "All ya did was fall on your face! Let's see if we can get ya a real turn. Ya oughta be able to try til ya at least stand up once, right y'all?" He turned toward the boat for verification, and we all answered in agreement.

Della waited behind the boat while Bo swam out to gather up the skis and I readied the towline. A few minutes later, she was back in the skis and Bo was hauling himself into the boat.

"This time lean back a little bit more an' wait for the boat to pull ya up; don't force it," Bo yelled. "Ready?" he asked. Della answered with another thumbs-up, and Bubba hit the throttle.

We held our breaths again as the skis, with Della squatting on top of them, surged through the water. This time, she kept her weight back and stayed in position for several seconds. Then, amazingly, she stood up. She was shaky, and it wasn't the prettiest skiing we'd ever seen—but, by God, she was up, and we started cheering. The mixture of shock and pleasure on her face was indescribable and made us cheer all the more.

The ride only lasted a few seconds. I think she got so excited she fell over, ending her ride with a pretty impressive barrel roll. Bubba brought us around as Tully hollered and waved the flag. Once again, Della came up laughing and Bo nearly walked on water in his haste to get to her. They were practically dancing in the water when we pulled up alongside. Bo swam out to round up the skis while Della, smiling and breathless, clambered into the boat. Scott helped her in and gave her a hug, congratulating her on how quickly she was catching on. I swallowed past the sour lump in my throat and gave her a warm hug of my own. It wasn't Della's fault I was having my first crush. I wasn't about to hold it against her.

In the water, Bo was swimming back with the skis. He wanted to try to slalom, so he handed the second ski to Scott. I dropped the tow bar over the stern and Bubba eased forward to pay out the line. Bo grabbed the tow bar and got himself set. When he signaled, Bubba pushed the throttle forward and we were off.

Bo wasn't as graceful as Scott—he never was—but there were few things Scott could do that Bo couldn't. Within seconds he was up and skimming along the surface of the water. It was obvious he was struggling a little to keep his balance, but he stayed up and was soon winding his way back and forth behind the boat. After a few minutes, Bo signaled that he was done. Bubba throttled down and Bo let go of the rope . . . and promptly went flipping and tumbling across the water before slowing enough to sink beneath the surface. He came up spitting and sputtering, furious that he hadn't ended his ride as gracefully as Scott had. Accompanied by our laughter, he filled the air with near-expletives as Aubrey waved the flag and Bubba brought the boat around to pick him up.

***

And so it went. Moon River was kind and forgiving the entire day, and we were able to ski until sunset. We were all still learning, some of us quicker than others, but every single one of us managed to stand up at least once, and we were all feeling pretty pleased with ourselves by the time we were done.

Scott delivered us back to Morgan's dock and we walked home together from there. Bubba, always our official timekeeper, kept our pace up to a brisk walk, but the stars were already beginning to wink on by the time we parted ways. It had been a great day, and we were all exhausted. I couldn't help but wonder if I was exhausted enough to sleep instead of ramble.

I wasn't.

CHAPTER 16

As much as we loved the river, summer meant much more than motorboats and crab traps. Summer also meant baseballs, gloves, and bats.

It had long been a burr in my backside that I couldn't be one of the "boys of summer." In those days, baseball was strictly "No Girls Allowed." Our gang disputed this rule when talking among ourselves; wasn't I the first baseman on our school's number one kickball team? Hadn't I been shoulder to shoulder with them in everything we ever did? It just didn't seem fair that I should be left out, but that's how things were back then. Playing on a real Little League baseball team wasn't something my mother would've let me do anyway. So I made up for it the only way I knew how: I turned into the biggest Little League fan the world had ever known. When my boys played, I turned into Bo.

The boys all played on the Cresthill Baptist Church team. Their positions were different from when we played kickball: Bo was at shortstop; Bubba hunkered down to catch; and Scott, who had the golden arm, was on the mound. I always planted myself firmly right smack dab in the center of the bleachers, where I could see all the action, egg on the crowd, and razz the umpires when they made bad calls. This year the only difference was that Della was planted right next to me, ready to do whatever was needed to help support our boys.

Most of the games were played at Meridian Park, a relatively new facility on Meridian Road, although the end-of-the-season play-offs would be played at Ambuck Stadium downtown. There were four diamonds at Meridian Park, so you could get your fill of both baseball and softball pretty much anytime. Any field not in use for a real game was typically full of kids playing pickup games, so I always took my glove so I could at least play for fun if I got the chance.

There were also large swatches of grass surrounding the fields that were perfect for warming up and for playing pepper and hot box. I always grabbed a catcher's mitt and headed with Scott for one of those areas first; I'd been helping him warm up his arm for as long as he could hurl, and I wasn't about to change that now. Lately, warming him up meant having red, stinging fingers when we were done, but I didn't mind that one bit. I was pretty proud of the heat my best friend could bring.

Della and I rode with Bo and his folks to the first game of the season. It was also going to be the first game Della had ever seen, so Bo and I tried to teach her as much as we could on the way. She was excited to be going with us and to be learning something new, and when she first saw Bo in his uniform—white with red trim—she made such a big deal about how handsome and grown-up he looked that he blushed bright crimson and could hardly speak. I grinned at Della and elbowed Bo, which made him blush even deeper.

When we got to the park, Bo ran ahead to check in while I hurried over to the grassy area closest to our team's designated diamond. Scott was there with a catcher's mitt waiting to warm up with me. Della had to run to keep up, and when she saw Scott in his uniform, it was her turn to blush and get all befuddled. He did cut quite a figure, and I understood her feelings, although I didn't like them. It was okay, though; I was the one who got all his attention while he warmed up. When we were done, Scott thanked me, winked at Della, then ran to the dugout. We followed behind at a slower pace as I tried to shake the feeling back into my catching hand.

When we reached the bleachers, we found Bo's folks sitting next to the Bashlors and the Stricklands. They had saved our seats and gotten us some soft drinks and popcorn. (It was too early in the year for "bawled" peanuts.) Della and I sat down in front of them and were soon munching away and discussing exactly how bad a whooping our boys were about to put on the other team. "We" took the field first, and Della was nearly bouncing in her seat by the time Wimpy Harden, who was one of the umpires, stepped into place behind the plate and called, "Play ball!"

Scott was bent over on the mound, carefully scrutinizing the pitches Bubba suggested from behind the plate. Scott shook off the first two signals, then nodded. His wind up and delivery were flawless and as beautiful a thing as you could ever wish to see.

"Steee-raaaaaaaaack!" Everyone smiled and laughed at that; nobody called strikes like Mr. Wimpy; you could hear him all over the park. Our section of the bleachers cheered for Scott as Bubba tossed the ball back to him. He bent over again and chose a pitch. Another wind up and delivery and the batter swung, grunting and twisting around like a pretzel, as the bat met nothing but air.

"Steee-raaaaaaaaack!" Mr. Wimpy's call rolled across the field. Bo went nuts at shortstop, and we joined him from the stands.

On the field, Scott decided on his next pitch, wound up, and let it fly. This time the batter connected solidly and the ball sailed toward left field. Bo was playing a little deep and leaped into the air like a crazed Superman. He came down with the ball looking like an ice cream cone the way it was perched on the end of his glove, but he held on and we had our first out. Scott grinned at him and gave him a nod. Bo sent the ball on a trip around the infield while the next batter stepped up to the plate.

Within seconds, Scott was bent over watching Bubba's signals. Della and I were hollering and cheering as loud as we could while Bo started revving up in the field: "That's one! That's one, y'all! Okay, big Scotty, you got this! You got this!" Then to the batter: "Hey, battuh-battuh-battuh! Suh-WING, battuh-battuh-battuh!" Bo spit in the dirt and took a defensive stance.

This time the batter put the ball right over Scott's head, splitting second base. He made it to first, and Bo let everyone know what to do: "That's okay! That's okay! We got this! Awlright, y'all, let's turn two, now! Let's turn two!"

I had to take a few seconds to explain to Della that Bo was referring to making a double play. Then I had to explain what a double play was. Behind us, I could see that Bo's father was getting a kick out of listening to me school Della in the finer points of baseball. His eyes had the same sea-green twinkle Bo's got when he was tickled about something.

The next batter was a lefty, so everyone in the field adjusted their positions accordingly. I heard a slight murmur run through the bleachers; many pitchers had a hard time pitching to lefties. I sniffed at their comments. They had obviously never seen Scott pitch.

On the mound, Scott wound up and smoked one right down the middle.

"Steee-raaaaaaaaaack!" We all went nuts in the bleachers, and I shot a smug look at the people who had doubted Scott's ability.

On the field, Bo was, of course, being Bo. "Woohoohoohoohoo! Atta way, Scott! Atta way! Put 'im another one jus' like that! Let 'im hit! Let 'im hit! We gotcha, man! We gotcha!"

Scott put the next one low and inside, and the batter sent the ball straight to our second baseman, who scooped it up off the ground and hurled it to second base.

My cousin may not have always been the most graceful person in the world, but on the ball field he was poetry in motion. Bo stepped on the bag a heartbeat after he caught the ball, leaped high into the air to avoid the base runner, who was sliding into second beneath him, then side-armed the ball to first while he was still in the air. It was a beautiful thing to see, and the batter was out by a mile.

Everyone in the stands went bonkers, especially Bo's folks. I jumped up and down and screamed, then turned to Della. "That," I said, "was a double play!"

On the field, our boys were jumping and yelling, and Bo was enjoying all kinds of congratulations and slaps on the back as the team headed to the dugout. Scott smacked him on the butt as he ran by, which made Della's mouth drop open. She looked up at me with wide, surprised eyes.

"That's only okay when they're playing ball," I explained.

"Well, who'd-a-thought?" she exclaimed, then started giggling so hard in her warm, deep voice that everyone around us joined in. They'd all noticed that she was just learning about the sport, and the combination of that voice and her reactions to the game had all of us laughing.

***

It wound up being a pretty good game. Scott pitched very well, and Bo made some amazing plays. Even Bubba got to snatch off his catcher's mask and chase down a couple of pop-ups and foul balls. By the time the game ended and the teams lined up to congratulate each other, we had won thirteen to ten. Our boys had done us proud, and we couldn't wait until the next game.

Della had learned pretty much everything she needed to know to enjoy the game, Scott's arm had held up well, and Bo hadn't embarrassed his mama. All in all, it had been a great evening. To celebrate, we hit the 7-Eleven for Icees and Slush Puppies, then dropped Della off at home, promising her she could go to the games with us every Tuesday and Thursday night. I was next to be dropped off. I leaned over the seat to hug my aunt and uncle, then grabbed a quick squeeze from Bo.

"You were awesome tonight, cousin!" I gave him a big, proud smile.

"Thanks, Rache!" Bo answered, grinning widely. "See ya tomorrow. Sleep tight!"

Yeah . . . like that was going to happen.

CHAPTER 17

Those early summer days were wonderful and filled with river adventures, baseball games, and all kinds of church activities, not to mention the annual Fourth of July fireworks display at Memorial Stadium.

I spent every possible waking hour with Della and our boys and, of course, my mother took me shopping for clothes and accessories every chance she had to get me ready for school. She was terribly excited that I would be attending Calvary Baptist Day School in the fall, so the shopping excursions were much more exhilarating for her than they were for me, but I tried to at least appear thrilled about my fast-approaching new life and all the trappings that came with it. I knew how hard my father worked to make the money necessary to get me where I needed to be, and I appreciated that. It just wasn't something I could think too much about while maintaining my sanity.

Meanwhile, my love affair with the night continued; in many ways, I believe it was my late-night excursions that helped preserve the balance between sanity and depravity. The gentleness of the night, the calm, the solitude—all seemed to heal any damage the previous day had inflicted upon my tender mind. Just walking out of my front door and becoming part of the night was a balm to my soul.

Each night, I walked out to our mailbox, turned right, and headed toward Crumrine's Farm, whose property was adjacent to ours. The Crumrine family had run a real working farm for years but had gotten more into boarding horses the past decade or so. I had always enjoyed going there and watching the farriers and the veterinarians as well as talking to the owners. I had a soft spot for horses; they seemed so noble. But I learned pretty quickly not to include the farm as part of my walks. Horses can be loud and shrill when startled, and then there were the farm dogs, who alerted to any movement or sound on the property they didn't recognize. The idea was to not be noticed, and that was hard to do with dogs and horses bellowing and trumpeting when they realized you were there. So I would cut across the field next to the school and wander up and down Beckman Avenue and, unlike Owen Godwin, cut through the woods and walk out to the docks, though I never walked all the way to the river.

I found that by looking through my neighbors' windows as I passed, I came to know many of them in new and unexpected ways; windows, it seemed, were like portals into other worlds. For instance, Mrs. Morgan wore a dressing gown and fuzzy pink slippers and enjoyed a glass of sherry just before she retired. Nudgie Harden watched wrestling and old movies and, shockingly, sat in her living room most of the night reading encyclopedias, *National Geographic*, and *Reader's Digest*.

There were other neighbors whose names I didn't know who had their own after-midnight predilections: I learned which ones preferred Carson over Letterman. I discovered one neighbor who sat alone and played Solitaire all night and another who had friends over to eat Chinese food and play poker. One man had a ham radio and spent the entire night talking with other operators all over the world, while another man had a stage set up in his living room with microphones and amplifiers; he sat up most of the night playing the guitar and singing country music. Then there was the young college student who spent hours peering at the stars through a telescope.

All of these people began to feel almost like family as I came to know them better. Of course, I set certain boundaries for myself. If certain intimacies seemed imminent, I would avert my eyes and walk away, and every so often I would have to turn my back on someone who was simply melting down, crying about a turn their lives had taken, or who was tormented by the results of bad decisions or some form domestic violence. These were things I could do nothing about, so I refused to allow myself to become a part of them emotionally. My life was hard enough without adding the woes of others to my own. I was, after all, only a kid.

Eventually, I became a little bored with seeing the same people doing the same things night after night. I longed for something new, if not more exciting. One night when I reached our mailbox, I turned left, and that left turn nearly cost me my life—and certainly led to the dramatic and heart-wrenching chain of events that were to come.

That night, I began to learn how curiosity killed the cat.

CHAPTER 18

It had been a long time since I'd seen Owen Godwin. I always kept
an eye open for him, making sure our paths never crossed. I decided
I could be safe walking to the area where he lived as long as I was careful. He wouldn't be there anyway if he walked the dirt roads most of
the night, as I suspected he did. The left turn at my mailbox took me
toward Bo's house and Cresthill Baptist Church, but I cut across the
church parking lot just before I reached Bo's driveway, crossed Whitfield
Avenue, and started down the little dirt road that would take me to the
Round and Round. Once I'd crossed that, I turned left just this side
of the natural arch that opened to Beckman Avenue across from the
Hardens' house and followed the small dirt lane that led to the homes
of the Godwins, the Tuckers and the Sikeses. I hadn't decided on any
particular destination, but the river seemed a good place to go, so I
headed toward the docks.

The river bank was a study in diversity. There were marshes everywhere, but in some places they ended at trees, in other places they
ended at scrub brush, and in still others they ended at large expanses

of semi-hard packed sand. To get to the docks that belonged to the Tuckers and the Sikeses, you had to walk past the Tuckers' house on the right, then past the Sikeses' house on the left. After that, the land sloped down toward the river. Beyond the houses, you had to follow a narrow footpath that crossed over a small brook, cut through scrub brush and oak trees, and crossed a wide expanse of sand.

The sand was interesting because it was pockmarked with small round holes only inches apart. In each hole lived a little fiddler crab, and there seemed to be about a million of them. These crabs had one little claw and one huge, menacing-looking claw. If you stood very still, the fiddlers would come out of their holes and stand at the openings, waving the giant claws back and forth in a beckoning motion. These were the males; they did this hoping to attract a mate. The motion made them look like they were playing a fiddle, hence the name. I'd always gotten a kick out of standing very still in the middle of the sand and watching them wave. After a few minutes of standing there, I would move suddenly and all the fiddlers would disappear into their holes. It was amazing; now you see them, now you don't. It always made me laugh. Sometimes, I made a game out of seeing how many I could step on before they dived back into their holes. The crunch of their little bodies under my feet simultaneously made my stomach lurch and gave me a thrill. On this night, walking in this new direction, I wanted to see if the fiddlers came out in the moonlight. I cut between the houses and headed for the sand.

It took me a minute to realize that some of the noises I was hearing weren't normal sounds of the night. I slowed and listened more closely. I could definitely make out some dragging and thumping sounds accompanied by grunts and heavy breathing. Then, as I got closer, I could hear gruff voices. When I reached the spot where the footpath opened out onto the sand, I stopped short.

There were three men out there, working hard and fast at something, but I couldn't quite tell what it was. I took a step closer, trying to hear and see better.

It was the Sikeses. Rupert "Foxy" Sikes was a widower. Rumor had it that he was a shiftless, heavy drinker who never did an honest day's work in his life if he could avoid it. He was always filthy, had a scraggly beard, and smelled like a moldy old whiskey barrel. He had three grown children named Gary, Derry, and Sissy, who were just as dirty and scraggly as he was.

From neighborhood gossip, I'd heard that Sissy was a sweet but slow girl with a lisp ("Hi, I'm Thithy!") who had pretty much been forced to take over the roles of wife and mother when her own mother had died. Foxy forced her to stay in the house and out of sight at all times. She cooked and kept house, and, from what I'd heard, did any and every other thing her father demanded of her, including awful, unmentionable things that, at the age of eleven, I was just beginning to grasp. I'd only seen her a few times; she'd always had a strange, blank expression on her face, and she was covered in bruises. I remember asking my mother why somebody didn't do something to help her. Mama had immediately shushed me and told me that people didn't get in the middle of other people's business. She said if I saw something like that I was to turn and look the other way; it was just how things were done. I couldn't wrap my head around that, and it gave me a stomachache when I thought about it too much. So I chalked it up to one more thing I would never understand, and I learned to turn my back and walk away.

Now, as I stood at the head of the path, I could see Foxy, Gary, and Derry working harder than the neighborhood rumormongers would have ever believed possible. There was what appeared to be a large pile of tarps wrapped around bushel-sized bundles on the end of the dock where, I could only assume, the three men had deposited them after bringing them up from the river. The three of them were now pulling the tarps off the dock and depositing them onto the sand. There were three wheelbarrows sitting near the dock; it looked as if the men would be loading whatever was in the tarps into the barrows and pushing them up to the house. I looked more closely, hoping to make out what was in the bundles while trying to figure out why the Sikeses were out here in the middle of the night working so hard. Fascinated, I continued to stand there watching as they began to load the wheelbarrows.

Suddenly, before I could react or even scream, someone grabbed me from behind, clamped a hand down over my mouth, and began dragging me—none too gently—backward up the path, away from the beach. Too shocked and frightened to struggle, my body felt frozen with fear, although my mind was going a mile a minute. I could not for the life of me figure out who would want to abduct me like this—or for what reason.

I was dragged all the way back through the trees and over the small creek, but just before the path came out next to the Sikeses' house, whoever had me cut behind some bushes and pulled me down a tiny footpath I hadn't even known was there. We came out of the woods next to the Godwin house, where I was released and spun around to face my kidnapper.

It was Owen Godwin.

CHAPTER 19

I hadn't seen Owen Godwin since the night he'd stopped in front of my house to breathe in the night air—the night I began my ramblings. Now here we were together, me kidnapped and dragged to his house, and no one knew I was here. I was too terrified to move.

He grabbed me by my upper arms and bent his tall, lanky frame so he could stare into my face. In the moonlight, his eyes were a strange, silvery, washed-out brown, wide and wild, and his thinning dark hair was damp and limp from the humidity. He shook his head rapidly and his lips twitched in his effort to speak.

"No! No! Can't be here! Can't! Shouldn't be here! Shouldn't ever! No-no-no-no-no!" He seemed to be caught on a loop. "Gotta go! Gotta go now! Gonna see things you shouldn't! Gonna see what can kill you! Can't be here! Gotta go! Gotta go and not come back!" He released my arms and took a step back.

"M-M-Mr. Owen," I stammered. "I don't understand." My arms were aching where he'd been squeezing them ("squozen!"). "What am I not supposed to see? What's going to kill me?" I knew I should be running, but I was still too terrified to move—and more than a little curious.

Owen took another step back and half turned away, seeming unwilling to be near me any longer than necessary. He wrapped his arms around himself and began to rock back and forth as he spoke again.

"Not good! Not good, what you saw! Better if you kept walking the other way. Should've stayed by the farm and in the woods. Should've kept visiting the people in the houses. Shouldn't have walked over here. Shouldn't have ever!"

I was thunderstruck—he knew! He knew I'd been walking, where I'd been going, and who I'd been watching. But how? I had never seen him there in the dark. I'd been certain he was nowhere around! I was so quiet and careful; I was sure I would've known if he was there. But he'd seen everything. He knew everything.

I was flabbergasted; why had he waited so long to kidnap me, and why had he released me like this and backed away if I really were being abducted?

"Mr. Owen," I asked, "why have you been following me? And why didn't I see you? Why did you drag me away, tonight of all nights?"

Owen Godwin was still rocking, and now he began shuffling from one foot to the other, like a small child who needed a bathroom. "Little girl. Small girl." Owen moaned as he spoke. "Too young to be out so late. Too small to take care of yourself. Too easy to hurt someone so little. And you don't know. You don't know! You don't!" He took another step away from me.

I held out my hands and tried to speak soothingly. "Mr. Owen, please," I implored. "Just tell me why I never saw you. I was being so careful. Why didn't I ever see you? Why didn't I know you were there?"

He continued to rock and mumble, then he spoke. "Don't know the night. Don't see how things are in the dark. Need to learn better. Need to learn so you can hide. Hide and not get hurt. Don't want to see you get hurt! Can't let you get hurt. Can't! WON'T!"

I was floored! He had been watching over me, protecting me?

Three feet away, Owen Godwin stopped rocking and mumbling. He turned to face me and his strange, washed-out eyes gazed deeply into mine as he spoke.

"Crickets are your friends. Frogs are your friends. Shadows are your friends. Trees are your friends. They warn you. They hide you. Learn to listen. Learn to see. Learn from the dark. *Become* the dark!" His eyes glinted in the moonlight as he stared down at me.

"I don't understand." My voice was quivering. "I don't know what you mean!"

Owen Godwin straightened up. "Look! Listen! Learn!" Then he stepped to his right, into the shadows beneath an oak tree, and was gone.

I was stunned. I knew he was right there, but he was absolutely invisible. I began to spin in circles, looking around wildly.

"Stop!" His voice floated to me from the shadows to my left. "Look! Listen! Learn!"

I stopped turning in circles and stood silently, eyes wide as I concentrated on the sounds around me. I heard the breeze that was coming off the river as it whispered through the oaks and moved through the Spanish moss. I heard the pine trees squeaking and groaning and growing in the night. And I heard crickets, millions upon millions of crickets, all around me in the woods. Then, from my left, came a soft rustling and the crickets there went silent. Seconds later, Owen Godwin stepped out of the woods at the exact spot and, watching me closely, crossed over to the woods to my right. Continuing to look at me, he stepped under the trees and disappeared into the shadows . . . and the crickets there fell silent.

It hit me like a freight train: the crickets went silent when someone was there! To my left, where Owen Godwin had first disappeared, they were singing away merrily again, but to my right, where I knew he now stood, it was dead silent. I listened more closely and heard a rustling sound I never would have noticed before, and I realized he was moving through the darkness, coming around behind me, and as he moved, the crickets around him grew silent. I knew where he was whether I could see him or not. To my right, where he'd just been, the crickets were breaking back into song.

I waited until the rustling and the silence were directly behind me, then spun around. "You're right there!" I practically shouted. "The crickets told me! You are right there!" I pointed where I knew he would be and, sure enough, Owen Godwin walked out of the shadows. He was almost smiling, but then he frowned and stepped right up to me.

"Now you know! The shadows hide you. The crickets help you. Crickets sing! Crickets sing, you're safe! Crickets stop singing, you run! All the animals, all the creatures, keep you safe. Tell you when to run. Show you where to run, when and where to hide! If you walk, you better listen! But no more. No more walking down here! You don't come down here! You die down here! You die! Stay by the houses! Stay in the woods! You don't come down here! You don't die down here!" It sounded like some strange, demented mantra. "You die here! You die here! You die!"

Owen Godwin scowled and took another step toward me. He bent and grabbed my arms again. He gave me a shake. "Now, go!" He bared his teeth and shook me again. "You go and you stay gone! Don't come here. Never come here! Don't die here! Don't! You stay gone. Stay gone! Now go!" He pushed me away, toward the small lane that would lead me back to the Round and Round.

"B-but I don't—" I began.

"GO!" He screamed and stepped toward me as though to grab me again, and I took off like a rabbit.

I don't know if I'd ever run so far so fast, but I didn't stop until my feet hit my front porch. I crept quietly into the living room, locked the front door behind me, and tiptoed back to my bedroom. Even though dawn was still hours away, I undressed, crawled into my bed, and pulled the covers up over my head. I was fearful and awestruck by what had just happened, and I knew it would be a long time before sleep would come. When it finally did, my last conscious thoughts were about seeing things I shouldn't see. I wondered what those things might possibly be. What might I see that would make me die? What was Owen Godwin so afraid of? He seemed to believe that my curiosity could kill me. Or would it? Everyone knew he was touched. What could really be so dangerous? Somehow, I had to find out. Whatever it was, I had to know.

Sleep took me.

CHAPTER

It was nearing the middle of July and our gang had spent almost every day together, either on the river or at Meridian Park when the boys played ball. The only breaks I'd taken from that were the school-shopping sprees my mother took me on. Now, as midsummer arrived, our usual routine was about to change.

The baseball team had a scheduled "by" the second week of July, which meant they had no games scheduled. The Bashlors and the Stricklands had both decided this would be the perfect time to go on family vacations. Scott would be spending the week with his parents at Disneyworld in Orlando, Florida; the Stricklands were going camping and fishing somewhere in the mountains near Brevard, North Carolina. That left Bo, Della, and me to our own devices, and there really was only one thing we could do.

It was time to visit the Big Hole.

Although we'd passed by the Big Hole many times on our way to and from Morgan's dock, we had never stopped to play. Della had been asking me about it ever since Nudgie Harden told us its history, but the river was too alluring, and I just hadn't gotten around to taking her. Now the time seemed to have come.

Bo and I had gone over to Della's so we could figure out what we were going to do while the rest of the gang was gone all week. Mrs. Rooney was still taken with Bo and always made sure he got plenty to eat when he was there, so of course Bo wanted to stop by Della's every chance he got. On this particular occasion, we were sitting around the kitchen table eating freshly churned vanilla ice cream with homemade peanut brittle broken into it. Bo was in heaven and Mrs. Rooney was happy to keep him there.

As usual, he got right to the point.

"So, I think the Big Hole would be the place to go today." Bo spoke around a huge mouthful of ice cream. "We ain't been there since summer started an' I've really been itchin' to get in there with my bike."

I had been thinking the same thing, but then something occurred to me. "Della." I turned to her. "I've never seen you on a bicycle. Do you have one?"

Bo stopped chewing and turned to stare at her, his eyes big. My cousin wasn't as observant as I was, so I guess he hadn't noticed that we always walked everywhere.

Della swallowed her ice cream and turned away. She seemed more than a little uncomfortable and I wondered, having been so withdrawn most of her life, if she'd ever been outside long enough to learn to ride. She was silent for a heartbeat, then turned back to face us. "I don't own a bike," Della answered defiantly, "and right now I don't have any plans to." Her face had gone red and her eyes were moist, and I wondered why not wanting a bike could be so upsetting to her. I decided not to press her for details.

"It's okay if you don't have a bicycle, Della." I tried to calm her. "Lots of kids don't. You can just borrow one of ours; we'd be happy to share. Right, Bo?"

Bo, his mouth full of ice cream and peanut brittle, bobbed his head enthusiastically.

Della looked at Bo, then at me before lowering her head. She sat there with such a sad, humiliated look on her face that Bo actually stopped chewing and glanced my way to see if I was as confused as he was. I hadn't seen her like this since the day we met, on the way home after Nudgie had saved us from the two Yankee boys at the Magic Oak Tree.

After several seconds of silence, Della finally lifted her head and spoke. "I'm sorry, but this is a bit of a sore subject for me." She sighed, then continued. "I had a bike a few years ago, a pretty pink one. I got it for my birthday. My daddy worked with me all day, teaching me how to ride it, and he and Mama were so proud of me because of how fast I learned. But when I took it out the next day to ride with the other kids, they all laughed at me." Her voice broke at the memory.

Over by the sink, Mrs. Rooney was watching us out of the corner of her eye, her lips pinched together. This was obviously a sore subject for her, as well.

Bo, of course, was immediately up in arms. "Whadaya mean they all laughed atcha? What a buncha creeps!" He looked ready to murder those kids; over by the sink, Mrs. Rooney looked ready to kiss him. "Why would they do a mean thing like that?"

"Because . . ." Della paused, then went on in a rush. "Because I'm a peanut, squirt, munchkin, all the names people call me because I'm so small and they think it's cute. They think it's funny. They think it doesn't hurt me!" Della looked up at us; her eyes were brimming at the memory. "I'm so little the only bike that fits me is one for a much younger girl. The other kids laughed because I was on a baby bike and I couldn't keep up with them on their normal-sized bicycles. I pedaled and pedaled as fast as I could, but the faster I pedaled, the more they laughed." Tears were running down her face. "I finally gave up trying to keep up with them and went home. I wanted to forget it, to put it behind me, but after that, whenever I was at school or tried to go out and play, the kids teased me and called me 'Training Wheels' and laughed at me some more." She looked up at Bo and then at me, begging us to understand. "It was horrible, the way they made me feel. People had always treated me different because of my size; that and the constant teasing hurt me so much I just stopped wanting to be around anyone, and I never went outside to play again, until we moved here." She swiped at the tears on her face. "Anyway, every now and then, when my family goes to the store, I sit on bikes to see if I've grown enough to fit on a regular-sized one; I haven't yet."

Della looked so forlorn that my heart ached for her. I didn't know what to say, so I just reached over and took her hand and gave it a "squoze."

Good ol' Bo! He jumped up from his chair so fast it nearly toppled over. He was around the table and had her in a bear hug so fast she gasped and started giggling.

"You jus' let me catch somebody laughin' at you, Della!" Bo was all worked up, his green eyes sparking. "It'll be the last thing they remember before wakin' up in traction!" He gave her another hug before turning her loose. No sooner did he let go of Della than Mrs. Rooney had him gathered up in a big bear hug of her own.

"Thank you, Bo! Rachel! Thank you both so much!" Mrs. Rooney had tears in her eyes as she reached to hug me, too. "I am so grateful to both of you for being such wonderful friends to our Della. She has needed that for so long." She began to cry in earnest.

Nothing makes a kid more uncomfortable than a crying adult. Bo and I looked at each other, then down at our bowls of ice cream. Neither one of us knew how to act.

It was Della who broke the awkward silence; she started laughing. "Wow! Talk about a conversation killer!" She laughed again. "That was just pathetic! I think I hear violins!"

With that, we all cracked up, even Mrs. Rooney. Bo, being who he was, happily dove back into his ice cream like nothing had happened. I smiled and joined in the laughter, but I was also resolved that no one was ever going to laugh at Della Rooney again, not as long as I was around.

After we finished our ice cream, Bo asked us to wait at Della's house while he ran back home and grabbed some things he'd forgotten. Mystified, we agreed, and he tore off toward his house. It was about fifteen minutes before we saw him headed back across the schoolyard, and when we did, I was stunned; he was walking back pushing his bike with one hand and mine with the other. I was furious! Had he not been paying attention to what had just been said? Then I saw what else he had with him and I understood what he had in mind. I smiled hugely.

"Bo DeLoach," I said under my breath, "you are a genius!"

CHAPTER 21

It was easy to see that Della and her mother were both a little hurt and confused when they saw Bo walking toward us with the bikes. I knew they would feel a certain sense of betrayal until they understood what he had in mind. I would've felt the same way had I been in their place. I thought I'd better pacify the situation before they jumped to the wrong conclusion.

"I know this looks bad, Bo bringing the bikes over after what you just told us," I said. "But you know Bo better than that by now. Wait until you hear what he's got in mind, Della. Not only are you going to have loads of fun, but Bo is about to make you the coolest, most popular kid at the Big Hole!"

I could tell by Della's face that she had her doubts, but she stood quietly and waited for Bo to arrive.

"Okay! Y'all are gon' like this!" He was so excited that he started talking before he got to us. "We came up with this idea last year an' it worked purty doggone good." Bo looked at Della. "Ya know how when we go tubin' ya lie down on the inner tube an' the boat pulls ya across the water?" Della bobbed her head. "Well," Bo continued, "this is the same thing, 'cept you're on land instead o' water an' instead o' bein' pulled by a boat, you're pulled by bikes. Ya get it?"

Della thought about it, then her face lit up. "I do get it," she said, then frowned. "But how do you keep the inner tube from popping and going flat when it hits rocks and roots and stuff?"

Bo grinned at her. "That's the part we had to figure out last year," he answered. "See this plastic tarp?" He gestured toward a small blue tarp that was folded over the inner tube looped over the seat of my bike. "An' these blankets?" They were folded over the seat of his bike. "The tarp has these big, metal eyelets all around the sides. What we do is fold the blankets up around the inner tube til they're real thick, then fold the tarp real tight around them, like a big, plastic pillowcase. Next, we thread this rope . . ." He pulled a rope out of his shirt. ". . . through the eyelets to keep the tarp closed. Ya gotta make sure to leave both ends o' the rope long enough to tie to the two bicycles. Then ya lie down on top, hold on real tight, an' the bikes pull ya jus' like you were tubin' on the water!"

Della got the idea immediately and jumped up and down, clapping and laughing.

Her mother was less enthusiastic. "Bo," Mrs. Rooney said, "that sounds a little dangerous to me. I'm not sure I should let Della do that."

"Mother!" Della was appalled. "It'll be fine! You know Bo and Rachel would never let me do anything dangerous!"

Bo was quick to set her mind at ease. "It really is okay, Mrs. Rooney. We'll be real careful. I promise! We ain't gon' run her into any trees or anything. We all took turns doin' this last summer an' nobody ever got hurt, not even once!" He looked so earnest that Mrs. Rooney couldn't help but laugh.

"Oh, Bo," she said, shaking her head. "I know you would never let Della get hurt. I guess I'm just being overprotective." She looked at all the trappings of our land tube. "Why don't you put it together and practice here in the yard before you go anywhere else? I think I'd feel better if I could see how it works and be sure Della knows what she's doing by the time you take her to that Hole place."

We all giggled at the way she referred to the Big Hole, but she actually made a lot of sense. Bo got the tarp laid out and ready, then pulled the inner tube off my bike seat. Next, we folded the blankets around the tube, creating a thick pallet. When that was done, we folded the pallet inside the tarp and Bo started threading the rope through the eyelets. Della and her mother watched us in fascination.

"Well, who'd-a-thought?" Mrs. Rooney exclaimed when we were done. And that's where Della got her catch phrase, I thought. Mrs. Rooney continued, "It's amazing what you kids today come up with! That is ingenious, Bo!"

Bo practically glowed under her praise. I smiled and shook my head at him.

Della's house had a very small front yard and there was a concrete driveway, so it didn't seem like the ideal place for her to practice land tubing. Besides, the schoolyard was just across the road, and it was huge and nothing but grass. It was where our gang had practiced the summer before. I suggested we walk over there instead.

Mrs. Rooney, Della, Bo, and I crossed over to the Hesse Elementary playing fields with the bikes and the rig, then Bo and I got busy attaching the ropes to our bikes.

Last year, when we'd first tried this, the ropes kept getting tangled up in the back spokes. It was pretty frustrating. But my daddy came up with an idea for keeping the ropes away from the tires. He welded and shaped a heavy, flat piece of metal that attached just below the bicycle seat and curved up behind the rider. There was a ring on the end of it that the rope threaded through. This held the rope above the tire so it would never get fouled. He attached the first one he made to Bo's bike to see if it would work. Scott volunteered to ride the land tube, and Bo jumped on the seat. They were off like a shot, both of them laughing and hollering at the tops of their lungs. Bo swerved and turned and Scott slid back and forth sideways behind him, but no matter what they did, the line never fouled. We all cheered when we saw how well it worked, and everybody begged my daddy to make metal rings for each of the bikes. He laughed, pleased with his invention, and was happy to comply. Within a couple of days, all of us were set up to pull the rig. It worked pretty well, too, except no one could get up enough speed to give Bubba a really good ride; he was so much bigger and heavier than the rest of us. That's when Bo and Scott came up with the idea of using two bikes. We reconfigured the ropes and attached them to Bo's and Scott's bikes. They counted to three and took off with Bubba behind them. It worked like a dream. Of course, we all had to try it then, and after that we never pulled with one bike again.

Now it was Della's turn to try the land tube. If she was as proficient at this as she was when she tubed on the river, it would be a breeze. Last year, all the other kids went nuts over our invention and couldn't get enough of it. I knew if we rode up to the Big Hole pulling Della, they would go nuts all over again and she would be the most popular kid there. I prayed she would be able to stay on now and that her mother wouldn't get so nervous that she'd forbid Della to ride it. I shot Bo a look and gestured to keep the speed down. He gave me a nod, and I knew he'd been thinking along the same lines.

It only took us a couple of minutes to get everything set up. When we were done, Bo and I jumped on the bikes and Della plopped down on the pallet.

"Okay, munchkin—" Bo said, and I smacked him on the shoulder. "Oh! I mean Della," he amended. "Let us know when you're ready, jus' like on the river. When you wanna stop, jus' holler."

Behind us, Della sat up. "It's okay if all of you call me munchkin and peanut and stuff. I know when you say it you're not teasing me," she said, smiling at us.

"That's right, munchkin!" Bo smiled. "We say it outta love . . . I mean LIKE! I meant to say LIKE!" His blush was beyond crimson, and he quickly turned to face forward on his seat.

Della and I looked at each other and got the giggles. A few feet away, Mrs. Rooney joined in.

Bo, still red-faced, tried to regain some semblance of composure. "Awlright! Y'all jus' knock it off now!" He gripped his handlebars and propped his right foot up on the pedal. "Can we please jus' do this? Cheese an' rice!"

Still giggling, Della stretched out on the pallet again and I twisted back around on my seat. Off to one side, Mrs. Rooney was obviously still a little nervous, but she was trying very hard to keep it to herself. Della pulled herself forward into a better position, grabbed the rope, and shouted that she was ready.

Bo let loose a rebel yell, and we were off.

CHAPTER 22

Bo and I had become pretty proficient at staying side by side when we were learning to pull the land tube the summer before, and with Della on the rig behind us, we were careful to implement everything we'd learned. At first, just to give Della a feel for tubing on land and to set her mother's mind at ease, we stayed on a straight, slow course but, seeing how well Della was riding and hearing her shouts for more speed, we were soon pedaling as fast as we could. As we neared the end of the playing field closest to the school, Bo yelled for us to turn to port and we swept left. Coming back onto the straightaway, he directed a slalom run and we began to sweep gently from left to right.

Up ahead, Mrs. Rooney appeared to be experiencing a mixture of pride and anxiety. As we swept past her, we heard Della shout, "Hey, Mama!" She sounded so excited. "Look at me! Look at me!"

I threw a quick glance back over my shoulder and saw that Mrs. Rooney was smiling and waving to her daughter. That's it, I thought, we're in! We reached the end of the schoolyard nearest Cresthill Baptist Church, and Bo called out another turn to port. As we approached

Mrs. Rooney, he called for a stop and we slowed to a halt, making sure we cut our speed gradually enough that the rig didn't run up and collide with our back tires.

Della was up and off like a shot as soon as we'd stopped. "Oh, Mama," she cried out as she ran to hug her mother. "That was so much fun! Did you see how good I was? It was just like being on the water!"

Mrs. Rooney returned Della's hug. "You certainly were good, honey! I'm so proud of you. Wait until I tell your father!" They stood hugging each other for a moment before Della pulled away and smiled up at her mother.

"So, is it alright if I go with Rachel and Bo, Mama?" she asked. "Please! I want to meet all the kids at the Big Hole and show them how good at this I am!" Della's dark eyes were shining with excitement.

Mrs. Rooney ran her hand through Della's hair, smoothing it down, then laid a gentle hand on her daughter's cheek. "Of course you can go," she said. "You were so good at it, I'm not even going to worry." She smiled over at Bo and me, still seated on our bikes. "And I know Rachel and Bo will take good care of you." We bobbed our heads at her.

"Oh, thank you, Mama! Thank you!" Della clasped her mother in another huge bear hug.

And as easy as that, we were off to the Big Hole.

***

Unlike many Georgia dirt roads, which were comprised of hard red clay, Beckman Avenue was mostly soft, powdery sand, so after walking across Whitfield Avenue, we put Della right onto the land tube and took off. At the Magic Oak Tree, we veered to the right, then headed down the path through the woods toward the Big Hole. On the way,

Bo and I discussed how best to have Della make her big entrance and came to what we felt was a great way to get everyone's attention while making her unforgettable. It was risky and Della would have to be both careful and lucky, but it was going to be an amazing thing to see . . . if we could pull it off. When we reached the edge of the woods near the Big Hole, we stopped and waited for the perfect moment.

There were kids everywhere, digging caves, running through on foot, sliding on flattened cardboard boxes, riding bikes. It was bedlam of the very best kind!

Bo turned around and told Della to hang on tight because when we took off, it was going to be fast. Then he and I watched for a break in the traffic. Timing was going to be everything.

It took almost a full minute, but finally there was an opening in the stream of kids riding in and out. Bo let loose one of his shrill rebel yells, and we took off. Every head turned to watch as we tore out of the woods and hit the Big Hole. I sent up a silent prayer that we wouldn't lose Della along the way as we dropped down into it at full speed and came barreling up and out on the other side. I could hear the land tube sliding behind us right up until Bo and I left the ground as we exited; then I heard nothing as the land tube, hopefully still carrying Della, followed us into the air. A split second later, we hit the dirt. I heard the land tube slam down behind us as Bo screamed for a tight left turn, which caused the tube to sweep hard around to our right and pull up next to us rather than behind us. Bo called for a full stop, and we all slid around until the bikes and the tube were lined up side by side, facing the Big Hole. Sending up another quick prayer, I glanced quickly to my right, and there was Della, kneeling on the land tube with both fists in the air. She cut loose her own rebel yell and Bo and I joined her.

Immediately, every kid there started cheering and screaming as applause broke out all over the place. I don't know how we pulled it off, but it was beautiful and I was willing to bet we wouldn't be able to do it again in a million years! And just like that, Della was surrounded by admiring kids asking her name and wanting to try the land tube.

Smiling exultantly, I reached over and punched Bo in the shoulder. "Great job, cousin," I said. "That couldn't have gone any better!"

He spit in the dirt and grinned back at me. "I knew this was a good idea!" He looked so proud of himself that he was practically glowing. Then he winked at me and whispered, "An' I bet we couldn't do it again if our lives depended on it!" We laughed together and slapped a high five, then turned to help decide which of the kids was going to go land tubing next. We made sure everyone knew Della had the final say. Beside us, she was laughing and making more friends than she probably ever thought she'd have. She turned and smiled at us, and I'd never seen anyone glow with as much happiness as she did at that moment.

That was the day Della Rooney became Queen of the Big Hole.

For the rest of the day, Della was at the center of a swarm of kids, and Bo and I got to see her truly shine. Her sweetness and fairness in divvying out turns on the land tube along with her compassion toward the smaller children were heartwarming, and everyone there fell absolutely in love with her. Even though we'd brought her there to play, I don't believe she rode the land tube again after the initial ride in; she was having too much fun sharing with the other kids.

When twilight approached and it was time to leave for home, every one of the other kids begged her to come back soon, and a few even hugged her! Bo and I were thrilled for her and promised to bring her back as soon as we could. After some final goodbyes, Della clambered onto the land tube, Bo and I mounted our bikes, and we headed off through the woods toward Della's house. We could hardly wait to tell Mrs. Rooney about our day, so we pedaled as fast as we could.

I personally had my own reasons for wanting to hurry; tonight, I was going back to spy on the Sikeses.

CHAPTER 23

There was a large oak tree just off the path near Fiddler Crab Beach. It was set back behind several large bushes and piles of deadfall, and I could tell it would be hard to get to, but I'd noticed in the past that it not only had a set of Paul Harden's ladder rungs nailed onto the trunk, but also had a small platform built into the branches about twenty feet up. I'd never tried to climb the tree because I'd never really wanted to be on the Sikeses' property, even though the Tuckers shared the beach with them and had often said I could use it.

Foxy and his sons had a hard edge to them that frightened me, especially after a close call I'd had with Gary when I was eight years old and too young to understand that some men might try to touch little girls in ways they shouldn't. Since then, I rarely came to this little beach and did so only when the rest of the gang was with me. But now that I'd set my mind to spying on the Sikeses, this platform seemed like the perfect vantage point, so it was my destination.

I had no idea when the Sikeses headed out to do whatever it was they did, and I had no way of knowing whether Owen Godwin still followed me at night, but curiosity was burning a hole deep down inside of me, and I couldn't help myself; I had to find out what those Sikeses were up to.

As soon as I was certain my parents were asleep, I headed out into the night.

***

It was clear and hot out and I was sticky with sweat in no time flat. I paid particular attention to the crickets and frogs chirruping around me as I moved through the darkness, knowing they would warn me if anyone approached. They surrounded me with their night songs all the way to Fiddler Crab Beach. No one was anywhere to be seen when I arrived, so I wasted no time climbing up into the tree and settling myself on the platform. Below me, I could hear the fiddler crabs exiting their holes and blowing bubbles in the dark. The sound was hypnotic, and I actually dozed off.

I have no idea how long I was in that tree, but eventually I was roused by the sound of a boat motor approaching from way off in the distance. Eventually, I could tell by the sound that it had stopped at the end of the Sikeses' dock. When the motor turned off, I heard deep, gruff voices floating to me over the marsh, and it wasn't long before the voices grew closer and louder. I sat up and faced the river.

Sure enough, Foxy, Gary, and Derry appeared on the dock, coming out of the darkness from the direction of the river. Each of them was dragging what appeared to be several square bundles wrapped in tarps.

As I continued to watch, Derry, who was in the lead, shoved his load off the dock and onto the sand, then ran toward the tree where I was perched. My heart hammering, I hunkered down as low as I could get as he pushed his way into the bushes beside the tree and, one by one, rolled out three wheelbarrows I hadn't noticed there in the dark. He then rushed back to help his father and brother drop their loads onto the sand.

I let out the breath I hadn't known I was holding.

Amid all sorts of grunting and cursing, I watched as the Sikeses pulled their loads over to the barrows. Once there, they opened the tarps, revealing bushel-sized bundles wrapped in what appeared to be waterproof plastic. They loaded some of the bundles into the barrows and quickly wheeled them up the path toward their house. Through the tree branches, I could see them in the distance unloading the barrows into the back of their truck. Then they quickly wheeled them back down to the beach to load up more bundles.

It took them four trips, and by the time the last of the bundles were wheeled up to the truck, I was a nervous wreck; but they never discovered me hiding in the tree. When they were finally done and had driven off in the truck, I climbed down and headed for home. I was sorely disappointed that I hadn't discovered their secret. Although there had been plenty of gruff words and inappropriate language tossed about, nothing had been said that gave me a clue as to what was in those bundles. I was very frustrated but nowhere near ready to give up.

I would just have to come back the next night.

CHAPTER 24

I awoke the next morning to thunderclouds and rain, and I could tell we weren't going to be able to go back to the Big Hole as we'd planned, so I dialed up Bo to see what else we could come up with. I suggested that we get one of our mothers to drop us off at Weiss Theaters; it had been quite some time since we'd been to the movies. Bo immediately started talking about some movie that had just come out about a giant, man-eating shark. I'd read about it and seen the trailers; it was suppose to be pretty good, so after arranging for Bo's mother to drive us, I called to invite Della to come along. She was just as excited as Bo had been, and I remembered thinking on the first day we'd met that she was a huge movie fan.

I grabbed my clothes and headed into the bathroom to get ready only to be surprised by the arrival of Mother Nature. I sighed as I reached for the unopened box of feminine napkins my mother had bought for me months before. She'd given me "The Girl Talk" when I was ten, so I knew what was happening, but I wasn't happy about crossing this particular threshold in my life.

When I was dressed, I closed my eyes, took a deep breath, and went out to tell my mother about my latest milestone. She, of course, was thrilled that I'd "become a woman" and giggled about all the new topics of conversation and womanly things we would now be able to share. For her sake, I pretended to be just as giddy as she was at the prospect, but I was in a sour mood by the time Bo's mother drove up and honked the horn, especially after having to hear my mother's warnings about checking myself often and not letting myself get too wet in the rain. She winked conspiratorially at me and handed me one of her purses as I went out the door. I knew what must be inside and gritted my teeth as I smiled and waved to her over my shoulder.

"Since when do you carry a pocketbook?" Bo asked from the front seat as soon as I got into the car. I glared at him and he quickly turned back around to face the front.

I could see his mother looking quizzically at me in the rearview mirror as we pulled out of the driveway. I knew she and my mama would be getting together while we were at the movie to discuss what was going on with me; that's what sisters did.

I shook my head and decided I'd better make an attitude adjustment by the time we picked up Della. Bo got over things pretty quickly, but I knew it would break Della's heart if I was short with her. By the time she climbed into the car a few minutes later, I was in a slightly better mood. Della, as always, was excited at the prospect of spending yet another day with Bo and me. She chatted happily with Bo and his mother all the way to the theater and seemed not to notice my reticence.

After Bo's mother dropped us off, we paid $3.50 each for our tickets (the most any of us had ever spent to see a movie!), headed to the concession stand for buttered popcorn and Cokes, then sat whispering and giggling in the dark while we waited for the movie to start. When the screen finally lit up, we munched popcorn and watched the trailers. I loved the "Coming Soons," but Bo was squirming in his seat like he was sitting on an ant bed. He was giving it all he had trying to be patient, but it was obviously a losing battle. Beside him, Della was stifling giggles as she watched him struggle to behave.

Finally, the screen was filled with a fish-eye view of something large moving through the water amid the spooky sound of brass horns playing the same two notes over and over, faster and faster. I glanced at Bo, then over at Della. They were both already engrossed, so I settled down in my seat and lost myself to the sights and sounds.

It was like nothing any of us had ever seen; several times we actually screamed out loud. At one point, a torn-up, decapitated head missing an eyeball popped out of a large hole that had been bitten into the hull of a sunken boat, and even Bo jumped and screamed like a girl; he didn't even realize he'd done it, and I was too scared to remind myself to tease him about it later. Della, I noticed, watched most of the movie through her fingers!

After much blood, gore, and suspense, the movie ended and we left the theater. Della looked a little green around the gills, but Bo laughed at the ridiculousness of a real shark getting that big and doing all the things the one in the movie had done. I felt it was mostly bravado on his part. Every kid knew that all movies were based on at least some small grain of truth. It would be interesting to see how brave he was the next time we went waterskiing on Moon River.

When Bo's mother picked us up, she announced that she would be treating us to lunch at Shoney's. While the others looked at the menu, I slipped off to the ladies' room to check on the status of "things." It turned out my mother had been right to caution me about doing this often; I'd nearly had a problem! I handled my business, washed my hands, and returned to the table, trying to ignore my aunt's knowing look. (She had obviously been speaking with my mother.)

The waitress came over then, and we all ordered Big Boy burgers with onion rings and thick chocolate shakes with mounds of whipped cream and a cherry on top. For dessert, we all had huge slices of strawberry pie topped with more whipped cream. It was all delicious, and Della and I were almost as happy as Bo by the time we were done. I left the restaurant in the best mood I'd been in all day.

We stopped to drop off Della first, and Mrs. Rooney met us at the car to say hello and to thank Bo's mother for inviting Della along and treating her to lunch. She then invited Bo and me to come in to play board games and stay for dinner. Although the rain had stopped, it was still pretty wet out, so Bo and I happily accepted. We three kids ended up playing *Monopoly* and *Clue* while Mrs. Rooney busied herself preparing dinner. She, of course, had every intention of spoiling us as usual, so we knew whatever she was making would be fantastic. As she sliced vegetables and boiled potatoes, we regaled her with details of the movie. By the time we finished, she was nearly as green around the gills as Della had been—which was, of course, the whole point! We got the giggles watching Mrs. Rooney's reactions, and she finally flapped her hands at us and begged us to stop. That broke us up even more, and our giggling got her going, so pretty soon we were all laughing. That seemed to happen an awful lot at Della's house, and it was probably why Bo and I enjoyed being there so much. Well, that and all the food. I know that was high up on Bo's list of reasons why he liked being there.

All in all, it had turned out to be a great day—much better than I'd originally thought it would be. That summer just seemed to be like that for all of us.

Later that evening, after thanking Mrs. Rooney for dinner and saying our goodbyes, Bo walked me home, then headed on to his house.

I was stuffed from all the good food we'd had that day and wondered if it would make me drowsy enough to sleep. For the first time that summer I hoped not; I really wanted to know what was in those bundles the Sikeses were transporting. I'd decided to borrow my father's pocketknife when I left the house that night. I figured there would be just enough time for me to cut through the plastic on one of the bundles while the three men were wheeling the first load up to the truck. I could grab a quick peek at what was inside, then scramble back up the tree before they came back for the next load. I figured it would be easy as strawberry pie.

I should've known better.

CHAPTER 25

There was only a half-moon riding low in the sky that night when I set out for the tree at Fiddler Crab Beach. I considered this a good omen, considering my plan to discover what was in the Sikeses' bundles. It would make it harder for me to be seen while I carried out my sleuthing. The beach itself was bright under the little bit of silver moonlight, but it was pretty close to pitch black under the tree.

Knowing there would be very little light where I'd be, I had opted to wear overalls so I'd have lots of material covering me in case I ran across any unseen poison ivy—not to mention, I'd have deep pockets. I had brought along not only my father's pocketknife, but also a small penlight to help me see. I didn't want to chance losing either one before I could return home and put them back where I'd gotten them. It would generate too many questions if they came up missing. I had also stuffed one of Bo's old baseball caps into one of the pockets. If it was windy down by the water, I could tuck my hair up under it to keep it from blowing into my face and tickling my nose. The last thing I needed to do while I was there was sneeze!

When I arrived at the tree by Fiddler Crab Beach, I quickly climbed the old, improvised ladder. There was a moment of concern when I thought I felt one of the rungs near the top move under my foot, but it held, and I forgot about it as soon as I reached the platform. As before, I settled myself in to wait. The night was beautiful, the scents were heavenly, and the sound of the fiddlers blowing their little bubbles was mesmerizing. Once again, I dozed off.

After what seemed like only moments, I was jarred back to consciousness by what I thought must have been a gunshot. I froze as fear coursed through me. Had I been discovered? Did the Sikeses realize I was spying on them? Calming myself, I realized the sound of the shot, if that's what it was, had traveled to me from across the marshes. Whoever was firing a gun was out on the river somewhere. I took a deep breath and again settled myself back on the platform, eyes and ears open for whatever might happen next. A moderate breeze had begun to blow, so I pulled out Bo's old cap and put it on, carefully tucking all the loose tendrils of my hair up under it.

It wasn't long before I heard the roar of a boat motor, accompanied by the inevitable onslaught of cursing and swearing, floating to me from the direction of the river. I flattened myself out on my stomach to wait. Sure enough, within minutes the sound of approaching voices as well as things being dragged reached me. Tonight, however, there seemed to be a sense of urgency to the sounds, and the three men who eventually appeared on the dock seemed to be moving much more quickly than they had the night before.

I was soon able to make out individual voices, and what I heard caused my blood to freeze in my veins.

"Dammit, Daddy, I know'd you was needin' to do somethin', but didja hafta kill 'im?" I recognized Gary's deep voice. "There jus' ain't no turnin' back from 'at!"

I could tell it was Foxy who let loose the stream of expletives that followed. "Maybe I jus' shoulda let 'im live so he could brang out more cops jus' like hisself!" Foxy sounded furious! "Then we could all go tuh prison together! Be cellmates an' whatnot. Is that what y'all want? Three hots an' a cot in Reidsville for the nex' twenty years or so?"

I heard Gary swearing again as the men dragged their bundles toward the end of the dock.

"Derry!" Foxy, who was in the lead, shouted back to his youngest son. "Soon as we hit the beach, you run on along an' fetch the shovel from up the house."

"Yes, sir!" Derry didn't seem as willing as his older brother to argue with their father. Behind him, I could still hear Gary spewing expletives.

"Knock it off now, boy!" I could tell Foxy had just about had his fill of Gary's attitude. "You don't shut that hole in the front o' yer head, I'll put my fist in it, ya hear?"

Gary went silent. On the platform, I was hunkered down as far as I could get, my entire body trembling from sheer terror. Foxy had killed a man! I knew if I were discovered, I would certainly be next. In that moment, I wished I'd listened to Owen Godwin. I wished I'd never turned left at my mailbox. No, I wished I'd never started these midnight ramblings to begin with. I wished I was home, safe in my bed, listening to my father snoring in the next room. I wished I was anywhere but up in this stupid tree seeing things I was never meant to see. In that moment, I felt closer to death than I'd ever imagined I could be. I prayed silently for my life and swore to the Great Almighty that if He would just save me from these evil men and get me home in one piece, I would never go rambling again. Amen.

Across the sand, the Sikeses had reached the end of the dock. In the moonlight, I watched as Derry pushed his bundle off the dock, then jumped down after it. He ran across the sand toward the path, causing the fiddlers to dive into their holes. I held my breath and made myself as small as possible as he passed beneath me on his way to get the shovel.

While Derry was gone, Foxy and Gary dumped their bundles off the dock and hurried back toward the river. They arrived back at the beach about the same time Derry came back with the shovel; they were dragging a much larger, longer bundle wrapped loosely in a tarp. I couldn't quite make out what it was, but I was sure it was something I didn't want to see. In fact, I never wanted to see anything that had to do with the Sikeses ever again. I just wanted to go home.

"Awlright, let's get this SOB took care of an' get the blow up tuh the house fore anything else gits off-kilter." Foxy's voice rang out clear as a bell.

I had an unobstructed view of everything going on just across the little beach from where I lay hidden in the tree. "Derry, start shovelin' out a hole right up next tuh that marsh grass yonder. It'll be swampy, but it oughta letcha git deep enough." Foxy laughed then, an evil, conspiratorial laugh. "Can't go too deep with it, though, not if we want them crabs tuh git at 'im." He snorted. "We 'bout to have some well-fed fiddler crabs at this here beach!" He laughed like he'd just told the funniest joke in the world.

I shivered as I realized exactly what he was talking about, and I feared I'd become crab food, too, if I wasn't careful and very, very quiet.

Across the beach, Derry had a pretty good hole started. He continued to work in silence, but Gary still seemed in the mood to argue, despite his father's threats.

"Daddy, I don't like this, not one little bit!" He was practically whining. "I know'd we was riskin' some jail time, runnin' this coke like we do, but I didn't never expect to be mixed up in no killin', 'specially of someone from the Drug Enforcement Agency! We git caught now, it's a cell on death row shonuff!"

Foxy spun on his firstborn and grabbed him by the shirtfront. He let loose a long stream of curse words as he shook Gary violently and boxed his ears. Then he kicked the tarp-wrapped bundle off the dock and jumped down after it, dragging his son with him. After another hard shake, Foxy pushed Gary to his knees next to the bundle, reached down, and yanked the tarp away, revealing what lay hidden within. It was a dead body. I slapped a hand over my mouth to muffle the scream that tried to escape. Next to the dock, Gary looked ready to do the same.

"Lookit here! You see this, boy?" Foxy gave Gary another shake. "I ain't goin' tuh no prison cause o' this! Now, grab ahold an' he'p me tote 'im tuh the hole." Foxy was obviously angry with what he considered Gary's weakness and let loose another stream of expletives that left no doubt of how little he thought of his son. Gary looked like he was going to be sick, but he grabbed the tarp and helped his father move the body.

Over at the hole, Derry had dug as far as he could in the soft, swampy sand. He stepped back as Foxy and Gary dumped the body into the hole.

Foxy was grinning again as he knelt down and looked at where the face would be. "I'm thinkin' that'll learn ya tuh stick yer nose where it ought not tuh be stuck," he crowed. He looked back at his sons. "Git on over here, boys. I wanna show y'all somethin'."

Derry stepped right up and peered into the hole, but Gary looked as though he'd rather do anything but. I watched as he shook his head, took a deep breath, and stepped up next to his brother.

"The thing about a body dyin' is the way the person inside jus' disappears," Foxy explained. "It's like, now ya see 'em, now ya don't. You can look at a person when they's dyin' an' you can see when they ain't there no more. You can see 'em leave. There's no mistakin' the moment, an' it ain't like nothin' else you'll ever see in yer whole life.

It's all in the eyes. Ya jus' look intuh those eyes an' ya can see clear tuh the soul, right down intuh the very depths o' the person. Then, when they start tuh go, the eyes change. They look the same, but they ain't the same. All the sudden they's gone—jus' pure, smooth gone, like nobody's home inside their head no more. I saw a buncha people dyin' all around me back when I was in the war, an' they all went out the same way, no matter how they died. The eyes tell it all: they's right there, then they's nowhere." Foxy smiled the most terrifying smile I'd ever seen, his large yellow teeth glinting in the moonlight. He seemed to be relishing the memory. "I use' tuh love watchin' the light go out o' people's eyes! There's jus' nothin' on earth like seein' that! Yessuh, it's all in the eyes. First they look all shocked, like they ain't a'believin' what's happenin' tuh 'em. Then they take on a look like they's beggin' for help. Then they git this funny look tuh 'em, like they's disconnectin' from theyselves. That's the last thing that happens fore they's gone. They git that look like strings is bein' cut. Then their eyes change, go blank-like, an' they's just gone. They's jus' dead an' gone. An' then." Foxy's smile widened. "Oh, an' then it's like ya' lookin' at doll's eyes, like the person wasn't never even real tuh begin with. No matter what else ya see, ya end up lookin' intuh empty, lifeless eyes."

Suddenly Foxy lunged at Gary and grabbed him by the shirtfront again. "Come on an' have yerself a look, boy," he said as he shoved his son toward the hole in the sand.

"No, Daddy! Please! No!" Gary sounded like he was going to be sick; his breath hitched as he struggled against his father's hold.

"I said, look!" Foxy screamed and pushed Gary down until he was nose-to-nose with the body.

Beside him, Derry had started snickering at his brother's predicament. Obviously he was a lot less bothered than Gary by what their father had done.

"Better grab a peek while ya can!" Foxy said. "This here'll be the last time he'll ever be lookin' human, once the crabs git at 'im!"

Derry spoke for the first time. "Daddy, how come we didn't jus' tie a' anchor to 'im an' drop 'im over the side when we was over deep water?"

Foxy shot his younger son a look that left no doubt of what he thought of the boy's intelligence. "Because," his voice was dripping with scorn, "there ain't no water deep enough in this here river for that. Besides," Foxy added, "sunken bodies tend to come loose an' float tuh the surface. If that happens, we can kiss the whole shootin' match g'bye. This body gits found in the river an' there'll be no more pullin' crab traps full o' coke. Now, I don't know 'bout y'all two, but I kinda like all the money we been gittin' paid, an' I ain't 'bout tuh let nothin' nor nobody git in the way o' that!"

Up in the tree, my stomach started knotting up and churning; I was beginning to feel very sick. Foxy's last statement had taken my last vestiges of hope that I might still be able to squirm my way out of the mess I was in, even if I was caught. I took a couple of quiet, deep breaths and swallowed a few times, trying to control my nausea. I knew if I vomited they'd notice me for sure, so I had no choice; it was time to make my escape. I began to watch for an opportunity to slip away unnoticed. The Sikeses' attention was on burying the body, but I knew they would eventually finish dealing with that nasty business and start wheeling the bundles of "blow," whatever that was, up to the house; and that would take too long. I was certain I'd be sick before then.

I slid very carefully to the edge of the platform and sat up, trusting the shadows to hide me. I shot a glance toward the Sikeses and saw they were all still busy with their bad business. Very slowly I turned onto my stomach, backed off the platform, and searched for the first rung with my foot. Finding it in the dark, I slowly began to descend. It seemed I was going to be okay. All I had to do was climb down, quietly head back along the dark path that led to the houses, and slip through the bushes onto the tiny footpath Owen Godwin had dragged me down not so long ago. It should have been that simple.

But it wasn't.

CHAPTER 26

Descending as silently as I could, I eventually grasped the top rung with both of my hands as I stepped onto the fourth rung down . . . which promptly tore loose from the trunk of the tree and fell crashing to the ground twenty feet below, nearly taking me with it. As I dropped, I pictured myself twisted and skewered by the sharp branches of the scrub brush and deadfall below. An involuntary scream escaped my lips; then my overalls caught on one of the rungs and I was yanked to a violent stop, held fast by one of my shoulder straps.

Instantly, the men on the beach whipped around and began glaring into the darkness under the tree. Blessedly, I hadn't fallen far before getting hung up, and they didn't see me.

"Who's there?" Foxy snarled. "Come on outta them bushes, ya hear? Come out, sez I!" He and the boys continued to stare into the darkness beneath me. I was too scared to make a sound, even if I'd wanted to. I hung there in the dark, praying and trying to be invisible.

After what seemed like an eternity, I saw Foxy turn and murmur something to his sons. They nodded and headed off in two different directions, Gary toward the trees nearest the river and Derry up the footpath toward the house. Foxy turned and disappeared into the marsh grass directly across from where I hung. I shivered as I realized the two younger men were positioning themselves to surround me and flush me out so their father could spring out and grab me. I knew that sooner or later they'd find me hanging there and I would be at their mercy. I had to get out of that tree!

Very carefully, I twisted my body until I could grasp one of the tree branches above me. Holding on tightly to the branch, I pulled myself upward until I felt the strap of my overalls lift off the ladder rung. I was free! I climbed down as quietly as I could, then crouched at the base of the tree and listened to the sounds of the night.

All around me, the crickets and frogs chirruped happily. I stayed where I was, listening for that to change. Sure enough, a few seconds later the crickets and frogs behind and on either side of me grew silent, telling me where the two younger men were and which direction I should go. Staying as low as possible, I ran straight ahead, out onto the beach. I scurried to the center of the sand, dropped to one knee and waited in silence. All around the base of the tree I'd just left, the crickets and frogs were completely silent. I took a deep breath; at least I knew where Gary and Derry were. Now to find Foxy.

The night evoked a false sense of peace and serenity. In the distance, night birds were calling and crickets and frogs were singing, but it was still silent under the tree. Time seemed to stand still as I continued to kneel in the center of the beach. I was there, unmoving, for so long the fiddler crabs began to come out of their holes. I could hear them blowing their little bubbles all around me as they milled about in the moonlight. I concentrated hard on everything going on around me in the dark and thought I'd go insane if something didn't happen soon.

Suddenly, the fiddlers directly in front of where I crouched began disappearing into their holes, falling toward me like dominoes and pinpointing Foxy's location. I knew without a doubt that he was coming. The younger Sikeses were still behind me and had cut me off from the footpath. Now, with Foxy coming straight at me, there was only one direction left for me to run.

I jumped up and made a mad dash for the dock. I had to be careful not to fall into the hole where the dead body lay or trip over the bundles, which were still scattered on the sand where the Sikeses had dropped them. As I hoisted myself onto the dock, I could hear the men pounding across the beach after me. I leaped to my feet and sprinted toward the river. Within seconds I could feel the dock begin to sway and vibrate under my feet, so I knew the men had reached it and were now in hot pursuit. I prayed I could reach the water before they caught me. I had no idea what I was going to do at that point; I just knew I had to get to the river. That was as far as I could think. Behind me, in the dark, I could hear the heavy breathing of the three men closing in on me; the pounding of their feet sounded like it was right behind me. I don't think I'd ever run so fast before in my life, but I wasn't sure it was going to be fast enough. I could hear myself whimpering as I ran and would've sworn I could feel the hot breaths of my pursuers on the back of my neck. Then the dock beneath me disappeared and I was airborne. I took a deep breath only a second before plunging beneath the dark, briny water. Thank God, I had made it to the river.

The silence under the water was deafening. I wasn't sure how long I could stay under after having sprinted such a distance, but I did know I couldn't allow myself the luxury of bobbing to the surface to take a breath. Instead, I did the only thing I could think of: I turned right and, swimming underwater, headed for Morgan's dock, forty yards away.

I hadn't gone far when I heard the muffled sound of angry voices coming from behind me. I knew the Sikeses had reached the end of the dock and were scanning the water, hoping to catch a glimpse of me. My lungs began to burn and I knew I would soon need to come up for air. All I could do was pray that I'd swum far enough away from the Sikeses' dock for the darkness to hide me. I had to risk it.

I quickly bobbed to the surface and sucked in a huge gulp of air before diving back under and continuing toward Morgan's dock. In that split second, I'd witnessed a terrifying sight: Gary and Derry were climbing into their boat and preparing to search the river for me. I assumed they would sweep slowly back and forth and knew my only hope of escape was to reach the dock before they found me. I wasn't sure how far underwater I was and didn't want them driving the boat over me. The thought of a boat propeller slicing into my back urged me on to greater speed.

I needed to surface for another breath soon. Just when I thought I could go no farther without coming up for air, I noticed that the water around me had suddenly grown darker. I risked surfacing again to check my position and breathed a small sigh of relief.

The Sikeses were searching in the other direction and I had reached Morgan's dock.

Taking another breath, I dove down one more time and swam under the large blocks of Styrofoam that supported the floating dock. I surfaced in the small space at the center, knowing they wouldn't be able to see me there. I reached up, stuck my fingers into the spaces between the planks, and held on for dear life. Finally, for the first time since hearing the gunshot, I began to feel safe.

Then I remembered: I was on my period.

Suddenly my mind was filled with the images I'd seen in the movie theater earlier that day and in my head, I could hear the sound of horns playing two notes over and over, faster and faster. I began darting glances down into the dark, murky water all around me, and for the first time in my life, I felt I truly understood the meaning of the old adage "out of the frying pan and into the fire." I crossed my legs tightly, hoping to stem the flow. I wasn't sure how effective that would be, but I could think of nothing else to do, except pray.

I don't know how long I hung there in the water like bait on a fishhook while listening to the Sikeses trolling back and forth as they continued to search the river for me, but I felt this had to be the longest night in the history of the world. I had begun to relax a little, realizing I'd chosen my hiding place wisely.

I couldn't make out actual words over the sound of the boat motor, but I could tell by the timbre of their voices that the Sikeses were getting frustrated. I heaved a huge sigh of relief when I finally heard their boat bang against their dock and the motor cut off.

The first voice I could make out was Foxy's, cursing and spewing venom over the fact that I'd made good my escape.

Then I heard something that sent a shiver through me.

"Don't worry, Daddy." It was Derry. "I got me a look at the little SOB, an' I know who it is. We can still git 'em!"

"Ya hear that?" Foxy screamed out across the river. "We know who ya are, so ya better jus' keep yer mouth shut! Understand? Keep yer damn mouth shut! We may be comin' fer ya, we may not! It's up tuh you! Ya hear me out there? Keep yer mouth shut!"

My blood ran cold as I continued to hang there under the dock. What had I gotten myself into? Foxy might have said it was up to me whether or not they killed me, but I knew I was a liability. Once he'd given it some thought, they'd come after me; there was no way they'd chance leaving me alive, not with what I'd seen.

Then, before I could completely process everything, another problem—what felt like a huge one—presented itself: something very heavy bumped me in the stomach so hard I nearly lost my grip on the dock above me. In my mind, there was only one thing it could have been. I began to whimper as I again heard in my head the sound of horns playing the same two notes over and over. One dock over, the Sikeses were tying up their boat and discussing their options. I couldn't leave my hiding place until they had gone back to the beach or they'd see me for sure. I felt the water surge beside me as something very large moved past me. Whimpering again, I curled up, trying to make myself as small as possible, and prayed like I'd never prayed before.

Finally, I could hear the Sikeses tromping back up the dock toward the beach as they discussed what had to be done before the night was over; they still had a body and a load of bundles to deal with. I listened as their voices faded into the distance. When I was certain they were too far away to see me across the marshes, I submerged and swam out from under the dock. That was when I was the most frightened, I think, trying to get out from under the floating dock and make it up the ladder before I had another run-in with whatever was swimming around me in the water. When I'd finally pulled myself onto the dock, I lay face down, trembling and sobbing, both relieved that whatever had been in the water with me had left me alone and crushed by despair, knowing it was only a matter of time before the Sikeses came for me.

I could see the end of my life.

CHAPTER 27

The secret to me being me after that fateful night was to behave as though nothing bad had ever happened. Anyone looking at me would have seen a normal, almost-twelve-year-old girl who had never done or seen anything untoward. The rest of that week, I went to bed at a reasonable time every night (whether I could sleep or not), awoke each day ready to face the world with a happy, hopeful attitude, and strode forth into my future in what would seem to be wide-eyed innocence. But underneath it all was the knowledge that I was fast-approaching my demise; it was only a matter of time.

I knew the only way I could keep my mind off what was eventually going to happen to me was to concentrate on the happiness and well-being of the people around me; so the rest of that week, I spent as much time with Bo and Della as possible. We spent every moment swimming (They swam, I didn't. Stupid period!), crabbing, and playing in the woods and at the Magic Oak Tree. We lorded over every place we went; we were the almighty triune. There was no one who didn't know who we three were, especially Della, who had become a fixture at the Big Hole. She practically had her own little fan club there!

I have to admit, though, it was a great relief when Scott and the Stricklands got back from their vacations Saturday afternoon.

"So, what did y'all do while we were gone?" Scott asked.

Scott's parents were visiting the Rooneys, and our gang had gotten together to shoot baskets on the outdoor court at Hesse Elementary School. Bo, Della, and I bragged about that first trip to the Big Hole and our grand entrance on the land tube, and regaled them with scenes from the shark movie we'd seen. (I didn't say a word about my after-hours escapades or my run-in with whatever was swimming around under Morgan's dock with me.) The boys were all impressed by the stunt we'd pulled with the land tube, and everybody wanted to go back with us at some point to see the movie.

Being together again also meant that plans for the upcoming week needed to be made.

"I've got it!" Scott said as he caught the basketball Bo had passed to him. "We're coming up on a full moon. That means a spring tide, so the beach down by the Tuckers' house is going to flood that night. We should go down there then and go wop-boarding!"

I shivered. The Tuckers' beach was also the Sikeses' beach, and I definitely did not want to go anywhere near there, but I couldn't tell Scott that, or why, so I kept silent.

"We've got about a week," he went on, squatting down and using the basketball as a seat. "So we have time to plan and build some wop boards." Everyone nodded in agreement. "What we really ought to do," Scott continued, "is plan a campout!" He grinned at each of us as we sat down around him. "We should see if we can find someone to go with us as a chaperone, pitch some tents, and spend the night out on Bird Island. We can go out skiing and tubing all day, wop-board on the Tuckers' beach that night when it floods, then camp out on Bird Island afterward. What do y'all think?"

"Sounds like a plan, man!" Bo's eyes were gleaming. The Stricklands were nodding in agreement. I, of course, remained silent, although I smiled and nodded and pretended to be as excited as they were.

Bubba screwed up his face, deep in thought. "So . . . who do ya think might be willin' to take us campin'? Not very many grown-ups are gonna wanna pitch a tent an' sleep out on an island with no bath-room or nothin'." He cut his eyes at Della and me. "And since we got a couple o' girls goin', it prob'ly needs to be a female, ya know?"

We all sat in silence for several seconds, trying to think of who to ask.

"Well . . ." Della sounded hesitant. "I'm still new around here, so I don't really know too many people, but what about the youth director at church? I've overheard some of the older kids talking about her tak-ing them camping and crabbing and stuff."

Scott's grin lit up his face and made my heart beat fast. "That's a great idea, Della!" His praise made her blush.

"Oh, yeah!" Bo grew animated. "You're talkin' 'bout Ann Harden! She's Mr. Wimpy's daughter, Nudgie's big sister. Everybody jus' calls her 'the Kid' because she acts so young. She's always doin' cool stuff with the big kids from church." He laughed. "She's even got her own ski boat, kinda like Scott's, only orange an' white. She loves campin' an' crabbin' an' stuff."

"Sure!" Bubba agreed. "She's a whole lotta fun, too! She takes the big kids to movies an' coaches baseball an' basketball, and on Thurs-day nights all the big kids go to her house for Bible study and snacks. She even takes 'em rollin' on Saturday nights!"

Everyone laughed at that, even me. Only Della appeared to be confused.

"You ain't never heard o' rollin', munchkin?" Bo asked. "Well," he continued when she shook her head. "Ya get as many rolls o' tawlet pa-per as ya can, sneak over to people's houses in the middle o' the night an' throw the rolls all over. They unroll an' leave streamers all up in the trees an' over the tops o' the houses. Ya also unroll 'em all through the bushes an' wind 'em around the porch banisters an' the cars an' anywhere else you can think of. It's messy but all in fun."

"Well, who'd-a-thought?" Della's eyes twinkled.

"Yup!" Bo smiled wistfully at Della. "I can't hardly wait to get old enough to join the youth group!"

"It's settled then," Scott said. "We just need to talk to the Kid and see if she's willing to do it. If she is, we'll plan the campout around her schedule, but hopefully it'll be next weekend so we can wop-board on the spring tide. Meanwhile, we can get together at my house this week and build some wop boards so we'll be ready. I can ask my father to cut them out, and we can finish them."

We all nodded in agreement, especially Della, who, I knew, had probably never heard of a wop board before in her life. But by now she knew we'd teach her everything she needed to know and make sure she had great time learning.

We sat there a few more minutes, discussing cool designs for the boards and what all we might want to bring on the campout. It was Bubba, always our official timekeeper, who let us know when it was time to head for home. The Stricklands went off in the direction of their house on Kings Way, Bo and I crossed Old Montgomery Road, and Scott walked with Della across Whitfield Avenue to meet up with his parents at her house. I was surprised to realize that despite the dark things going on in my head, I was actually looking forward to the next few days: I would be spending them with Scott.

But then again, I thought with a frown, so would Della.

CHAPTER 28

We met at church bright and early the next morning, chattering away about the upcoming weekend. Scott's mother had offered to speak with Ann Harden after the service to ask if she would be willing to chaperone us on our campout, and we were all wound-up bundles of nervous energy waiting to see what she would say. Bo was so jittery I thought he might bring the entire building down around us, and even Scott was a little antsy.

Although we usually really enjoyed our class, Sunday school seemed to move at a snail's pace, and the church service afterward dragged on and on. Then, just when it looked like Brother Arms was finally ending his sermon, he decided we needed to sing every blessed verse of "Just as I Am." We were all spinning inside like little Tasmanian devils by the time he asked Wimpy Harden to pray us out, and I knew Bo's head was aching from how many times his father had thumped him on the back of it to warn him to sit still. As Brother Arms quietly walked down the aisle to take his position just inside the foyer doors, Mr. Wimpy offered up the closing prayer, and it had to be one of the longest in the history of our church. (Bo swore later that Mr. Wimpy said "our Father" thirty-seven times during that prayer!) As soon as we heard the final "amen," we hit the aisle and headed for the doors, stopping only long enough to shake hands with Brother Arms on the way out. Then we all gathered next to an azalea bush at the corner of the building so we could watch Mrs. Bashlor talk to the Kid.

It was several minutes before Scott's parents came through the doors and made their way down the steps. It took the Kid quite a bit longer; all the big kids cornered her after church every Sunday to check on what she had planned for them during the upcoming week. Scott frowned and mentioned the possibility that they might make plans for the weekend before his mother could talk to her, and I thought the top of Bo's head would blow off when he heard that.

Finally, the Kid appeared and Scott's mother walked over and began to speak to her. After a short exchange, the Kid called out to Nudgie, who was just coming down the steps, and waved her over. The three of them put their heads together and spoke intensely for a few more minutes; then there it was: the three of them were smiling and nodding. We all had to struggle to contain ourselves, and I thought Bubba was going to have to sit on Bo to keep him from blasting off like a rocket! Scott, always the coolheaded realist, warned us not to get our hopes up too high until we knew for sure, but even he was practically bouncing with excitement.

His mother turned and approached us, and we all held our breaths.

"Well," Mrs. Bashlor said with a smile, "I can see y'all already know what Ms. Ann said." Bo started to cheer and jump up and down until Tully and Aubrey elbowed him from either side, making him "oof." Mrs. Bashlor laughed, then continued, "She asked Nudgie to go along to help since there are so many of you, and she's going to put her motorboat in so everyone can be on the water at the same time.

We'll get together with her after church Wednesday night to finalize the plans, but it looks like the campout's a go!"

We all cheered, and Bo took a noisy lap around the churchyard. Then we all went over and thanked Nudgie and the Kid before hurrying around the building to meet up with our parents in the parking lot. We couldn't wait to tell them what had been said.

"Man-oh-man alive!" Bo was almost levitating as he rubbed his hands together. "I ain't a'believin' this! It's gon' be cool, y'all! It's gon' be so cool! Aw, Lawd! Aw, my sweet Lawd!" We all stopped and looked at him because we knew what was coming next. He bounced up and down a couple of times as he struggled to hold it in since we were at church, but it was impossible: "Cheese an' rice!" Bo exploded.

Della squealed and we all laughed, except Scott, who was pinching the bridge of his nose and trying not to smile. I wondered how we were ever going to make it through the week!

Then I remembered the Sikeses and wondered *if* I would make it through the week.

CHAPTER 29

I was awakened early the next morning by the ringing of the telephone in the kitchen. I heard my mama answer it, followed by the sound of her footsteps approaching my room.

"Rachel?" Mama asked. "Are you awake?"

"Yes, ma'am." I'm sure I mumbled; I had only been asleep for a couple of hours.

"Bo's on the phone for you."

I practically leaped out of bed. "Yes, ma'am!" I scurried down the hall to the kitchen, bouncing off a couple of walls and the kitchen doorjamb along the way.

"Mornin', lazy bones!" Bo was in a great mood. "You ain't already drug yourself up outta that bed? You're usually the first one to hit the floor in the mornin's!"

I laughed at his teasing. "I thought it might be nice to let you beat me for once."

Bo's laughter joined mine; then he grew animated. "I jus' got a call from Scott. His father got up early this mornin' an' cut out a bunch

o' wop boards for us before he left for work. Scott had already promised to rake the pine straw up for one o' the old ladies at church this
mornin', but he's free after that. He says he'll pick us up at Morgan's
dock between ten thirty an' eleven an' take us back to his house. We
oughta be able to finish the sandin' an' paintin' by the end o' the day!"
I could tell from the sound of his voice that Bo was bouncing up and
down as he spoke. "Anyway, I'm fixin' to call the Stairsteps to let 'em
know, then I'mma get ready an' come meet ya at your house. You call
the munchkin, okay?"

Bo hung up before I could answer, so I quickly dialed Della's
number. Mrs. Rooney answered and called Della to the phone.

"Hello! Rachel?" Della's deep, melodic voice was husky from excitement and her rush to get to the phone.

"Hey! Are you ready for another banner day in the life of Della
Rooney?"

Della's laugh was a gift. "You know it!" She sounded every bit as
excited as Bo. "I can't wait to find out what a wop board is! Oh, and
this will be the first time in my life I've ever gone on a campout. I'm so
excited I can hardly stand it!"

I couldn't help but smile. As always, she was just too cute and sweet.
And, of course, there was that voice!

"You're going to love it!" I was feeling pretty animated myself. "All
of us have gone camping with our parents before, but this will be the
first time us kids have gone together." I laughed again. "This will be
a weekend we'll always remember!" I suddenly realized I was actually
excited about something, and I laughed again.

Della's laughter joined mine. "My whole entire summer has been
like that for me!" She grew serious. "Honestly, Rachel, I don't know
what I would've done if I hadn't met you and the boys." Her voice
caught. "When we first moved here, I thought this was going to be
the worst summer of my life, but instead it's been probably the best

I'll ever have!" Her voice brightened. "I'm so glad you were up in the Magic Tree that day. Meeting you was the best thing that's ever happened to me." She paused before continuing. "I think it would even have been worth that flying lesson we almost got, little 'boyd'!"

We both laughed at that; then I told her about our plans for the day. We decided that Bo and I should meet up with her at her house in twenty minutes so we could all go to Morgan's dock together.

We hung up and I ran to throw on my swimsuit. I was just brushing my teeth when I heard Bo blow into the house like a tornado and start hollering my name. I grabbed a towel, shouted a quick goodbye to my mother, and we were off. Della saw us coming through her window and rushed out before we could knock. She was just as excited in person as she'd sounded on the phone, so we started out right away.

"Bo! Rachel!" Mrs. Rooney called out from the front porch. We turned around and Bo whooped loudly when he saw the huge picnic basket and gallon jugs of lemonade in her hands. He ran back, gave her a huge Bo DeLoach hug, and returned lugging the feast she'd prepared for us. Della and I relieved him of the jugs, we all waved and called out our thanks, and then we headed off toward Beckman Avenue.

This was definitely going to be a banner day.

CHAPTER 30

When we arrived at the Bashlors' house a short time later, it was just as Scott had said: His father had taken the time that morning to cut out several plywood wop boards, one for each of us. They were lined up on newspapers on the floor of the gazebo at the end of their dock, waiting to be finished. Beside them on the floor were an electric grinder, sheets of sandpaper, sanding blocks, cans of paint, several paintbrushes in various sizes, and sheets of stencils.

Bo took one look and cut loose one of his shrill rebel yells. Beside him, Della was jumping up and down, squealing and laughing. That made me laugh because I knew she had no idea what she was looking at; she was just reacting to Bo's enthusiasm. Behind her, the Stricklands were shouting and slapping high fives. Scott just stood there beaming with pride and enjoying our joy and excitement. The Bashlors, I thought, had to be the most awesome people I knew, although the Rooneys ran a close second.

After transferring Mrs. Rooney's picnic lunch and lemonade from the giant basket to the outdoor kitchen refrigerator, we trooped back into the gazebo to inspect the wop boards more closely. Della's brow was furrowed in concentration as she tried to figure out what she was looking at.

Scott chuckled at her expression and began to explain. "Wop boards operate under the same principles as skateboards," he said. "You're riding along, standing on a board. It's that simple. But, whereas skateboards are rolling on wheels, wop boards are skimming along the surface of the water. Understand so far?"

Della nodded, still frowning.

Scott continued, "There are basically two shapes: round and elliptical." Scott saw Della's expression and chuckled. "Elliptical is an elongated circle, sort of the shape of a bathtub. I guess the wop board's not truly elliptical, though, because the back end is cut straight across, but we'll call it that anyway."

Della nodded seriously, soaking it all in.

"Okay," Scott went on, "the round ones are about eighteen inches across. The elliptical ones are eighteen to twenty inches across and thirty inches long. My father cut four long boards and three round ones. What we have to do is taper the edges with the grinder so the boards will skim across the water better. Leaving a flat edge will cause them to drag against the water and make for a rougher ride or even flip you over, and you don't want that. We also grind the corners on the backs of long ones to round them off. The next step is to sand the board all over, top and bottom, so there aren't any splinters when you stand on them. After that, we wipe them down with a damp cloth. Then the only thing left is to pencil on whatever design you like and paint it. That's it!"

Scott put an arm over Della's shoulder and guided her over to the boards while I gritted my teeth and tried to keep smiling. This crush thing was getting ridiculous!

"What do you say, fellas?" Scott looked around the group. "Shall we let the squirt pick out her board first?"

The boys all smiled and nodded. So did I, although "fella" wasn't a word I could use to describe myself anymore.

Della took her time choosing a board. She seemed torn between round and elliptical, but she finally went with round. It seemed to fit her small stature better. Once her choice was made, the rest of us descended en masse on the remaining boards.

The rest of the day was spent grinding and sanding, designing and painting. We only stopped once when Bo reminded us that we had one of Mrs. Rooney's picnic lunches waiting for us in the outdoor kitchen, but we got right back to work as soon as we finished eating. When we were finally done late that afternoon, there were seven amazing wop boards drying on racks. Each one of us was bouncing as we chattered away about whose board was the coolest and which one of us was going to show the most skill. The excitement level was so high that none of us minded the sore muscles, raw fingers, and splinters that came with all the grinding and sanding we'd done.

We could hardly wait for the weekend!

CHAPTER 31

The rest of the week fluctuated between dragging and flying by. Tuesday morning we took the land tube to the Big Hole. That night the boys had a game and Scott pitched a no-hitter, thanks in part to some amazing plays by Bo. After the game, a coach from one of the local private schools spoke with both Scott's and Bo's parents about the possibility of them attending his school so they could play baseball there. He thought they both showed real promise and said he wouldn't be surprised if, with the proper training, they'd each be able to go to college on a baseball scholarship, then maybe even have a shot at the pros! All of us were excited at the prospect but none as much as me: This coach was from the school I would be attending in the fall, which meant Bo and Scott might be going there with me! I was practically jumping up and down at the prospect.

On Wednesday we swam off Morgan's dock (I had a sketchy moment when I first jumped in, remembering that something very large had been in the water with me the last time I'd been there); then we went to church that evening. We met with Nudgie and the Kid afterward to firm up the plans for the weekend. The big campout would be Friday night and, besides going wop-boarding, we were going to spend all day Friday and Saturday on the water! The Kid also had some sort of surprise planned for us Friday evening. We could hardly wait and were all acting like a bunch of bouncing Bos.

Thursday arrived with me trying to sleep in after my usual restless night. I was awakened by the ringing of the phone followed by my mother calling my name down the hall. I yawned and stretched, then headed to the kitchen.

"Hello?" I stifled another yawn as I answered.

"Rachel!" Della's voice, filled with excitement, was even more husky than usual. "Wake up! I have the most wonderful news."

I shook off the last of the cobwebs. "Really? What's going on? What's happened?"

On the other end of the line, Della laughed musically. "My parents are so excited about our campout, they want to make sure we have everything we need." She sounded absolutely thrilled. "My father actually took the day off from work, and they're taking me shopping for a tent and a sleeping bag and a cooler and . . . oh, just everything!" I could hear light, rhythmic thumps in the background and knew it was the sound of her feet hitting the floor; Della was jumping up and down in her excitement.

"That's fantastic, Della!"

"Rachel, we want you to come shopping with us and help pick out what I need. We really aren't sure what all to get since we've never camped, and I figure you and I can be roommates in the tent, so it would be great if you'd come, too!" Della, in her excitement, sounded like she was about to go Bo on me. It was adorable. "Oh, please come! We really need you!"

How could I say no to that? I told Della to hold on while I let my mother know what was going on and got her permission, then assured

Della I'd be right over as soon as I could get ready. Apparently, everyone was too excited to waste a single second, so the Rooneys offered to pick me up in fifteen minutes. Della was squealing when she hung up, and I wondered if she could wait even that long!

I let my mother know to watch for the Rooneys, then returned to my room, quickly dressed, and dashed to the bathroom to brush my teeth. I was pulling my hair into a ponytail when my mother called down the hall to let me know the Rooneys had arrived. I gave her a quick peck on the cheek, ran out the door, and climbed into the backseat of the Rooneys' station wagon, settling myself in next to a very excited Della. Mr. and Mrs. Rooney both turned to give me a smile and say hello, and we were off.

Sears was, in Mr. Rooney's opinion, the best place to go for anything under the sun, so we headed for the Oglethorpe Mall. Della chattered excitedly about the upcoming weekend and all the things we might want to buy for the campout. She seemed to want to get every single article of camping equipment known to mankind, so I kept having to remind her that the Bashlors, the Stricklands, and the Kid already had pretty much everything we'd need, except for the few things Della might want to bring for herself. All the boys had tents and sleeping bags; Scott and the Stairsteps had volunteered to bring a camp stove, cooking and eating utensils, and lanterns, and Nudgie and the Kid were bringing coolers filled with ice and drinks. The Rooneys were sending food so I suggested we limit our shopping to a small cooler, a two- to four-person tent, a sleeping bag, and maybe an air mattress for Della; but everything I said seemed to go in one ear and out the other. The Rooneys were all just too excited to really listen.

Once we reached the sporting goods department of Sears, it got even harder to rein everyone in, but we all finally managed to come to an agreement: Della would need a sleeping bag, an air mattress, and a tent, and it wasn't a bad idea for her to have a lantern for the tent and a flashlight in case nature called in the middle of the night. I lost the argument about whether or not they got to buy me a pretty new sleeping bag and air mattress of my own, but I managed to get them to put back the camp table with built-in seats, the camp chairs, and the portable barbeque grill—although it was a close call. I also let them win the argument over the size of the cooler; the Rooneys had decided to send along sandwich fixings, and I had to concede that a larger cooler would come in handy for more than just this campout. I shook my head and grinned as Mr. Rooney, smiling hugely, chose the largest cooler in the store and balanced it precariously across the top of our shopping cart. When he smiled like that, he looked just like Della.

When we finally left Sears, we loaded our purchases into the back of the station wagon and headed out. We'd only traveled a couple of blocks when the Rooneys surprised me by pulling in for lunch at Duff's Smorgasbord. Mrs. Rooney said lunch was on them; it was just a small gesture to thank me for all of the wonderful things I'd done for Della that summer. I assured her it had been my pleasure because the whole gang loved Della so much, but Mrs. Rooney insisted that it had all started with me. As I got out of the car, Mr. Rooney took my hand and added his thanks to his wife's. Della, her eyes glistening, waited for her father to release my hand before she grabbed me around the waist and gave me a big "squoze." I wasn't sure how I was supposed to feel about all of that, but, thanks to my mother, I knew exactly what to say and how to behave.

Still, I was a little uncomfortable all the way through the meal, but I decided it was from guilt; I was the only one in our gang who was getting spoiled that day, and I knew that Bo in particular would've loved the buffet.

Too bad he's missing out on this, I mused, taking a huge bite out of a fried chicken leg.

***

Later that evening, we all headed over to Meridian Park to watch our boys play ball. Earlier in the season, Della and I had bought matching baseball jerseys, white with red trim, just like our boys wore. We always parked ourselves in the center of the bleachers, where we could make the most noise and keep the crowd revved up.

Sweet, shy, quiet little Della had become a beast in the bleachers, and I was hard-pressed to keep up with her cheers and chants. I was constantly shaking my head and marveling at the monster I'd created.

As usual, we sat with my aunt and uncle, the Bashlors, and the Stricklands. Scott's mother had brought bags of "bawled" peanuts from home, so we sat munching away all through the game, occasionally throwing the shells in the direction of the field when we didn't like a call or straight up in the air when we got excited. As usual, Bo played like it was the final game of the World Series while Scott was, of course, magnificent. There was just no beating our boys that season, and Della and I were both beaming when the game ended and "we" had soundly trounced the other team. Scott's parents were gracious when some of the other parents congratulated them on his pitching ability, and several people complimented my aunt and uncle on how talented Bo was as a ballplayer. More than one person said they thought he might have a real shot at going pro someday. I had to agree with them; my cousin truly was that talented.

As excited as we all were to be at the ballpark, we couldn't wait to get home and go to bed. The sooner we went to sleep, the sooner we would wake up to campout day! We were meeting Nudgie and the Kid at 9:00 a.m. on Morgan's dock to pack all the camping equipment into the boats and take it over to Bird Island, and we all still had an awful lot to do. The Stairsteps raced to their car as soon as the game was over, and even Scott seemed anxious to leave. Bo, Della, and I bounced in the backseat all the way home and didn't even ask to stop for our usual postgame Icees and Slush Puppies. Our excitement level was sky high.

I had a feeling I wasn't the only one who wouldn't be able to sleep that night.

CHAPTER 32

Morgan's dock was humming with excited energy at nine o'clock the next morning. No one could believe that Friday had finally arrived. Scott roared up in his ski boat right on time (according to Bubba), and the Kid pulled up in hers a few seconds later. Both boats were soon filled with tents, sleeping bags, backpacks, lanterns, coolers, and a camp stove, and the Kid had even brought a couple of large crab traps to drop while we swam, tubed, and went skiing. It was going to be an epic weekend and we could hardly contain our excitement.

"Okay, folks, this is the plan." The Kid wasted no time getting down to business. "First, I have to pick up Nudgie. We put the boat in by the Morgans' house, then she drove the truck around to the Tuckers' so it'll be easy to get to later. She should be at the end of their dock by the time we get over there. Next, we're going to drive over to Bird Island and get the boats unloaded and set up camp; that way we don't have to do it tonight. Then we'll drop the crab traps and spend the rest of the day in the water. Around three thirty we'll pull the traps, then head to my house for supper; Daddy's grilling chicken and steaks for all of us, and Mother is cooking the crabs along with corn on the cob, potato salad, and hushpuppies. At full dark, we'll head back to the Tuckers' beach and go wop-boarding for an hour or so, then head back to Bird Island for the night. Is that cool?"

We all jumped up and down and cheered, and Bo almost fell off the dock into the water, he was so excited. On top of everything else we had to look forward to, we were also having supper at the Hardens'. Mr. Wimpy and Ms. Frances were well known for their weekend steak and seafood feasts, and we knew we were in for a treat.

We couldn't get aboard the boats fast enough.

Bird Island was located directly across the water from Morgan's dock and took no time at all to reach. After picking up Nudgie, we drove into the narrow channel that separated the island from a large patch of marsh grass and pulled up onto the small sandy beach. Everyone pitched in, and the boats were soon empty. The boys got busy clearing an area well above the high-water mark and were soon assembling the camp stove and setting up the tents. Nudgie and the Kid excavated a shallow hole at the center of camp so we'd have a nice, safe fire pit for later while Della and I set out in search of enough pine straw, pinecones, and driftwood to keep a fire burning all night. We also cut several long, sturdy green sticks from the trees around the campsite to use as cooking utensils; according to Nudgie, there might just be some s'mores in our near future! We had also heard that the Kid was a master storyteller and had a long list of local legends and ghost stories to scare us with.

I don't think any of us expected to get much sleep that night, and that was alright with us.

We were back out on the river in less than an hour. Scott had the skis in his boat; the Kid was going to pull the tubing rig with hers as soon as she dropped the two crab traps. All the boys opted to start with skiing, but Della and I climbed into the boat with Nudgie and the Kid so Della could see how a real, commercial-sized crab trap was set. She leaned in close and studied the trap while Nudgie explained how it worked. Meanwhile, the Kid motored us out to mid-river and headed past Morgan's dock, in the direction of Land's End.

"These particular crab traps hold twelve dozen crabs," Nudgie began. (We were dropping two, and I couldn't for the life of me understand how we would ever be able to eat 288 crabs!) "As you can see, they're made out of a thick wire mesh that resembles chicken wire. This," she said, indicating a small wire door that accessed an empty wire cylinder in the top of the trap, "is the bait well." We watched as she filled it with bait fish. "Okay," Nudgie continued, "see these cone-shaped openings on the sides that reach almost all the way to the bait well?" Della nodded, intrigued, and Nudgie grinned at her. "The crabs smell the bait, crawl up the side and into the openings, then fall down into the trap when they try to reach the bait. The shape of the trap on the inside prevents them from crawling back up and out. Understand?"

Della chewed her lip and nodded, then looked up at Nudgie and frowned. "I get how the traps work," she said, "but once they're in the water, how do you get them back out? When we kids have crabbed, we tied the traps to a dock, but you said we're going to drop them from the boat, then go tubing. So . . . how do we get them back?" Della looked confused.

The Kid looked back at us and laughed, her blue eyes twinkling. Nudgie grinned again, then reached over and picked up two empty one-gallon bleach bottles and two large coils of yellow ski rope. The ropes had knots tied in them every eighteen inches, and the bottles were painted bright yellow with huge black "Hs" printed on the sides.

"That's a great question, Della," Nudgie said. "What we do is tie one end of these ropes to each of the traps and the other ends to the handles of these bleach bottles. Next, we pick a spot in the middle of the river that's handy for crabbing but not in the way of skiing and tubing. Then we just drop the whole kit and caboodle over the side. See? The caps are on the bleach bottles so they'll float. We'll be catching crabs the whole time we're playing in the water. When it's time to go back to our house later, we'll just grab the floats and pull up the traps. That's why we tied knots in the lines, to make them easier to grab hold of and haul up. Get it?"

Della's eyes sparkled with understanding. "Well, who'd-a-thought?" She smiled at Nudgie, then at the Kid. "I sure am learning a lot this summer about living on the river!" She was exultant, and we couldn't help but laugh at her expression; she was still just too cute.

"Excellent, Grasshopper!" Nudgie handed her one of the coils of rope and a bleach bottle. "Now, let's see you tie these to one of the traps so we can drop them and get ourselves into the water. The boys are already hard at it." She tipped her head toward the other side of the river, and we all looked up just in time to see Scott fly by pulling Bo on the slalom ski. They all hollered and made faces at us, and we shouted and gestured right back at them. Bo gestured so energetically he nearly pitched face-first into the water!

After they'd passed, Nudgie handed me the second rope and bleach bottle, and Della and I had them tied to the traps and dropped over the side in no time flat.

"Alright, folks," the Kid pushed the throttle forward, "let's get in the water!"

We all cheered and clapped, Della cut loose with a rebel yell that would've made Bo proud, and we were off. Once we were far enough away from the crab traps, the Kid idled down while Nudgie dropped the towline and tubing rig over the stern. The Kid pulled forward to pay out the line, then Nudgie turned to Della and me.

"Okay! Who's first?" she asked.

No sooner had I pointed to Della, who was already wearing her life vest, than Nudgie picked her up over her head, shouted, "Sink or swim!" and launched her as high and far out over the water as she could. I felt my mouth drop open and saw that all the boys, who had come around just in time to witness the event, were wearing the same expression. None of us had ever been that spontaneous or rough with Della, and we waited apprehensively for her to surface, hoping she'd handle it well. Bo, who had already pulled himself back into Scott's boat, seemed especially concerned and appeared ready to go in after her.

Only a second or two passed before Della exploded up out of the water, big-eyed and sputtering. She coughed and choked, then squealed in surprise and delight, her husky, musical laughter rolling across the water.

"Oh, wow!" Della laughed again. "I was NOT expecting THAT!" She beamed up at Nudgie, who was grinning over the side at her. "That was so much fun! I think I want to get into the water just like that every time from now on."

We all burst into relieved laughter, and the boys gave her their own special ovation by shouting and pounding on the gunwale of Scott's boat.

"Atta way, peanut!" Scott called out proudly, and the rest of the gang joined in with their congratulations. Bo in particular was hollering and seemed about ready to join her in the water.

Della waved both arms at them, then swam over and mounted the tube. "Okay, Ms. Kid! I'm ready, and don't hold back!" she shouted.

The Kid smirked and shook her head as Nudgie laughed and teased her about her new, proper nickname. Then the Kid pushed the throttle as far forward as it would go, the line pulled taut, and we were off.

It turned out the motor on the Kid's boat was a lot more powerful than Scott's, and Della was soon skimming along at speeds she'd never experienced before. It made me a little nervous for her, and when we passed the place where the boys were still floating and watching, I could tell from their expressions that they felt the same way. But Della was a trooper and rode like the miniature powerhouse she was. Within seconds we were all fist-pumping the air and cheering her on.

The Kid veered to starboard, then pulled hard and fast to port, trying to break Della's grip on the rope and send her tumbling across the water, but Della hung on like she was glued to that rope. The Kid accelerated, decelerated, and even crisscrossed at full speed back and forth over her own wake, making the tube bounce and slam down forcefully, doing everything she could think of to throw Della off. Nothing worked; Della hung on like a tick! Several minutes passed before she signaled that she was done.

The Kid idled down as we pulled abreast of Scott, and everyone in both boats came unglued. Della pulled herself up to a kneeling position and raised both fists into the air while screaming at the top of her lungs. We all screamed back. This time, Bo lost complete control and launched himself into the water. Within seconds, he had her around the waist and was boisterously bouncing her up and down in the water to the accompaniment of hoots and hollers from both boats. When the celebration was over, Bo hauled himself up and over the side of our boat, wanting to take a turn of his own behind the Kid's much-faster boat.

"You can still go first, Rache! I don't mind waitin'!" he said, beaming at me. I had to smile. Good ol' Bo. He just grew sweeter and sweeter the older he got. It occurred to me then that my cousin was growing up to become one amazing man. I wondered what kind of girl he might end up with someday. I sniffed at that and thought to myself that whoever she was, she would never be good enough for my Bo. No one would.

I watched as he reached over the side and gently helped Della into the boat.

CHAPTER 33

We spent the next several hours taking turns on the skis and the tube, stopping just long enough to scarf down sandwiches and guzzle sweet tea at the campsite before getting right back to it. Everyone had some amazing rides behind both boats, and even the Kid took a turn on the tube. It was so much fun that we weren't even aware of the passage of time. So when Bubba glanced at his watch and called out that it was almost three thirty, we were shocked!

The Kid started issuing orders: "Alright, let's go, folks! Pull in the rigs and ropes. Nudgie and I are going to haul in the traps; you boys go grab the two big empty coolers from the campsite. We'll meet up at the Tuckers' dock and dump the crabs into the coolers. Then we're all going to have to pitch in carrying them up to the truck, okay? Now, let's move! We don't want to be late for supper!"

Everyone scurried around, coiling ropes and putting away rigs and skis. The boys fetched the two largest coolers from the campsite and brought them to the Tuckers' dock. At Scott's suggestion, they had also brought the wop boards so we wouldn't have to go all the way back to camp to retrieve them later. Meanwhile, Della and I rode along with Nudgie and the Kid so we could watch the crab traps being pulled. The Kid's boat had a walk-through windshield with seating in the bow just like Scott's, so Della and I scrambled forward and took our seats there. The Kid climbed in behind the wheel and Nudgie sat directly behind her. In no time at all we had circled Bird Island and were headed back toward Land's End to retrieve the traps.

"I think I should tell y'all that Ann and I have a little competition going," Nudgie called up to us. "She drives past the floats while I lean over the side and scoop them up. I haul them into the boat while she circles around. The trick is for me to do all of that without her having to stop. Usually when we do this, I have the trap emptied and ready to drop back into the water by the time she reaches the spot I just pulled it from. But since we're doing this just for supper tonight, I won't be dropping the traps again. We'll just be circling for practice, then moving on to the next trap."

The Kid laughed. "And my job is to see if I can go fast enough to make her miss, but not so fast that she can't get the trap out of the water if she doesn't," she said.

Nudgie winked at us. "So far, I haven't missed!" She chuckled and we joined in.

"You'd better get ready," the Kid called out to Nudgie. "They're coming up on the right. And *don't scratch my boat!*"

Nudgie, who was midway between the wheel and the stern, nodded and positioned herself on the starboard side, leaning far out over the water. Della and I clasped hands and held our breaths as the Kid zoomed toward the first float. As we watched, Nudgie tensed up, the muscles in her back rippled, and she lunged toward the water. Next to me, I heard Della gasp, as it looked like Nudgie was about to pitch headfirst over the side of the boat. Then her back stiffened and she straightened up, clutching a yellow bleach bottle. The Kid slowed and turned gently to starboard while Della and I cheered as Nudgie quickly pulled up the trap and hauled it into the boat.

"Ha!" The Kid grinned back at Nudgie. "I almost had ya that time!"

Nudgie made a face at her sister. "Yeah? Well, better luck next time!"

"You mean THIS time!" the Kid shot back as she zoomed toward the second float.

Della and I giggled at their friendly wordplay. Since both of us lacked siblings, this sort of interaction was new to us. It gave us a glimpse into what it would be like to have a brother or sister.

The second trap was coming up fast. Once again Della and I held our breaths, and we were nearly bouncing in our seats from the excitement. I had my fingers crossed; next to me, Della whispered, "Come on, Nudgie! You can do it!"

As before, Nudgie leaned over the side, tensed up, then lunged far out over the side. This time, the Kid cut the boat sharply to starboard just as her sister reached for the float, and Della screamed as Nudgie pitched so far over the side that we really thought she was going to fall out. But she hooked her knees under the wooden trim that ran around the interior of the boat and, with a colossal effort, straightened up. Nudgie whooped loudly as she held up a bright-yellow bleach bottle. The Kid shook her head and smirked as she watched her little sister haul in the second trap.

Nudgie grinned back at her. "That was a close one, Ann!" she shouted. "I'll give ya that!"

The Kid shook her head again and turned toward the Tuckers' dock. Within minutes, we were tied up behind Scott at the floating dock, the crabs were transferred to the two large coolers, and the boys were practically running up the dock toward the beach with them.

Della and I, carrying the wop boards, were right on their heels. No one wanted to be late for supper.

Once we reached the beach, we hurried up the path toward the Tuckers' house, where Nudgie had parked the truck. (I ducked my head and tried to stay hidden behind the boys as we hurried past the Sikeses' house, which earned me a quizzical look from my cousin.) When we reached the truck, Nudgie lowered the tailgate, and we all jumped in. The Kid climbed in behind the wheel and started the engine. Only one thing remained to be done:

In the back of the truck, Bo raised both fists into the air, screamed "Yeeehaaaaw!"—and we were off.

CHAPTER 34

We could smell the barbecue before we even got to the Harden house. When we drove up, the first thing we saw was Mr. Wimpy standing in front of the grill, checking the coals. He turned and smiled, his blue eyes twinkling with the same gleam we'd seen in the Kid's eyes all day. Now we saw where she'd gotten it.

As soon as the truck stopped, we all bailed out of the back and the boys yanked out the coolers of fresh crabs. Ms. Frances had a huge pot of water seasoned with salt and Old Bay already boiling over a fire pit in the backyard, so we dragged the coolers over to it. As we turned toward the house, the sliding glass doors opened and out came all of our parents! They were carrying gifts, and Mr. Rooney held a birthday cake.

"SURPRISE!" the parents shouted, and they all started singing "Happy Birthday" to a very red-faced Della, who turned and buried her face in my chest. When the song was over, us kids milled around her, giving her hugs and wanting to know why she hadn't told any of us it was her birthday.

"Because," Mrs. Rooney answered for her, "our Della is too shy, but I knew all of her friends would want to celebrate with her, and this was the only way we could do it." She smiled, and Della threw herself into her mother's arms.

"Oh, Mama!" Della, still blushing, seemed unable to decide whether to laugh or cry. "I can't believe everyone did this for me!" She turned and smiled at us through her tears. "I wasn't expecting this, and I'm not sure how to act. I've never had a birthday party before."

"Do *what?*" Bo was incredulous. "Cheese an' rice, Della! How does that even happen?" He shot her a lopsided grin. "Well, ya won't never be able to say that again, now, will ya?" He grabbed her up and swung her around while everyone laughed.

The men gathered around Mr. Wimpy at the grill while Ms. Frances, using a long pair of tongs, began dropping crabs into the pot of boiling water. The other ladies had deposited the gifts and cake on one of several tables that had been set up under some pine trees, and had then disappeared back into the house to help with whatever still needed to be done in the kitchen. Us kids walked over to the tables to inspect the gifts, admire the cake, and generally keep out from underfoot while the adults finished preparing the meal.

Just beyond the tables we could see a pear tree, a plum tree, two different kinds of fig trees, and a huge scuppernong grape arbor. All were heavy-laden and ripe for the picking. Bo's eyes grew huge as he stared at all the fresh fruit, and I have to admit that my mouth was watering, too.

Nudgie walked over to join us and chuckled at the expressions on our faces. "Go ahead and help yourselves," she said. "There're also pomegranates over by the corner of the house, peaches by the pump house and loquats around front. Just don't ruin y'all's appetites. Supper'll be ready soon."

Bo leaped into the air and hollered before disappearing behind a leafy green wall of grapevines. The rest of us scattered to sample our own favorite fruits. Della and I ended up gravitating between the figs and the plums.

"This is wonderful!" Della said, biting into a fig. "Imagine being able to just walk out into your own yard and pick your own fruit!"

I nodded in agreement as I took a huge bite out of a plum. It was juicy and delicious, and I closed my eyes in bliss as I chewed and swallowed.

"Maybe," she continued, "I could get Mama and Daddy to plant some fruit trees around our house." She licked the juice from her fingers and smiled up at me. "Then you and Bo could come over anytime you wanted and help yourselves!"

I chuckled. "If you let Bo come over and eat fruit whenever he wants, you'll never have any. You've seen him eat!" We both laughed at that.

Across the yard, the Kid and Nudgie were helping Ms. Frances dump huge piles of steaming crabs onto the tables. The rest of the ladies were setting out large serving dishes of corn on the cob, hush-puppies, and potato salad while the men helped carry heaping platters of grilled chicken and steak.

Mr. Wimpy yelled, "Come an' get it!" and Bo almost tore a hole through the grapevines trying to get to the tables. Everyone laughed at his antics, but I knew exactly how he felt; nothing makes you as hungry as a day on the river.

Once everyone was seated around the tables, we bowed our heads and Mr. Wimpy said the blessing: "Our Father, we just thank Thee for these and all Thy many blessings. We ask in Christ's name, Amen."

"Amen," we echoed and dug in.

***

Two hours later, the meal was finished, the gifts had been opened, the cake, which had been served with Heavenly Hash ice cream, had all but been demolished (mostly thanks to Bo), and everyone was still gathered around the tables, relaxing and talking. It had started to cool off after the heat of the day and the weather was perfect. I was full and content and sitting quietly next to Della, who was still feeling a little overwhelmed as she once again inspected her birthday gifts.

Always aware of his location, I noticed that Scott was speaking quietly with his parents at the next table, and I felt familiar butterfly wings when he walked over and took a seat across from us. Bo, who was forking the last of the cake into his mouth (where did he put it all?), slid over to make room for him.

"What a meal!" Scott said. "This was really great of the Hardens and our folks to do all of this for us."

"Yeah," Della agreed, "especially what they all did for me for my birthday! I still can't believe it." She shook her head in wonder.

Scott smiled at her, making her duck her head and blush; I could feel an entire flock of butterflies fluttering around in my stomach. "Yeah, well . . . that's what I'd like to talk to you about, peanut," he said. Della looked up at him, her expression quizzical as he continued, "I feel really bad that I didn't know it was your birthday so I could've done something special for you myself." Scott held up a hand to stop her when Della began to protest. "I actually have an idea of how to make up for that, and my parents have agreed. Next Saturday night we're going to the Savannah Yacht Club to attend some sort of annual dinner and dance, and I remembered how, at the beginning of the summer, we all promised to introduce you to all sorts of new adventures." He grinned and dropped her a wink. "Personally, I don't like going to these kinds of things—they can be pretty boring—but my parents enjoy mingling and networking, plus all proceeds go to charity, so it's something we never miss out on. I was just wondering if you'd like to go with us. I'd sure appreciate having someone to talk to all evening, and you could experience something else you've never done before. It would be a belated birthday gift."

Della's eyes were huge and her mouth was agape. She seemed unable to speak. Next to her, I could feel the butterflies inside of me dying as I hid my clenched teeth behind a smile.

I answered for her. "She would love to go, Scott!" I gushed. "Who wouldn't?" I turned to Della. "Come on! You have to say yes." I widened my smile. "Oh, Della, I'm so excited for you!"

Across from me, my cousin stopped mid-chew and gave me a confused look. He appeared ready to speak, so I kicked him under the table. He ducked his head, shoveled the last bite of cake into his mouth, and glared at me as he chewed.

Sitting next to me, Della took a deep, trembling breath and, blushing crimson, graciously accepted Scott's invitation. He smiled at her and promised to have his mother call hers with all of the pertinent information. Then he and Bo walked over and joined the Stairsteps to discuss wop-boarding.

"Oh, Rachel!" Della appeared to be in shock. "I can't believe what just happened. Dinner and dancing at the Savannah Yacht Club! Who'd-a-thought? It's going to be amazing, like being a princess for the evening, just like Cinderella!" She sighed. "Can you imagine?"

Oh, yeah, I thought. I can imagine. I can imagine quite well, thank you very much. I smiled as warmly as I could, but inside of my chest, my heart felt like a block of ice. Oh, yes, I thought, I can imagine better than anyone. Della's birthday was today but next Saturday she would still be celebrating . . . with Scott. My smile widened automatically as she threw her arms around me and "squozed" me tight. Oh, I can imagine just fine. I "squozed" her back. Next Saturday was going to be wonderful for her. Next Saturday would be a night she would never forget as long as she lived. Next Saturday would be a dream come true for her. I forced another smile as I gritted my teeth even harder and fought down the sudden desire to "squoze" the life right out of her.

Next Saturday was MY birthday.

CHAPTER 35

Fiddler Crab Beach was almost completely underwater when we arrived that night. We had stayed at the Hardens' house until well after nightfall, shooting baskets and playing board games while waiting for the sun to go down and the tide to come in. Now it was completely dark out except for the light of the full moon, which had turned everything a ghostly silver. It was almost like being on a different world.

"Okay, folks, I have one more surprise." The Kid held up a large paper bag. We all gathered around her as she reached inside and pulled out a handful of glow-in-the-dark necklaces and bracelets. "I thought these would look cool in the dark, and they'll keep you from running into each other in the dark," she said.

We all whooped and laughed as we each grabbed several. In no time at all, our entire gang was glowing in the dark.

"This is it!" Scott was practically bouncing; I'd never seen him so excited. "Before we start, does anyone have any questions? I know Della's never done this before." He smiled at her and I was glad it was dark so I didn't have to flash another fake smile. My jaw was starting to ache from clenching my teeth so much.

Nudgie stepped forward. "Actually," she said, "I've never done this, either." She held up a wop board. "This board is my brother, Paul's, from when he was a kid. I found it on a shelf in his woodshop. I'd sure appreciate some pointers."

Scott grinned at her, then spent the next several minutes explaining technique and balance. When he was finished, he stepped to the edge of the shallow water that covered the beach, dropped his board onto it, and took several steps back. We all held our breaths as he took off running and leaped onto the board. A huge cheer rose as Scott smoothly and gracefully skimmed across the surface of the water, his glow-in-the-dark accessories leaving colorful traces of light behind him. He stepped off into the waist-deep water when he reached the marsh grass, turned, and gave a mock bow as we applauded again. It was a flawless ride, and even I was smiling as he waded back to where we all stood, waiting.

As soon as Scott reached us, a rebel yell sounded behind me and Bo tore past, threw his board onto the water, and leaped onto it, all in one fluid motion. He skimmed across the surface of the water, stepped off just as gracefully as Scott had, and turned to face us, grinning from ear to ear.

There was a split second of silence, then everyone was shouting and laughing as we dashed toward the water. In no time at all there were wet, screaming kids skimming across the surface of the water in every direction. The Kid told us she wasn't much of a wop-boarder and took a seat on the edge of the Sikeses' dock, where she could keep an eye on us and watch the fun.

Nudgie, meanwhile, was right in the thick of it. "Hey! I think I got it," she called. "Watch this, y'all!" We all turned to look as Nudgie, who was standing at the footpath, took off running, leaped onto her board, and promptly went tumbling head over heels into the shallow water. She came up laughing and sputtering. "Okay, maybe not," she said.

"Way to go, Grace!" The Kid took the opportunity to tease her little sister. Nudgie just grinned and shook her head as she prepared to try again.

Over on the Tuckers' dock, Scott and Bo had their heads together, and I wondered what was in the works. They dropped their boards onto the water, then turned and headed down the dock toward the river. Stopping after about twenty feet, they turned back toward the beach. By now, we'd all noticed them and were waiting to see what they would do. Scott shouted off a countdown, and they both took off running. A murmur ran through the group when we realized what they were about to attempt.

Scott and Bo, timing themselves perfectly, leaped from the dock and hit the boards in tandem. Side by side, they skimmed across the surface of the water all the way to the footpath, where they gracefully stepped off the boards onto dry land. They turned and gave each other a leaping high five while the rest of us came unglued. Over on the Sikeses' dock, the Kid cheered right along with us. My own applause was cut short when I glanced beyond the boys.

In the shadows on the edge of the footpath, directly behind Scott and Bo, Foxy Sikes stood, watching. There was no mistaking the hateful, angry glare he shot in our direction. Our presence on the beach was probably interfering with his nighttime enterprises. I swallowed hard, turned to retreat toward the docks, and promptly ran into Nudgie, who was standing behind me, frowning toward the footpath. She'd obviously seen him, too.

"Those guys give me the creeps!" Nudgie's frown deepened. "There's something about them that's just not right. Y'all kids know to stay away from them, don't you?" She looked down at me, and I nodded. "Good," she said. "Keep it that way!" Nudgie put her arm around me protectively and shot one more glance toward the footpath as we walked back to the docks.

Out on the beach, the rest of our gang was wop-boarding all over the place. Bubba was trying to set up some sort of relay race competition, and Scott was trying to see who could travel the farthest. It was pandemonium of the very best kind. Bo was just being Bo, shouting and laughing and challenging everyone to everything. Apparently, wop-boarding was one of those things he was just naturally talented at.

I glanced over at Della, who had teamed up with the two younger Stairsteps. Della seemed to be another one of those kids who was naturally good at things. She was picking this up just as quickly as she'd picked up tubing and skiing. I smiled at her; she grinned back and gave me a wink, and I felt the tension from earlier in the day drain away. I knew it wasn't her fault Scott had forgotten my birthday while worrying about hers. I ducked my head sheepishly as I remembered how jealous and angry I'd been. Della was a sweetheart, pure and kind, and would never do anything to hurt anyone else. I mentally scolded myself and swore to be more forgiving and understanding. I knew better than to feel that way! Cheese an' rice, as my cousin would say.

I waded out to where Della stood, ready to challenge her to a competition of some sort while burying the hatchet at the same time, a hatchet she didn't even know existed.

The smile on my face was as genuine as I could make it.

CHAPTER 36

It was after midnight by the time we finished wop-boarding, made our way down to the boats, and motored across to Bird Island. As soon as we disembarked, the Stricklands scurried about, lighting all the lanterns that had been hung around the campsite, while Scott saw to getting a campfire started. Della and I helped the Kid pull the wop boards out of the boats and set them up against the trees to dry, while Bo happily helped Nudgie unpack the graham crackers, marshmallows, and chocolate bars.

Everyone retreated to their tents to change into dry clothes; then we all gathered around the campfire, where the Kid was waiting to tell us some of her stories.

"Okay, folks," she began. "This is the story of John and Mary and explains why most people are afraid to camp out on Bird Island. John and Mary were two young, star-crossed lovers who could never be together."

"Oh! Sort of like *Romeo and Juliet!*" I exclaimed, already enthralled.

"That's right!" The Kid grinned at me. "John was the son of a wealthy plantation owner, while Mary came from a family of lowly sharecroppers. They probably never should've met, but Mary worked in the rice paddies down near Land's End and John used to fish and shrimp up and down the banks of the Vernon River. One day, their eyes met across the water and they fell hopelessly and irrevocably in love."

The Kid took a moment to pop the top on a can of RC Cola as we all waited breathlessly for her to continue. Bo began to rock back and forth as the Kid took her time tipping the can back, taking several long swallows, obviously drawing out the suspense.

"Well," she finally continued, "the families were *not* happy when they found out these two young lovers professed to have feelings for one another. Each of their fathers took a firm stand and forbade the two from ever seeing each other again."

Beside me in the firelight, Della gasped and put her hands to her face. "Oh, those poor kids!" she cried out shakily; the tears in her eyes glistened in the firelight.

"Yup," the Kid went on. "But as much as they tried to be obedient, it wasn't long before John and Mary realized they just couldn't live without each other. They met in secret and devised a plan: On a prearranged day, John would take his boat out as usual, but instead of fishing and shrimping, he would land on Bird Island, where he would wait. At sunset, when all the other workers were leaving the rice paddies, Mary would make her way down the riverbank to the very spot where Morgan's dock now stands, where she would call out John's name. Then she just had to wait for John to row across and pick her up. They knew that once they were together, nothing would ever keep them apart again. They would run away and live happily ever after."

"Oh, how romantic," Della sighed.

"It was a good plan," the Kid agreed, "but Mother Nature had plans of her own. On that fateful day, as planned, John landed his boat on Bird Island and waited for the sun to go down. Once it had, he listened for his lady to call out to him.

"On the other side of the river, Mary finally made her way to the designated spot. 'John! John, my love!' she called out across the water.

"'I'm here,' he answered. 'I'm coming!' He climbed into his boat and began to row across." The Kid lifted her RC can again, drawing out the story. She took her time swallowing.

"Oh, please, Ms. Kid," Della begged. "What happened next? Did they get away? Did they live happily ever after?"

The suspense was killing me, Bo was squirming like he had an itch he couldn't scratch, and anticipation was causing a low murmur to echo around the fire.

The Kid slowly finished the RC, then tore open the wrapper of a Snickers bar. She took a bite and smiled at Della before continuing. "Alright, CD, folks, CD!" The Kid's eyes took on her trademark twinkle.

"CD?" I whispered.

"It's short for 'calm down,'" Nudgie explained quietly.

"Okay! You kids know how quickly the weather can change out here." The Kid grew serious as we all nodded. "It's always been that way. Well, John had just rowed out of the channel and into the main waterway when a storm blew in. Dark clouds billowed, thunder clapped, and lightning bolts tore through the air. Then the sky opened and the rain came down so hard that the two lovers could barely see each other.

"Midway across, John's boat was swamped. He threw himself overboard and began to swim toward the bank. Lightning flashed and Mary saw the boat sink so, screaming his name, she leaped into the river and began to swim toward the spot where his boat had gone down. Treading water, she spun in circles, crying and calling his name. Meanwhile, John was still making his way to the last place he'd seen Mary. He screamed her name each time he lifted his face from the water. The clouds blocked what little bit of moonlight there might have been, and the rain poured from the sky harder and harder, until visibility was down to nothing. Soon, the two young lovers had lost all sense of direction and had begun to swim in circles."

The Kid shook her head sadly. "And that's how it happened: There in the inky darkness, with the storm raging and the water swirling all around them, John and Mary were lost to each other. Their bodies were never found, and their families never knew what had become of them. But . . ." She paused for effect as she looked each of us in the eye. "People say when the moon is full and the night is quiet, just like tonight, you can hear the two young lovers calling to each other across the water: 'John!' 'Mary!' And they are destined to do so forever."

When the story was over, the Kid leaned back and cocked her head, listening to the sounds of the night. We couldn't help but join her. All around us, it was as silent as a cemetery.

Then Nudgie shouted, "S'mores!" and we all jumped about three feet into the air. That got us laughing, and we were soon telling jokes and sharing funny stories as we toasted marshmallows and assembled our treats.

Finally, at about two in the morning, the Kid sent us off to our tents. We had a full day of tubing and skiing to look forward to the next day, so we needed to get some rest. Della and I ducked into our tent. She seemed to fall asleep as soon as her head hit the pillow. When her breathing grew deep and even, I stood and quietly slipped out into the night. When Della and I had been gathering firewood earlier that day, I'd noticed a large tangle of driftwood tree roots overlooking the river and had thought that it looked like a good place to sit and pass the night.

I turned toward the other side of the island and walked into the dark.

CHAPTER 37

"Now, why am I not surprised to see you here?"

I nearly jumped out of my skin as I stifled the scream that wanted to tear past my lips.

Nudgie was sitting on the driftwood tree roots. She gazed up at me, her eyes glinting in the moonlight. She beckoned, inviting me to join her. "I guess I'm not the only insomniac in the group," she said as I settled myself beside her. "I do understand, though. Life starts to get a little complicated once you reach a certain age. It can be hard to sleep."

I nodded and sat quietly, listening to the night. The world was silent around us. It was amazing how peaceful and quiet the river was at this time of night. The full moon shared the sky with a smattering of stars and a few errant, wispy clouds as it dipped toward the tree line; and the only sounds were the occasional lonely calls of night birds, the lapping of the water against the land, and the soft whisper of the wind as it moved through the marsh grass. I'd never come down to the river on my ramblings. I hadn't realized what I'd been missing. It felt magical. I sighed, leaned farther back into the driftwood, and closed my eyes.

I must have dozed off because I was jarred awake by a loud thump and a stream of obscenities. I gasped and started to lurch to my feet, but a hand on my arm stopped me.

"Shhh!" Nudgie had her lips to my ear. "Don't move and don't speak," she whispered and sat back very slowly.

Out in their boat, less than twenty yards away, the Sikeses were pulling up one of their crab traps. Foxy was cursing and railing at his sons about the lateness of the hour, trying to make them move faster. Apparently, they had a deadline to meet.

"Well, it ain't our fault, Daddy!" Gary argued back. "How was we s'pose to know them brats was gon' be out on the beach half the night?"

Foxy spewed more obscenities as the boys worked to lift the trap from the water. Inside was one of the plastic-wrapped bundles. Derry pulled open one side of the trap and removed it.

"I 'bout had it with all yer excuses, boy!" Foxy bellowed as he boxed Gary in the head. "An' I 'bout had it with them kids, always pokin' their noses where they ought not tuh be poked an' gittin' in the middle o' things they ought not tuh be in the middle of!" He let loose another stream of obscenities. "I'm 'bout tuh put a stop to it, though, an' I know one little brat that ain't gon' like how I do it. Yessuh! Somebody's 'bout tuh have a real bad day!"

I swallowed hard at that; I knew exactly who he meant. I shivered, and Nudgie put an arm around me.

Keeping as still as statues, we continued to watch as the Sikeses finished their work and motored around the island, out of sight. When they were gone, I sighed audibly and nearly melted with relief.

"I wonder what that was all about," Nudgie said. In the moonlight, I could see the frown on her face. "Those sure weren't crabs they were pulling out of that trap." She looked down at me. "But I guess some things are better left alone and ignorance is bliss." She gave me a reassuring smile.

I swallowed again before I spoke. "They scare me, Nudgie. I get a bad feeling from them, like they're going to hurt me or do something awful to me. I just want to stay as far away from them as I can." I shivered again, and Nudgie gave me a quick squeeze.

"Well," she said, "staying away from them is a pretty good idea, I'd say. From what I've heard, they're involved in some pretty shady stuff. Getting too close to them could be a dangerous thing."

I nodded and cleared my throat. "Nudgie?" I spoke hesitantly, and she looked down at me again. My voice was quivering slightly, and I took a deep breath to compose myself before continuing. "Do you think those Sikeses would kill a kid? I mean, I know they're dangerous, but do you think they'd actually murder a little kid?"

Nudgie turned to face me. "Rachel," she said, "I don't know what they're capable of. I only know they're ruthless. There's something about them that's just not right. I learned a long time ago to stay as far away from them as possible. You and your friends all need to do the same, and y'all need to talk to Della about them because she's new to the neighborhood and doesn't know any better. And warn her about Owen Godwin, too. I've never seen it, but I've heard he can lose his temper and go pretty crazy at times. I'm not so much afraid of him as I am cautious. But you never can tell, so it's probably best if you tell Della to stay away from him, too."

I nodded. That was true. It would never occur to Della that there might be evil lurking just around the corner. I shivered again, then looked back up at Nudgie. "I've been thinking a lot about death." I hadn't meant to say that to her, but it just sort of slipped out. I swallowed before continuing. "I mean, I wonder what it's like, how it feels, if it hurts, you know?"

I remembered how the dead man on the beach had looked and how Foxy had described watching the life leave a body when someone died. And I thought about dead eyes: empty and black, Foxy had said, like a doll's eyes. Ever since that night I'd been plagued by the images in my head, both remembered and imagined. It was all I could think about. I knew I was in mortal danger and felt it was just a matter of time before the Sikeses came for me. I wondered what it would be like to die. I was even starting to wish I could see death up close so I could understand it better and maybe not be so afraid when it finally came. I blinked back tears and hoped Nudgie wouldn't notice.

"I guess that sounds pretty weird, huh?" I laughed nervously.

"Not really." Nudgie smiled down at me. "You're at that age when kids start to understand more about the world around them. It's natural to wonder about things like that." She laughed. "I remember a few years ago, when I realized people actually die and are gone for good, I was terrified to let my mother out of my sight! Every morning she'd drive me to school and I'd try to think of things to say that would keep her there with me for just a few seconds longer. She always ended up looking at me like I was nuts, but I was really just scared something would happen while I was at school and I'd never see her again. It seems silly now, but at the time, I was terrified."

"Why do you think you felt that way?" I couldn't believe she was sharing this with me. "I mean, did something happen to you to make you that scared?" I wondered if maybe I wasn't the only one who'd had some sort of run-in with the Sikeses or someone else who was just as bad.

Nudgie sat quietly for a moment before answering. "I'm not sure exactly. A couple of things did happen that affected me pretty deeply, one being particularly awful." She looked at me intently, frowning slightly. "I'm not really sure I should be talking to you about this."

"Oh, please, Nudgie! It would make me feel so much better to know I'm not the only one who feels this way."

Nudgie seemed to weigh my words, then she nodded. I held my breath as she began to speak, fearing the slightest sound or movement would cause her to change her mind. "When I was really young," she began, "my grandparents died—first my granny when I was six, then my grand-daddy Bill when I was eight. The whole family went to both funerals, but my parents wouldn't let me go. It really hurt to be left out like that. I mean, I loved my grandparents as much as anyone else did and I would miss them too, so it made me feel really bad, like I wasn't truly a part of the family or something. Then it occurred to me that maybe there was something they didn't want me to see, something that would hurt me or scare me. Maybe death was too horrible for a child to experience." Nudgie smiled and shook her head. "So, of course, I became completely fascinated with death. When one of my father's dogs died, I had to get a look at it before he buried it. When he went hunting, I had to see the deer and the quail before he butchered them. It was some sort of sick fascination. I noticed, though, that all of the animals and birds had the same shocked look, the same expression of disbelief—"

"The same eyes?" I couldn't help interrupting. "Like doll's eyes?"

Nudgie looked over at me, blinking in surprise. "Well . . . yeah," she said, "that's exactly what they looked like." She shook her head before continuing. "Then, about four years ago, one of the boys at school suffered what's called a ruptured aneurysm, right there in class in front of everybody. That's where one of your blood vessels grows a balloon on the side of it. The bigger it gets, the thinner the walls of the vessel get until it bursts and all the blood runs out. I'll never forget it. It was the week before school let out for Christmas vacation and we were decorating the room. I was making a red-and-green construction-paper chain for the tree, and the boy was probably only six or eight feet away from me." Nudgie smiled sadly. "I had a little crush on him and was always watching him, so I saw the whole thing. I won't describe it to you, but it has to be the most horrible thing I've ever experienced. This little boy—my friend, my first crush—practically died right in front of me! I guess I went into shock or something because as soon as I realized something was wrong, I blacked out. I literally have no memory of anything that happened after that. I don't remember the ambulance coming for him, I don't remember leaving school or going home or anything else about that day.

"The boy and his family went to our church, so as soon as she heard what had happened, my sister Ann rushed to the hospital to be there with the family. Mama stayed home with me; I guess she was worried about what I'd been through that day and wanted to keep an eye on me.

"Anyway, at ten o'clock that night, I heard the back door open and my mother ask for an update. Then I heard Ann's voice saying that my friend was dead. The doctors hadn't been able to save him." Nudgie trembled at the memory. "A cold chill ran through me, and I remember it felt so strange to think of a little kid being dead. Little kids are supposed to run and play and get scraped and bruised, but they aren't supposed to die. They just aren't.

"I stayed awake almost all night trying to wrap my head around the fact that my friend was gone. He was dead and gone, just like that. It seemed so wrong, and it took a very long time to become real to me. I'll never forget how fast it happened or the way he looked when he fell or the sound his head made when it hit the floor. Honestly, I don't think a day has gone by since then that I haven't thought about him and how he looked lying there on the floor of our classroom. A thing like that gets under your skin and eats away at you. That's when you realize life isn't as safe as you've always believed. Bad things happen, even to little kids.

"It was right about then that I started being afraid to let my mother out of my sight, and it was right about then that I started being unable to sleep at night." Nudgie bit her lip. "Death is a frightening and powerful thing, and it's not a pretty thing, but it does have a way of fascinating and captivating you. So, no, it's not weird at all for you to be thinking about it. Just try to make sure it's not the only thing you think about. That would be more than just weird." Nudgie looked at me intensely.

"That would be crazy."

CHAPTER 38

"What a weekend! I knew this was going to be great!"

It had all been perfect, and Scott was beside himself: skiing and tubing, Della's surprise party, wop-boarding, the campout, and now we had just concluded another full day on the water and were bringing everything from the campsite over to the Tuckers' dock. Once there, everyone pitched in to separate Scott's camping gear from everyone else's. Then we had to load Scott's things into his boat and help run everything else up the dock to the Kid's truck. She had decided to leave her boat in the water so she could go out in it over the next week.

"Aw, yeah, y'all!" Bo was just as excited as Scott. "I think we oughta do this every summer!"

"Sure, Bo! That's a great idea. The Annual Bird Island Campout!" Scott was smiling and his eyes sparkled behind his aviator sunglasses, making the flock of butterflies in my tummy take off in unison.

The Stairsteps agreed and Della jumped up and down, her feet turning the floating dock into a bass drum. I smiled along with everyone else but, remembering Foxy Sikes's words the night before, I wondered if I'd still be around next summer.

The Kid grinned and said, "That could be a definite possibility, folks!"

Nudgie nodded and we all cheered.

"But for now," the Kid went on, "let's get all this stuff loaded up so everybody can get home and get ready for church tomorrow."

With that, we grabbed the things that needed to go up to the truck and took off toward the beach. By the time we reached the end of the dock, we were practically running.

Della, carrying her tent and sleeping bag, was in front and reached the beach first. She leaped off the dock, the rest of us right on her heels, and took off toward the footpath. She disappeared into the shadows under the trees then suddenly reappeared, staggering backward and falling on her bottom, the tent and sleeping bag flying out of her hands and landing in the sand beside her. The rest of us skidded to a stop, surprised and confused, unsure of what had happened. We looked up just as Foxy Sikes stepped out of the shadows.

He scowled at us, then turned his anger on Della. "You bes' be watchin' where yer runnin', girl," he snarled. "This here's *my* footpath an' you an' yer li'l friends don't need tuh be chargin' up 'n' down it, actin' like its yer's!"

Della, still on the ground, gasped and crab-walked backward as Bo and Scott stepped up to stand between her and Foxy. I melted back to stand behind Bubba while Aubrey and Tully helped Della to her feet.

"Excuse me, sir," Scott said, trying to be reasonable, "but this footpath also belongs to the Tuckers, and we have their permission to be here."

Foxy Sikes ignored him; his eyes were now glued to Bo, who was glaring back fearlessly. It looked for a moment like it was going to get ugly. Then the Kid stepped up and placed herself between Foxy and my cousin. But before she could say anything, Foxy shot Bo one last angry look, then turned and stalked back up the footpath toward his house.

"That's why Sikes is short for 'psycho,'" Bo declared loudly.

I could tell Foxy had heard this remark by the way his shoulders tightened up.

"Bo," I cautioned him, "you really shouldn't antagonize him like that."

"Whadaya mean?" Bo was incredulous. "We have permission to be here! An' he shouldn't have hollered at Della that way to begin with! Cheese an' rice!"

"It's okay, folks," the Kid said, trying to smooth it over. "We just had an incredible weekend. Let's not let one stinkin' old snake in the grass ruin it for us."

"Yeah," Scott agreed. "This was still the most awesome weekend ever! Nothing can change that, right?"

The boys cheered and we continued up to the truck. Nudgie slipped up to walk on one side of Della, who had bent to retrieve the tent and sleeping bag she'd dropped, while I stepped up on her other side. It was obvious that Della was shaken by her first run-in with Foxy Sikes, and I knew this was the perfect time to warn her to stay away from him.

"You okay, shortcake?" Nudgie was doing her best to make Della smile. It worked . . . a little. "Rachel and I were going to talk to you about the Sikeses and let you know to stay away from them. I guess we waited too long."

Della sighed. "It's okay, Nudgie. I just wish he hadn't been so mean. I didn't run into him on purpose. He really didn't have to push me down like that!"

I raised my eyebrows. I hadn't realized she'd been pushed. It was a good thing Bo hadn't realized it, either, or things would've really gotten out of hand. We continued up the path while Nudgie explained a little more about the Sikeses as well as Owen Godwin. When she was done, I was pretty sure Della would never come down to Fiddler Crab Beach without having at least one of us with her.

By the time we reached the truck, the boys already had the tailgate down and were loading everything into the back. When they were done, Scott waved goodbye and headed back toward the Tuckers' dock, where his boat was moored. The rest of us piled into the truck bed while the Kid slid behind the steering wheel. She drove each of us home since we all had camping gear to carry. We were exhausted, sunburned, and extremely happy and, ultimately, no one gave Foxy Sikes a second thought.

No one, that is, except me.

***

Later that evening, after a hot shower and an even hotter supper where I recounted all of our gang's weekend escapades to my delighted parents, I climbed into bed and settled in, expecting to face my usual sleepless night. Surprisingly, I fell asleep right away, but I can't say I rested well. My dreams were plagued by images of dead children and of running away from people who were trying to kill me, and everywhere I turned there were eyes—empty, black doll's eyes staring at me like they had secrets to tell, secrets I couldn't quite make out, secrets I didn't want to know.

The night seemed to stretch on forever.

CHAPTER 39

The next morning at church, it was easy to tell from the sunburns and sun-bleached hair which kids had gone on the campout and which adult had chaperoned. Everyone in our Sunday school class wanted to hear all the details and wanted to be a part of The Second Annual Bird Island Campout. The event appeared ready to turn into a huge blowout for all the kids our age. Scott, of course, being Scott, immediately offered up the use of one or two more of his family's boats to accommodate the growing number of participants, and our Sunday school teacher suggested we extend it to a two-night campout and turn it into a Bible-based retreat. It sounded like it could really become something big, which prompted Scott to suggest that we move the location from tiny Bird Island on the Vernon River to the larger, group-friendly Pigeon Island on Moon River. That way, he pointed out, more people would be able to attend and we'd be camping close to his house, which would make it more convenient if we needed to use more than one of his boats—not to mention it would allow us to reach his house quickly and easily if we needed to. You never knew when someone might get sick or hurt, and what if a storm blew in?

Our teacher, who was very excited at the prospect of a youth retreat, promised to discuss the matter with the pastor and the Board of Deacons to see if we could add it to next year's church calendar of events. Then, after saying an opening prayer, he opened his Bible and started the lesson.

An hour later, when the bell rang and Sunday school was over, all the other kids chattered excitedly about next year's big campout as they headed over to the sanctuary. Our gang gathered outside to discuss this new turn of events.

"Wow!" Scott's expression broadcast his feelings. "That got really big really fast! I had no idea so many kids would be interested in camping out like we did."

"Yeah," Bo agreed, frowning slightly. "But it almost feels like we done lost control over our own personal little thing! I mean, it jus' wouldn't have been the same if we'd had to stop halfway through everything to go back to the campsite to study our Bibles an' pray an' stuff. No offense to the church or nothin'—y'all know I'm all about goin' to Bible studies an' youth retreats an' whatnot; I'd never miss one! But this campout was s'pose to be ours, jus' for us, an' I'd jus' as soon keep it that way, not turn it into some big ol' religious event! That'd be changin' the whole purpose of it. I know it'd sure ruin it for me, ya know? I mean, cheese an' rice!" He spit into the dirt.

Bubba nodded in agreement. "I gotta say, I'm agreein' with Bo." His younger brothers were nodding along with him. "No offense, Scott. We all know how much ya love your ministerin' stuff, but this was s'pose to be our own private thing, jus' for our gang—not that a weekend Bible retreat wouldn't be fun. Me an' my brothers wouldn't never miss out on somethin' churchy, y'all know that, but that's not what this was s'pose to be about. I'm with Bo: I feel like we done lost control, or like somethin's 'bout to be taken away from us!"

Scott, being a natural leader and mediator, stepped forward and put a hand on Bo's and Bubba's shoulders. He smiled as he made eye contact with each of them. "I understand exactly how you both feel," he said, "and I have to admit that I agree with you."

Bo and Bubba looked like you could've knocked them over with a feather.

"This was our idea and our own special event that we planned for ourselves. It wasn't meant to include all these other kids or have anything to do with church. That being said, there's no reason why we can't plan two separate campouts every summer: one for the church group and one of our own. That's what I'm thinking, anyway." Scott smiled as he clapped Bo and Bubba on their backs.

"Hey!" Bubba's face lit up. "Now, I like the sound o' that. We'd get two summer campouts 'stead o' one!" Behind him, the two younger Stairsteps grinned and slapped high fives.

"That's right," Scott agreed, "and since we'd hold the youth retreat on Pigeon Island, it would be like Bird Island was still all ours, and we wouldn't have to share any part of our campout with anybody else. Besides," he glanced at Della, "part of the reason we got together was to celebrate the peanut's birthday. That hasn't changed, right?"

Della blushed beneath her burn when Scott winked at her, and I found myself once again hiding my gritted teeth behind a smile as the boys voiced their agreement.

"Man-oh-man alive!" Bo was rubbing his hands together, already gearing up for next year. "That sounds cool, y'all! Jus' think: *two* big campouts! An' maybe we could even turn it into somethin' bigger someday, like maybe a youth trip up to Stone Mountain an' Six Flags or somewhere like that. All kinds o' big things could come out o' this!" Bo's sea-green eyes were gleaming as he bounced up and down on his toes. Then he made a failed attempt at a whisper: "Cheese an' rice!"

Scott smiled and shook his head, and everyone laughed as we headed into the sanctuary for church.

After church, the boys huddled up off to one side of the churchyard to make plans for the next few days. I was about to join them when I heard my mother call my name. I sighed deeply as I turned toward her. She always left me alone to enjoy the Lord's Day, so I knew she must be arranging something that involved me. I noticed she was standing with Della and Mrs. Rooney, so whatever she was planning involved them, too.

"Rachel Anne still needs a few more outfits and accessories before school starts in a few weeks," my mother was saying as I walked up, "so I think we should all go shopping together tomorrow." My mother giggled girlishly. "We'll make a day of it! We'll help the girls pick out some cute things, maybe have them put on a little fashion show for us right there in the dressing room area! Then we can all go out for luncheon. It will be an absolutely fabulous day!"

Della and her mother were smiling and nodding.

"Rachel!" My mother was practically gushing. "The Bashlors have invited Della to attend the annual charity ball at the Savannah Yacht Club next weekend, and she hasn't a thing to wear! I'd planned on doing some more school shopping with you tomorrow, so I've invited her and her mother to join us. We can help her pick out the perfect dress, shoes, and accessories for the event and have just a wonderful girls' day out together. Won't that be fun?"

All I could do was smile; it was all I had in me. I won't lie and say I was happy for Della. The ball was Saturday, and Saturday was my birthday. I felt it should be me going. It was as simple as that. Ever since Scott had invited her, I'd been trying to find it in me to be happy for Della. It had been a struggle, but now I had to not only smile and pretend to be happy for her, I had to help her pick out an outfit! The unfairness of it left a sour taste in my mouth. My jaw hurt from all the teeth-clenching I'd been doing lately, and it was hard to swallow past the lump in my throat.

Della, of course, was clueless. She was bouncing and giggling not only at the prospect of attending the ball but of spending a girls' day out with me. She had no idea I was upset. She didn't know Saturday was my birthday or that I had the hots for her date to the ball. I knew she never would have agreed to go if she'd been aware of any of that. Della loved me, pure and simple, and she would never do anything that she thought might hurt me. She loved me with every ounce of her little being, and it was this fact that left me feeling monstrous.

I had begun to question what kind of person I was, to be able to do and feel some of the things I was experiencing lately. I could feel myself winding up tighter and tighter inside, and I wondered if I would eventually melt down or just "go slug nutty," as my cousin feared. Or maybe I wouldn't live long enough to go crazy. There were the Sikeses, after all, and my fear of them lurked on the perimeter of my every thought. They were coming for me; God help me, I knew they were. I swallowed and clenched my teeth even harder as I wondered whether I would die or lose my mind first.

I continued to smile.

CHAPTER 40

Monday morning dawned bright and clear. I knew this because my mother had me out of bed at sunrise to see it. We were picking up Della and Mrs. Rooney at eight o'clock sharp, then driving to downtown Savannah to browse some designer shops. In her excitement, my mother had decided we needed to be there when the stores opened for business. I wasn't nearly as excited, to put it mildly, and tried my best to get out of going.

There had been small skirmishes between my mother and me ever since my feet hit the floor that morning, but the final battle was waged over breakfast; I believe it was the Tang that finally put me over the edge.

"But Mama, I really do have enough clothes already. You've been shopping for me ever since school let out. There's absolutely nothing else I need!" I shoved the untouched glass of Tang away.

"Rachel." Mama would not be deterred. "One can never have enough outfits! Now, the matter is closed." She lifted her coffee cup to her lips.

"But I really wanted to hang out with the boys today." Yes, I was whining. "Scott has something to do this morning, but they're riding their bikes at the Big Hole later!"

"Rachel Anne!" Mama slammed her coffee cup down on the table and gave me *the look*. "You are going shopping with us today, and that is final! You spend entirely too much time with those boys as it is. It's time you stopped being such a little roughneck and started behaving more like the young lady you are." Mama's lips were pinched into a thin line. "Now, go to your room and get ready. And wear a dress—"

"A dress?" I interrupted.

"A dress!" Mama was adamant. "We are shopping for proper dress attire, and you need to be wearing the correct slips and undergarments for trying them on. Now, get!"

I shot an angry look back over my shoulder as I headed to my room.

"Rachel Anne Holland!" My mother was shocked by my behavior; I had always been a compliant, obedient child. "Don't you give me that look! You come back here this instant, young lady!"

I didn't even slow down.

***

It was a horrible day, and it seemed to pass at a snail's pace. My mother had begun giving me a good talking to as soon as I came out of my room dressed and ready to go, and had droned on and on until we left the house. I pasted on what was becoming my trademark fake smile as soon as we pulled into the Rooneys' driveway, ignoring my mother as she issued one last, quick warning to watch my smart mouth and sassy attitude.

Della, of course, noticed nothing, and I doubt Mrs. Rooney would have either if my mother hadn't given her a knowing look and mentioned that it was "almost that time of the month" while tipping her head in my direction. I mentally rolled my eyes but decided we could just go with that story if I wasn't able to maintain my happy-girl façade. Who knew? Maybe that actually was part of my problem. It *had* been about a month since Mother Nature's first visit.

***

We browsed through several shops downtown while listening to my mother bemoan the fact that we hadn't had time to make a trip to Atlanta. That, she assured Mrs. Rooney, was the VERY best place to go for formal attire. Mrs. Rooney and Della were perfectly happy with the stores downtown; they had never shopped for designer labels, so this was plenty of excitement for them.

Della was thrilled and could barely contain her excitement.

"Oh, Rachel," she gushed. "I know this is probably old hat to you, but this is a dream come true for me, like living in a fairy tale! I mean, who'd-a-thought?" she squealed as she bounced on her toes.

I probably would've found her reactions adorable if I hadn't been in such a sour mood. Della, as usual, didn't notice that anything was amiss. She was too excited to be shopping with us for the upcoming ball. Plus, I was getting pretty good at pretending to be happy for her.

We browsed and shopped and tried on what felt like every formal dress in downtown Savannah. By lunchtime, Della had a lovely wine-red ball gown with matching shoes ("My first pair of heels, Rachel!") and a clutch, not to mention the appropriate undergarments. Both of our mothers had gasped and Mrs. Rooney had gotten tears in her eyes when Della came out of the dressing room in that gown. The color really brought out her skin tones and dark hair and eyes, and I was reminded again of a beautiful gypsy princess. I was actually almost thrilled for her until I remembered who she would be dancing with the next time she wore that dress.

As for myself, my mother chose for me (She knew I couldn't care less; what did I need a ball gown for?), and I ended up with a cream-colored floor-length gown with matching shoes and clutch as well as a shorter, black cocktail dress. ("Every proper woman should have a little black dress for that special occasion," my mother had whispered to me loud enough for Mrs. Rooney to hear.)

Once the shopping was finally done, we discussed where we might have lunch. Della and I both clamored for pizza at Spanky's down on River Street, while Mrs. Rooney mentioned that she'd always wanted to try Mrs. Wilkes' Boarding House, but my mother was having none of it. We were, she insisted, a group of proper ladies out on the town, and as such, we would have luncheon befitting our social stature. Mrs. Rooney blinked in surprise at that, although she said nothing. I smiled inwardly when I saw the look on her face as she glanced in my direction. Yeah, I thought, welcome to my world.

We ended up dining at The Olde Pink House, which was fine. It just wasn't as much fun as it could've been. My mother corrected my posture and my manners, expounded upon proper table etiquette, and explained the layout and use of every piece of the table setting. I was already well versed in all of that; I'd been schooled on just this sort of thing from the time I no longer needed a high chair. I knew she was doing it to instruct Della on what would be expected of her at the ball, and I'm sure my mother thought she was being helpful and extremely clever, but it was a badly veiled attempt and left my mother looking both shallow and conceited. I was horribly embarrassed for her and dipped my chin to hide the blush I felt coloring my cheeks. I don't know if Della noticed, but I could tell from Mrs. Rooney's face that she hadn't been deceived at all. In fact, I could see that she was extremely insulted by my mother's assumption that she herself was not capable of schooling her daughter in proper etiquette. I was impressed by the level of grace and decorum she displayed in overlooking my mother's behavior, but that did little to assuage my embarrassment.

I lowered my head even further as I felt my blush deepen.

***

Della chattered away the entire ride home, which was a good thing considering the uncomfortable silence emanating from the front seat. She was still excited about her new dress and couldn't wait to show it to her father. When we dropped them off, she hugged my mother fiercely and thanked her profusely for the wonderful day. Mrs. Rooney, meanwhile, displayed only minimal gratitude, and it lacked any semblance of warmth. As soon as good manners allowed, she put an arm around Della and guided her to their front door. I doubted she would ever want to go shopping with my mother again.

"Well, I never," my mother huffed as we backed out onto Whitfield Avenue. "After all the help and advice I gave them today, I get THAT?" She tsk-tsked and clucked and complained all the way home and was still going at it when we entered the house. I wanted to scream at her to just shut up already, or maybe stick my fingers in my ears, and I even made an attempt to go hide in my room, but she followed me through the house, nagging and going on and on and on until I thought I would go insane.

The final straw came when Bo came running through the house and burst into my room with a huge smile on his face.

"Awlright! Y'all're back!" His eyes were sparkling, and he was practically dancing in place. "I just stopped at Della's. She's changin' clothes an' says she'll be ready to go by the time we swing back by to get 'er. Scott's all done with his mornin' errands an' everybody's ready to hit the Big Hole. We jus' been waitin' on y'all! We got the land tube hooked up an' everything!"

Yes! Just what I needed! I smiled hugely, my first real smile of the day, but before I could grab jeans and a tee shirt, my mother had spun on Bo and voiced the words I feared the most:

"Rachel Anne will *not* be going to that Big Hole or anywhere else with you boys ever again. I told her today that she was to start behaving like the lady she's meant to be. There will be no more Big Hole, no more tubing, no more climbing trees or camping or baseball games. These are not the sort of pastimes a proper young lady indulges in, and I will thank you to leave her out of your future plans and shenanigans. Now leave!"

Bo was thunderstruck. This was his aunt, his mother's sister. He had grown up in this house, had practically been a son to her, and she had never spoken to him this way. I could see the shock and hurt all over his face. Then I realized what she'd just said.

"Mother!" I shrieked and winced inwardly when I heard how much I sounded like her. "You can't do that! You can't take away my cousin, my boys!" (My Scott!)

"Rachel Anne, I've had just about enough of you and your smart mouth today." She was seething. "You will do as I say, and not another word! Bo, leave now!" She grabbed him by the shoulder and pushed him toward the door.

"NO!" I had never screamed at my mother before in my life, and she gasped and took a step back as though I'd slapped her. "You want to see someone leave? Watch this!"

I sprinted down the hall, through the living room and out of the house.

I didn't have a plan as I turned left out of the driveway, then hung a quick right, running through the breezeway between the sanctuary and the fellowship hall at Cresthill Baptist Church, but I knew

I couldn't go to the Big Hole or down to the river or even climb the Magic Oak Tree. Those would be the first places anyone who knew me would go to look for me and, wherever I ended up, I didn't want to be found. I dashed across Whitfield Avenue without even bothering to look both ways and tore down the dirt path toward the Round and Round.

By the time I passed under the arch of trees by the bank of mailboxes and came out in front of the Harden house, I had figured out a destination. I ran straight down Beckman Avenue, past the turn-off to the Big Hole, all the way to the Morgans' house. Normally, I would've turned left into his driveway, made my way down to the end of his dock, and gone on out to the river, but that was too obvious and I really didn't want to be found. Instead, I continued straight ahead past the Morgans' house and came to a stop at what appeared to be an impenetrable wall of scrub brush, thorn bushes, and palmetto trees. Very carefully, I picked my way through the tangled growth and, with only a few pricks and scratches to show for my trouble, came out on the other side. I stood looking at a place no other kids my age even knew existed. Ahead of me lay a long strip of white sand that led to a small peninsula. It was about a quarter of the size of Bird Island, and if you saw it from the water or from the area of land I'd just left, you would think it was an island set out in the middle of a field of marsh grass. I'd never heard anyone else mention it, so I was pretty confident that I alone knew of its existence.

I had found it one day when I was on my way to Morgan's dock. I remember wondering what was on the other side of all the stickers and bushes. It was one of my more adventurous days, and I was thrilled when I saw the tiny, hidden beach with the almost-island attached to it. It reminded me of *The Secret Garden* and, in my heart, I immediately claimed it as my own. I hadn't really gone there much, not only because it was so hard to get to but also because I was so rarely alone and really didn't want to share it with anyone else. Now, though, it was the perfect hiding place.

I was still breathing hard from my long run as I walked the length of white sand and stepped into the shadow of the trees at the far end. I knew that on the far side of the peninsula there was a tangle of drift-wood roots much like the one I'd shared with Nudgie on Bird Island two nights before. (Was it only two nights ago? It seemed like so much longer now!) I decided to go there to think. I knew it was set far enough back under the trees that no one passing in a boat would see me there, just in case anyone decided to look for me from the river.

My breath was coming easier by the time I reached the driftwood and I sat quietly, looking out over the water, waiting for what I knew was coming:

I covered my face with my hands and wept bitterly.

CHAPTER 41

The sun was setting, and it was already starting to grow dark by the time I started thinking about going home. I'd been sitting there on my makeshift driftwood chair for hours, and my joints popped when I finally stood to leave. I placed my hands on the small of my back and bent backward, stretching my muscles and trying to loosen up. I grimaced at the thought of making my way through the sticker bushes in the dark when I reached the end of the causeway, and I knew my dress and shoes would be ruined, but I found that, in the mood I was in, I couldn't care less. I shoved my way through and slowly headed toward home. I could only imagine the depth of trouble I would be in when I got there, and I was in no hurry to arrive.

"Rachel Anne! Where have you been?" My mother leaped out of her wingback chair and rushed toward me as soon as I came through the front door, but my father stepped between us and gathered me into his arms.

"Oh, thank God!" He held me tighter than he ever had before. "I was afraid we'd never see you again! Are you alright, pumpkin?"

"Yes, Daddy," I said as I collapsed against his chest, tears springing to my eyes. He held me close and let me cry. Behind him my mother, eyes red and swollen, stood wringing her hands. She appeared unsure of what to do.

My father held me in his arms for several minutes while I finished crying. Then he pulled away from me, held me at arm's length, and looked deeply into my eyes.

"Honey, I want you to think very carefully," he said gently. "Have you seen Bo since you left the house earlier?"

I frowned, confused. "Bo? No, sir." I shot an angry look at my mother. "I haven't seen him since Mama grabbed him and tried to push him out of the house. She said we couldn't see each other anymore. She told him to get out!"

I saw my father's jaw muscles flex in anger, but his eyes stayed tender and never left mine. Then his question sank in. I took a step back as I fought the fear trying to rise within me.

"Why do you want to know that? Has something happened to Bo?" I could hear the shrillness in my voice as fear began to set in.

My father took a deep breath before releasing me and straightening up. He placed a hand on my head and put on a weary smile. For the first time, I noticed the worry lines around his eyes. Had I done that to him?

"When you ran out of the house today, your mother wanted to go after you." He shot my mother a look the likes of which I'd never before seen on his face, and she lowered her eyes to the floor. "Bo stopped her and said he would go after you himself; he knew all your favorite places and thought he could find you and bring you back fairly quickly. He left . . . and no one has seen him since."

A wave of nausea washed over me as panic engulfed me and I struggled not to scream. Bo, *my* Bo, was missing. Deep inside, an angry voice told me to blame my mother, but I squashed it down. This was entirely my fault. This was the sort of thing I knew could happen if I didn't control my emotions at all times and pretend to be the perfect daughter and debutante. For once in my life, I'd allowed myself the luxury of expressing my feelings while fighting for what I wanted, and this was the result. Bo was gone. The room was spinning, and I thought I might be sick. I swallowed hard and took a deep breath.

My father leaned down and gave me a squeeze. ("Squozen!") "I just came home long enough to see if either of you had come back. I'm going back out to keep looking for Bo." He chucked me gently under the chin. "Scott and his father are out looking. So are the Stricklands, the Hardens, Mr. Morgan and Mr. Rooney, along with several of the men from church. Don't you worry; we'll find him." My father turned and strode out the door without a single glance in my mother's direction.

I heard him slam the car door and start the engine. It was dark enough now that he needed to use the headlights. They streamed through the living room windows as he backed out of the driveway.

"Rachel—" my mother began.

I spun on her. "Don't you talk to me. Don't you dare! YOU did this—you tried to take us away from each other, and now Bo's gone! I don't ever want to see you or talk to you again! *I hate you and I wish you were dead!*"

I ran down the hall and into my room, slamming the door behind me. I even locked it for good measure, something I'd never done before in my life. I stood for a moment, trying to calm down before giving up and throwing myself across the bed. I cried until I had no more tears, then I just lay there in the dark, feeling lost and helpless in the face of what was going on.

***

I'm not sure how much time passed, but I must have exhausted myself enough to sleep because the next thing I knew, I was coming awake in the darkness of my room. I experienced several seconds of confusion and disorientation as I blinked at the inky shadows and wondered what had awakened me. Then I heard it again:

Scritch-scritch-scritch.

My eyes traveled to the window, and I felt a cold shiver of fear run through me when I saw strange, silvery eyes staring back at me.

Owen Godwin.

I stifled a scream as he put a finger to his lips. I took a deep breath to calm myself, then walked over and opened the window.

"Mr. Owen!" My throat was raw from all the crying I'd done, and my whisper was shaky. "What are you doing here?"

"Must come," he answered in his strange way of speaking. "Must come now. Have to hurry, though. Have to!" He silently pulled the screen off my window frame and leaned it against the side of the house. "Come! May be too late, may not. But must come. Hurry!"

Everything in my being screamed at me not to go, but my body wasn't listening. I shocked myself by sitting on the sill and swinging my feet through the window. Owen Godwin reached up and lowered me to the ground from there. Then, before I could say a word, he turned and hurried off into the darkness. He didn't even look back to see if I was following him.

I was.

***

The night was bright from the light of the large, waning moon, and I had no trouble seeing where I was going. We hurried along the same path I'd taken earlier that day when I'd run away, but when we reached the arch of trees by the mailboxes, Owen turned left and headed toward

215

the river. We moved silently, not speaking at all as we passed his house. The kitchen lights were on, and I could see his parents inside seated around the kitchen table. We skirted the lights that streamed from the windows and lit up the ground, then hurried down the tiny trail that led through the trees to the Sikeses' footpath. In my concern for my cousin and my curiosity over where we were headed, I didn't even worry about crossing paths with Foxy and his boys.

Owen turned left when we reached the footpath and headed toward Fiddler Crab Beach but stopped just short of it. He spun around and stood staring at me, and I wondered why in the world he had come all the way to my house just to bring me here.

He finally spoke, his strange eyes blazing in the moonlight. "Told you! Told you to stay away. Told you there was danger." He lifted his hand and poked me accusingly in the shoulder with his finger; then he began to rock. "Little girl didn't listen. Little girl didn't hear. Too late now. Too late!" He began to moan, and tears leaked from his eyes and ran down his face as he rocked harder.

"Mr. Owen, please!" I felt something wet drip onto my face. Great—rain! As if my dress and shoes weren't damaged enough already. I glared into Owen Godwin's strange, crazy eyes. "Why did you bring me here? I can't be here right now. My cousin is missing and all the men are out looking for him. I need to be home so I'll know as soon as they find him!" Another drop landed on my face, then another. I angrily swiped at them with the back of my hand as I glared at Owen Godwin, who continued to rock and moan. I felt another drip and the wetness ran down my face and dripped onto my dress. I didn't even bother to wipe it off this time.

Then I heard another moan, one that did not come from Owen Godwin. His moans had turned to a shrill keening and he was holding himself around the middle as he rocked crazily, faster and faster. I looked all around, searching for the source of the new moaning, but it

216

was impossible to see into the shadows under the trees. Another drop of wetness landed on my face; this time I looked up to see where it was coming from.

It took a moment to process what I was seeing and still another to realize that the screaming I now heard was coming from me. The horror I saw hanging there twenty feet above me nearly drove me over the edge as another fresh spurt of wetness dripped off of it and landed on my face. Upside-down, bruised and bloody, horribly mangled and misshapen with a single, bleary, sea-green eye staring down into mine, the thing did not appear to be human. Then it moaned again and more blood dripped onto my upturned face. I screamed again and felt my stomach lurch as my heart tried to rip itself out of my chest. I didn't want to see what was suspended from the platform above me, but I was unable to tear my eyes away as I continued to scream and scream and scream at what was hanging there.

It was Bo.

CHAPTER 42

I've never liked hospitals. The sights, the smells, the sounds—they all seemed alien and frightening to me. In my limited experience, hospitals weren't somewhere you went if you wanted to get better. Hospitals were where you went to die. That had been true for both sets of my grandparents. I feared it would be the same for Bo.

I'd been there for hours. Bo had arrived by ambulance and had gone directly into surgery. He was now lying in a bed in the ICU. Down the hall, in the waiting room, we had all gathered to pray and wait for whatever news the doctors might bring. His parents were with him. I longed to be there, too, but hospital rules stated emphatically that no children under twelve were allowed. I sniffed and thought that it wouldn't hurt to overlook my age. I was turning twelve in less than five days, after all. I covered my face with my hands and thought back to the events that had taken place after I saw Bo hanging upside-down from the edge of the platform in that tree.

Everything had been surreal and had seemed to move in slow-motion. I hadn't been able to move or shout for help. All I could do was scream, my hands to my face and my nails digging furrows into my cheeks. It was my screaming that had eventually brought help.

Mr. Bashlor and Scott had been trolling up and down the river, searching the riverbank and shouting Bo's name. They'd heard my screams over the sound of the boat motor and Scott had known immediately that it was me. His father had quickly tied the boat to the Tuckers' dock, and with only the moon to light their way, he and Scott had run pell-mell up the dock and across the beach to where I was standing on the footpath. I'd been alone when they reached me; Owen Godwin had disappeared into the shadows as soon as I'd started screaming. I was unable to speak but pointed at what was hanging above me and saw Mr. Bashlor blanch when he spotted Bo. Scott was immediately dispatched to the Tuckers' to call for an ambulance, and I had never seen him move so fast. He had returned a few minutes later accompanied by Mr. Tucker, who had brought a ladder. It had taken some doing, but Mr. Bashlor, balancing precariously at the top of the ladder, was finally able to lower my cousin down out of the tree.

Bo had looked like death itself and was barely coherent when Scott and Mr. Tucker reached up to help gently guide him to the ground. His arms had been tied behind his back at the elbows, his right ankle had been pierced by something sharp, and a rope had been threaded through the hole and pulled between his ankle bone and the Achilles tendon. He had then been hauled up and hung by that rope ("Just like a deer," Mr. Bashlor had exclaimed later in disgust), and at some point his left leg had been twisted and pulled down until it had snapped and hung loosely against the side of his body. He had also been used as a punching bag before finally being hoisted high up into the tree.

The men were certain Bo had been in excruciating pain throughout the entire ordeal, but he'd been unable to scream for help because whoever had done this had stuffed something into his mouth to keep him quiet. Scott had pulled the makeshift gag out of Bo's mouth to help his breathing, and I had picked it up from where it had fallen. Now, sitting in the waiting room at the hospital, I pulled it out of my pocket for what must have been the hundredth time and turned it over in my hands. It was one of Bo's old baseball caps; it even had his name scrawled across the headband inside. I felt my eyes well up again as I remembered the last time I'd seen it. I'd thought it was lost to the river. I should have known better; I'd seen caps floating on the surface of the water many times before.

I recalled hearing Derry say that he had recognized the person who had been spying on them that night. He said he'd gotten a good look at them. I had been right, too; the Sikeses *had* come. They had bided their time, waiting for the perfect opportunity, and then they had sprung. I swallowed hard as more tears flooded my eyes and ran down my face.

They had come, but they'd taken the wrong cousin.

***

Bo's folks had asked the doctor in charge of Bo's case if he would come to the waiting room to explain the injuries and Bo's prognosis to the rest of us. There were just too many things wrong with him for them to remember, and they didn't want to leave anything out.

First had been the puncture and injury to his right ankle and Achilles tendon. As awful as it sounded, that was one of the more minor injuries. The tendon had, by some miracle, not been badly damaged, so it was just a matter of cleaning it, stitching it up, and putting a cast on it until the tendons and ligaments healed.

The other leg was a different story. The doctor spoke of "spiral fractures" and damage to Bo's epiphyseal or "growth" plates, which could cause that leg to grow at a different rate and to a different length than the right one. He would also suffer permanent weakness in his left leg, so if he recovered, Bo would almost certainly walk with a permanent limp, and running and jumping would be very difficult for him. (This bit of news nearly stopped my heart. I found myself remembering Bo on the ball field, leaping high into the air from second base while throwing the ball to first as he pulled off the perfect double play. He had been so beautiful to watch! Tears sprang to my eyes. We had thought he might even go pro someday. Now, it seemed, he would never play again.)

Next, the doctor explained that there were several fractured ribs, a ruptured spleen, bruised kidneys, and both shoulders were dislocated, not to mention numerous head and facial injuries. The right side of Bo's face was crushed, and there was possible damage to his right eye. There was no way to really examine and treat the eye, though, until the swelling went down enough to see into it. His nose was also broken, and both lips were split and had needed stitches.

The worst injury, however, was a fractured skull (I made a mental note to myself to look up "parietal bones" in the encyclopedia when I got home) that had resulted in swelling and bleeding in the brain. There was a good possibility there was brain damage, but Bo was in a coma, so there was no way to tell until he woke up so they could ask him some questions and gauge the damage . . . if he ever woke up. Bo was in critical condition, and there was no guarantee that he would even survive. Only time would tell.

The doctor painted a bleak picture, and everyone in the waiting room was reeling from shock at what had been done to this sweet, vibrant little boy. Across the waiting room, I saw Mr. Wimpy shake his head in anger and disgust, then walk over to join the other men from church in prayer. Meanwhile, the Kid rushed out to use the pay phone to call Ms. Frances and let her know what was going on so she could make the calls to update the church's prayer chain. Nudgie was sitting in a chair against the far wall staring into space, her lips moving in silent prayer while, two seats down from her, Scott slipped out of his chair and, tears streaming down his face, dropped to his knees to pray. His parents joined him on the floor and wrapped their arms around him as their prayers joined his. Mr. Rooney and the Stricklands were in the far corner of the waiting room, standing in a circle, holding hands and praying. Nearby, Mrs. Rooney was crying uncontrollably and clutching Della tightly to her breast as she rocked her like a baby. Della, meanwhile, was sobbing like her heart was breaking. Brother Arms and some of the deacons had approached Bo's parents when the doctor was done speaking and were now kneeling with them in the middle of the waiting room offering prayers of supplication, pleading with God to save this child. My parents were kneeling with them, and my mother held her sister as they prayed. (Obviously no one had told Bo's parents what role my mother had played in all of this, I thought viciously.)

For the first time since finding Bo strung up in that tree, there were no tears in my eyes. I stood off to one side, watching the others praying together and supporting one another while I stood apart, lost and alone. I wasn't sure how I was supposed to act or what I was supposed to do. I'd never had to face anything alone before. Bo had always been there with me, *for* me. Over the course of our lives, my cousin and I had done everything together, been there for each other, and shared everything every single day. I'd never gone through anything without him, and now that I had to, I found I didn't know how. I needed my cousin; I needed my twin.

I turned and silently slipped out of the room.

CHAPTER 43

The hospital room was cold and quiet, and the only sounds were the beeps and whooshing noises coming from the many machines that were hooked up to the small, still figure lying on the bed. There were so many machines and tubes and medical contraptions that it was hard at first to make out where they ended and Bo began. I cautiously approached the bed, afraid of what I would see but needing so badly to be with my cousin.

He was swathed in gauze from head to toe, and there were IV tubes in his arms, more tubes down his throat, prongs in his nose, and some sort of electrodes stuck to his chest. His one good eye, the one that had been staring down at me from the tree, was tightly closed now, while the other was hidden under what seemed like miles of bandages that were wrapped around his head. He had blankets tucked in around his body, and his right leg, encased in a cast, was propped up on some sort of foam wedge. His left leg was suspended in the air by a series of ropes and pulleys, while some sort of metal brace (traction?) appeared to be literally screwed through the skin and muscle directly into the bone.

It was an overwhelming sight, and for a moment I was afraid to move any closer. But then I reminded myself that this was Bo, *my* Bo, and I needed him near me now more than any other time in my life.

I approached the bed on silent feet and stood looking down at the broken form that was my cousin. Gingerly, I reached out and touched his arm. So cold! I gently chaffed it, trying to bring him warmth. I stood there for several seconds, willing him to wake up and talk with me. I needed him to drop me a wink and tell me he was fine, that it was just a scratch and he'd be up and at 'em in no time flat . . . but he just lay there almost lost in bandages as the medicine dripped into him and the air whooshed in and out, the machine breathing for him when he couldn't breathe for himself.

Man-oh-man alive, I thought. You would hate this, Bo, having to lie so still and not being able to move at all, having to be careful not to snag any of these wires and tubes. This would drive you slug nutty, man. Cheese an' rice!

I moved closer and bent down to put my face close to his. I caught a sudden whiff of blood but ignored it as I looked intensely at the one eye that showed through the bandages. Come on, Bo, please! Wake up and talk to me. I can't get through this without you. I can't!

My silent pleading was interrupted when a hand dropped onto my shoulder. It startled me so badly I nearly jumped right on top of Bo. I spun around and found myself looking up into the eyes of the doctor who had spoken to us in the waiting room.

"I don't believe you're supposed to be in here." Tall and thin, he spoke gently and his eyes were kind. "Come on, sweetheart. I'll take you back to the waiting room. There's really nothing you can do for Robert right now."

"Bo," I said softly as the doctor ushered me toward the door.

"What's that, dear?" He leaned down so he could hear me better.

I took a deep breath. "I said his name is Bo. When we were babies just learning to talk, our parents tried to teach me to call him 'Robert,' but all I could manage to say was 'Bo.' Everyone thought it was cute, so the name stuck." I looked back at the still form lying on the bed.

"His name is Bo; I named him and he is mine."

***

There would be no more news that night, so the number of visitors in the waiting room had dwindled. By two in the morning, the only ones still there were Brother Arms (he stayed the entire night, praying and offering spiritual support wherever it was needed), the Bashlors, and our family. The Rooneys had stuck it out almost that long but had finally decided it was becoming too much for Della, who hadn't stopped crying since word of Bo's assault had reached them. She'd been sobbing uncontrollably and was inconsolable. Her parents felt a change in atmosphere would be the best thing for her and, despite her pleas and protests, they had managed to convince her to leave, but only after I promised to call her right away if there were any change at all.

"Oh, Rachel," she had sobbed as she hugged me. "He's got to be okay! He's just got to be. Mama and I, we love him so much!" She "squozed" me so hard I could barely breathe, and clung to me until her mother came over, gently pulled us apart and guided her to the elevators. Della looked back at me over her shoulder the entire way; I could see my own overwhelming grief reflected in her swollen, red eyes.

We were still staring at each other when the elevator doors slid closed.

CHAPTER 44

I awoke cozy and warm in my own bed the next morning and experienced a few moments of confusion and disorientation (That was twice in two days!) before recalling a vague memory of my father carrying me like a baby down to the car at the hospital, then lifting me out of the car at home and taking me inside. I also recalled a moment of loathing when my mother had helped him undress me and tuck me in. (So much had happened that I'd never changed out of the dress I'd worn shopping. It was ruined now!) I still hadn't wanted her anywhere near me, but I'd been too exhausted at the time to complain.

My first coherent thoughts were of Bo. Now, in the light of day, everything that had happened the night before seemed like some horrible nightmare. There was no way my vibrant, leaping, bouncing Bo was actually lying in a hospital bed on the verge of death, hooked up to a bunch of tubes and machines like a pint-sized Frankenstein's monster. That could never really happen. I pushed down the flood of emotions that threatened to overflow as reality set in.

I swung my feet over the edge of the bed and stood on trembling legs. The room seemed to spin for just a moment, but I shook it off as I pulled on jeans and a tee shirt, stepped into an old pair of sneakers, then headed for the front of the house. I was hoping my father would be there, but he wasn't. I glanced out the living room windows as I passed through and saw that the car was gone. (He must have gone to work today; I'd hoped he'd stay home.) I continued on to the kitchen, where my mother stood at the stove stirring a pot of oatmeal. I glanced at the table and saw my old nemesis, the inevitable glass of Tang, sitting there waiting for me. I ground my teeth together as I picked up the glass, stalked over to the sink, and poured it down the drain. My mother turned and watched as I rinsed the glass and carried it to the refrigerator. She remained silent as I rummaged around, searching for the jug of chocolate milk. When I found it, I carried the jug and my glass to the kitchen table and set them down. I continued to ignore her as I filled my glass, then tipped it back and drank thirstily.

"Rachel—" my mother began, but her words were cut off when I slammed the empty glass down on the table so hard it broke in my hand. She gasped in alarm and seemed about to rush over to see how badly I was cut but stopped short when she saw the look on my face as I glared at her and continued to squeeze the broken glass. We stood across the kitchen from each other for several seconds; then I turned, threw the bloody shards of glass against the kitchen wall, and stalked out of the house. She made no attempt to stop me.

She couldn't have if she'd tried.

***

It was just beginning to rain and the thunder was booming ominously in the distance when I left my house and crossed Old Montgomery Road.

I glanced up at the roiling mass of angry, black clouds as I walked across the schoolyard, and thought that this storm was going to be a doozey.

I really hadn't thought about where I was going, but when I found myself entering the dugout at the kickball field, it felt like I'd come home. Everywhere I looked I could see Bo: He was there in the field, making phenomenal plays; rounding the bases after one of his monumental, countless homeruns; hanging from the dugout fence while he razzed the other team and cheered our team on. He was a special soul, a real one-of-a-kind force of nature, and I couldn't imagine living in a world where he didn't exist.

I stared at his spot at second base and thought that God would never be so cruel. He wouldn't create a Bo DeLoach and then just take him away. Our God, the One we learned about at church, the One we were supposed to trust and have faith in, simply would not do such a cruel and heartless thing. Our God was a God of mercy and miracles, and I had to believe He was about to work a big one now. Bo would wake up soon and he would be fine. He would recover, and our lives would go back to exactly the way they'd been before all of these horrible things had happened. God help me, I would make sure of that, I thought grimly. Bo would get well and come home, and he would be as good as new. He would tell the authorities that it was the Sikeses who had hurt him, and they would all go away forever. I would stay inside at night and never go rambling again. I would even go to bed on time, and somehow I would make myself sleep. And I would make it so it was just me and my boys again, I thought bitterly. No one else needed to be a part of anything.

I felt my mouth twist in anger as it occurred to me that nothing bad had happened until Della had come along. I had slept just fine at night before she showed up with her needy, whining, scared little self. I had never felt weird feelings toward Scott until she inserted herself between us and started hogging all his attention. And nothing that had happened to my cousin the day before would've happened if we hadn't taken her shopping for that stupid ball gown. That's what had started the fight between my mother and me that had culminated in the events that led up to Bo getting hurt.

I made a fist so tight my lacerated hand began to bleed again in earnest. In the mood I was in, it was easy to ignore.

I clenched my teeth. How could I have missed it? It had been Della all along. Della had planted herself in our lives starting from the moment we'd met. She had squirmed her way into every plan we'd made for that summer, and she had all but forced her way into our gang. I frowned again. I had told her I would introduce her to the boys and help her get through the last two weeks of school, and I had been kind enough to offer to include her in some of the boating and tubing excursions; but she had ended up going to every ballgame, every jaunt to the Big Hole, yesterday's shopping trip—absolutely everything. She had even turned our gang's special campout into a birthday party for herself and was about to steal my birthday from me! I frowned again as I thought of all the things that would've turned out better if I hadn't taken her under my wing the day we met at the Magic Oak Tree.

I should've let those two Yankee boys push her sneaky little butt out of that tree, I thought. Then none of this other crap would've happened. The mess we're in now started that day. This is all Della's fault! All of it! Bo could die and it's all because of *her*! It was Della who had run into Foxy on the footpath three days ago and made him so mad. *She* should have been the one who was beaten and tortured and left hanging in that tree! *She* should be the one lying in a hospital bed in a coma and wrapped like a mummy! *She* should be the one on the verge of death!

I raked my wet hair out of my eyes and felt my hand sting as the loose strands dug down into the cuts. I wish I'd never met Della Rooney, I thought. I hate her even more than I hate my mother! I have to find a way to get rid of her. I sneered, then smiled to myself. Oh, yes, Della would have to go. It was the only way I could protect Bo when he came home from the hospital. Somehow, I would have to make her go away. Then life would return to normal, everything would go back to the way it was supposed to be, and Bo would be safe. And Scott would be—

"Rachel?" Well, speak of the devil! "Rachel, what are you doing sitting out here in the storm? Don't you know how dangerous that is? You could be struck by lightning!" I looked up at Della, where she stood shivering next to me. She must have seen me through her living room window.

My smile widened. Of course, I thought. She saw me and realized that she had to come over here. She probably knows if she leaves me alone long enough, I'll figure everything out and then everyone will know what a manipulative little monster she really is.

I stood and turned to face her.

"Rachel?" My thoughts must have shown on my face because Della took a step back from me. "Rachel, what's the matter with you? You're scaring me a little." She continued to look at me; then her eyes clouded over and she gasped. "Oh, no!" She looked ready to cry. "Is it Bo? Has something changed? Is he. . . ." She was unable to finish the sentence.

"Bo's the same as he was last night. Don't worry, though. He's going to be fine. Everything is going to be fine. Bo just needs to rest. That's why he's in a coma, so he can put all his energy toward getting well. In fact, by the time he wakes up, he'll be as good as new."

Della's eyes shone. "Really? Oh, that's wonderful news, Rachel!" Her expression grew quizzical. "But if he's going to be fine, why are you sitting alone out here in the rain?"

I shrugged. "I just have an awful lot on my mind," I answered. "You know, whoever did this to Bo is still out there. The authorities have no idea who it could be, but if it happened to Bo, it could happen to any one of us."

Della trembled and looked around. "All the more reason for you not to be out here by yourself."

I smiled at her. "You're probably right, Della, but I just can't be trapped in the house today. I'm too antsy and I have too much on my mind." I looked up at the sky, blinking as the first raindrops splashed into my eyes. "Besides, I can't imagine that anyone else would be crazy enough to be out in this, so I think we're pretty safe right now. In fact," I stepped around her. "I think I'll take a walk."

I headed for Beckman Avenue.

"Rachel, wait!" Della ran to catch up with me. "Why don't you come to my house if you don't want to go home? Mama would be really happy to see you." I didn't slow down, so she continued her entreaty. "Please, Rachel. We really shouldn't be out in this weather. It's dangerous!" A flash of lightning and a loud clap of thunder added credence to her argument.

I just kept walking.

CHAPTER 45

O nce again, I had no idea where I was going. I just let my feet take
me wherever they felt like traveling. Somehow, I ended up back
at the thorny, hidden entrance to the causeway. Della had continued
to follow me, whining the entire time and begging me to turn around
and come back with her.

"Mama doesn't know where I am!" She sniffed and wiped the rain
out of her eyes. "I didn't even tell her I was leaving! I know she must
be worried sick by now." She shivered violently, and I could tell it was
from fear as much as from being soaked to the skin. "Please, Rachel! I
want to go home!"

Her begging was pathetic. Had she always whined so much?

I continued to ignore her as I pushed my way through the bushes
and brambles. I wasn't surprised in the least when she followed me.

I came out on the other side with only a few small scratches. Behind
me, Della battled her way through the undergrowth, then gasped at
the sight that lay before her as she stopped by my side. I looked down
at her and could see that she was badly scratched and scraped. I shook

my head in disgust, then looked back toward the sandy strip of beach, gray now in the gloom of the storm.

"What is this place, Rachel?" Surprise and wonder showed on Della's face. "You've never brought me here before."

"This," I answered, "is my special place. No one else even knows it exists, not even Bo. I come here when I need to be alone to think and I don't want anyone to bother me."

"Is this where you were yesterday when no one could find you?"

Oh! Smart girl!

"Yup, I was right here the entire time," I answered as I walked toward the peninsula. Della stayed glued to my side. It was easy to see she was freaked out about being out in the storm. A bright flash of lightning lit up the sky and thunder boomed so loud the ground seemed to shake. Beside me, Della jumped a foot in the air and began to whimper. I was surprised when I felt a twinge of pity and regret at how I was making her feel. It left me confused and torn. Why was I doing this to her? I shook my head, trying to clear my thoughts.

We reached the peninsula and walked under the cover of trees. The rain was falling much more gently here, as the canopy of leaves and moss acted as a natural umbrella. I led the way back to the tangle of driftwood and took my usual seat. Della sat down next to me and snuggled up tight to my side. After only the slightest hesitation I put an arm around her and held her close as she sighed with relief.

"Thank you, Rachel," she whispered. "I thought you were mad at me and I couldn't for the life of me think of anything I'd done to upset you."

I felt my heart melt. "I'm sorry, Della," I said. "I guess I'm just in shock over what happened to Bo, and I can't remember ever being so scared." I sighed miserably as I fought back tears. "I don't know what's been wrong with me lately. It's almost like there are two of me battling for control of my head, and I feel so black and hateful most of the time." I "squozed" her gently. "I know I haven't been as kind as I should've been. Please forgive me."

Della hugged me back hard, then looked up into my eyes. "There's nothing to forgive," she said. "I love you, Rachel."

I hugged her in earnest. "Thank you, Della." I tucked her head under my chin and sobbed softly into her hair.

Neither one of us was wearing a watch, so I don't know how long we sat there holding each other as the storm raged all around us, but there on the peninsula it seemed like we were in another world. The rain fell much more softly; the lightning and thunder surrounded us but never approached us, and there were no Sikeses trying to kill anyone, no crazy Owen Godwin wandering around, no obnoxious mother trying to force me into a life I didn't want, and there was no wounded, dying Bo. On the peninsula, the world was far away and all was well. I wanted to stay there forever.

Della, however, was having none of it.

"We really should think about heading back, Rachel," she finally said. "My mama is probably going crazy with worry by now. Yesterday was so hard on her. First you ran away, then Bo disappeared, then hearing what had happened to him, not to mention spending most of the night at the hospital not knowing if he was going to make it. You know how much my mama loves Bo. Now I've disappeared and, well, she must be going to pieces by now!"

I exhaled deeply. "You're right, Della. It was wrong of me to keep you here for so long. I'll bet your mama's about to have a cow." I stood up. "Come on, let's go."

We walked back through the trees the way we'd come, still protected from the majority of the wind and the rain. That changed when we stepped out of the trees and started up the causeway. The wind immediately began buffeting us, and Della, as small as she was, was blown sideways toward the place where the sand dropped sharply off into the prickly marsh grass and razor-sharp oyster beds. She screamed and pinwheeled her arms, fighting to keep her balance as I yanked her back just as she was about to topple over the edge. I put my arm around her and held her close to my body, trying to protect her from the storm. What had I been thinking, bringing her out in this weather? I could feel her tiny body trembling, and her sobs had an edge of hysteria to them.

"Hold on to me, Della!" I had to put my lips to her ear and shout to be heard. "Hold on and don't let go! I've got you!" She looked up at me and I saw her lips move, but I couldn't hear a thing over the storm.

When we reached the brambles, I held her as close as I could and took the brunt of the stickers and thorns myself. We broke through on the other side and ran as fast as we could up Beckman Avenue while all around us the lightning flashed and ripped the sky apart and the thunder seemed to be just one long, rolling boom.

I can't for the life of me figure out why I didn't just go to the Morgans' or the Hardens' to wait out the storm. At the time, all I could think of was that I had to get her home to her mama, so we battled and struggled against the wind and rain. We were only halfway to the Round and Round when Della fell to her knees in the middle of the road. I urged her to rise, pleaded with her, even tried to lift her up and carry her, but she wouldn't move. I hadn't seen her this terrified since she climbed the Magic Oak Tree the first day we met.

"Della, come on," I shouted over the wind. "You can't stay here like this. You yourself said it's too dangerous. Please! Get up!"

I could barely see her through the heavy sheets of rain that were pouring down on us while the lightning and thunder continued to flash and roar and rattle the ground beneath our feet. I could tell by the way her body was shaking against me that Della was crying hysterically, and I was afraid I'd never be able to get her to move. Then a lightbulb went on over my head.

I put my lips to her ear and shouted so she could hear me.

"Della! I have an idea. I can get you out of the storm for a few minutes, but you have to stand up and come with me. Please, Della! Get up and come on!" I didn't know if she'd heard me until she rose and leaned into me.

Thank God, I thought. I tucked her under my arm, doubled over, and pulled her into the woods to our left. I could feel the difference immediately. The trees acted as a natural windbreak and, as on the peninsula, the canopy of leaves and moss acted like an umbrella, filtering the rain just enough for us to see where we were going. I took the familiar path and within seconds we were standing at the edge of the Big Hole. All around us the storm continued to rage; the lightning and thunder were worse than I had ever seen it.

"Rachel," Della screamed over the sound of the wind. "What are we doing here? How is this going to get us out of the storm?"

Rather than answer, I took her hand and guided her down one of the bike trails that dipped into one end of the Big Hole. Through the rain, I could see the confused look on her face but, trusting me completely, she followed me. We stopped next to a large tunnel some kid had dug into the red clay overlooking the bike path. The small, bushy tree that was growing just out in front of it even offered a bit of protection from the wind.

I pressed my lips to her ear again and explained that this little cave was just big enough to protect her from the storm.

"But what about you, Rachel? That hole's not big enough for both of us. You'll still be out in the weather!"

This child was amazing! Della was terrified, but she still put my safety before her own.

"Don't worry about me," I shouted back. "Just turn around and back in." I bent over and looked into the recess. "I believe there's just enough room for you to stretch out on your stomach and still have your head fit just inside. I'm going to stay right here." I crouched down at the small opening. "See? The wind isn't as bad right up against the wall here. Now, come on; turn around and scooch yourself in."

Della appeared ready to argue some more but changed her mind when a bolt of lightning struck very near to where we were huddled. She spun around, put her hands on the ground and her feet in the hole, then wriggled back as far as she could. It was tighter than I thought it would be, but she just fit. I knelt down and blocked as much of the wind and rain as I could. In this position, my face was mere inches from Della's. I could have kissed her on the nose if I'd wanted to.

Della peered out of the recess and frowned. "I don't know if I like this, Rachel," she shouted. "It's pretty tight in here. I can barely move. I'm not even sure I could take a deep breath!"

"I know, Della, but it won't be for long," I assured her. "This storm can't possibly last much longer. Just try not to think about where you are. Think of something else, something happy."

"Okay!" Della thought for a moment, then smiled shakily. "I'm going to think about how magical everything will be at the ball Saturday night. It's going to be so wonderful!"

The smile froze on my face. The ball, I thought. Of course her happy thought would be about dancing with Scott at the ball. Once again, I felt my teeth clench behind my smile.

"I still can't believe I'm actually going! Nothing like this has ever happened to me before." She continued to smile, obviously imagining how wonderful it was going to be to spend an entire evening alone with Scott.

I fought the anger that was trying to twist my face. My Bo was lying in a hospital bed fighting for his life, and all Della could think about was being with Scott. It struck me as wrong, and I felt the rage rising inside of me as the storm, rather than abating, grew stronger and wilder around us. My hair was whipping wildly about my face as the rain came down even harder, plastering my already-sodden clothes to my body.

I saw Della's lips move, but I could no longer hear her. I leaned in closer and she took a breath and shouted again: "I said, I don't think this is such a good—"

Lightning flashed, the ground shook, and the world seemed to be ending. Right before my eyes, inches from my face, a waterfall of muddy water rushed over the ledge above us, followed by an avalanche of mud and muck. (Mudslide?) I reached for the wall on either side of Della's little cave to brace myself and my hands sank up to my wrists. As I yanked them out, I heard Della scream in terror. It took me a moment to find her, but then I saw the glittering of her eyes behind the muddy waterfall. She was whipping her head around and appeared to be struggling. I was dumbfounded and couldn't process what I was seeing.

Then she screamed again. "Rachel!" She choked and spit out a mouthful of mud. "Rachel, help me! I'm stuck and I can't breathe!" She struggled to pull in air. "Please, Rachel! Pull me out! Please!" Her brown eyes, always huge, seemed about to pop out of her head.

Meanwhile, I was lost somewhere inside of myself. It felt as though I was seeing what was happening, but I wasn't actually there. It was the strangest sensation I'd ever felt, like an out-of-body experience. I was watching one of my best friends fighting for her life, but I couldn't make myself move, just like I'd been unable to move when I'd seen Bo hanging in the tree.

Just inches away from me, Della was making a valiant attempt to free herself from her muddy prison. I could hear her gasping and wheezing as she tried to draw breath, but she was stuck fast, and I still couldn't make myself move. All I could do was stare into her eyes—her horrified, terror-filled eyes. They were all I could see of her as more muck streamed over the edge above us and ran down her face. She spit out more mud and made one last effort to free herself. Suddenly, she grunted hard and her hands thrust out of the mud just below her face. That broke whatever spell I was under, and I reached out and grabbed her hands. I still couldn't see her face, but the look of relief and hope I saw in her eyes was indescribable . . . until I "squozed" her hands and shoved them back into the mud as deep as they would go. I could feel her fingernails gouging deep into my own hands and wrists as she continued to struggle to free herself. Still grasping her hands, I leaned in as close as I could and stared into her eyes. I could see shock and confusion there now, and some other expression I couldn't quite decipher, something akin to heartbreak and betrayal.

I realized then that the darker side of me had won the battle inside my head as I continued to stare into those eyes, ignoring the storm as well as the gurgling and choking sounds coming from the mud right in front of me. Della coughed and a huge gob of muck and slime hit me in the face, but I ignored that, too, as I lost myself in those eyes.

In my mind, clear as a bell, I heard every word Foxy had said that night on the beach. It was all in the eyes, he had said. If you looked into their eyes, you could see them leave and it would be like they were never really there to begin with. After that, all that was left were the eyes. Lifeless eyes, empty eyes, like doll's eyes. I thought of Nudgie and how she'd seen her friend die right in front of her. His eyes had gone lifeless and empty, too.

Now, inches in front of me, I watched the very same kind of eyes being created. Della's eyes were devoid of everything but disbelief and hopelessness. More mud flowed over her from above, and her hands, which had been scratching and clawing at mine beneath the mud, suddenly squeezed down hard for several seconds, then went limp and grew still. I continued to stare into her eyes, waiting for what I knew would come. And then, finally, there it was: her eyes, huge and round, glazed over, and I swear I saw her leave herself. Those eyes emptied of everything that had been the person I'd known until absolutely nothing of her remained. Her spirit had flown, and there was nothing left inside. She was gone, and only her eyes—her lifeless, soulless eyes—were left. Empty eyes. Doll's eyes.

Della Rooney was dead.

***

I stayed where I was, frozen in place, still staring into those eyes, mesmerized and fascinated by what had just happened in front of me. I realized I was smiling in wonder as I continued to gaze into those empty, lifeless orbs. I was in awe of what I'd just seen, and I realized I'd never felt so alive.

I might have stayed there for hours, lost in those eyes and the power of what I'd just been a part of, but suddenly there was another huge flash and boom as lightning hit a tree just off to my left. The air around me crackled, and more water rushed down over the side as I felt the ground beneath me shift. I yanked my hands out of the muck and struggled to stand, only then realizing that my feet were stuck in mud nearly up to my knees. Another huge clap of thunder rocked the very earth around me, and the entire wall of clay collapsed and slid toward me. I fought tooth and nail against the flow, struggling to free myself and reach the safety of higher ground. It seemed to take a lifetime, but I finally dragged myself up and over the edge to my right.

Another clap of thunder sounded, the sky lit up, and in that second I saw the small tree that had been at my back shake violently as the roots tore themselves out of the ground and the entire thing fell, half-burying itself in the mud that had just slid down around it. More mud and water rushed down then and that entire side of the Big Hole came down, completely engulfing the tree and what now lay hidden beneath it. The only evidence of where the tree now rested was a few errant branches sticking up out of the clay. Nothing else remained, and there was no hint that anything else might lie there as well.

I was sure that beneath the tree, buried deep in the red Georgia clay, those eyes were still wide open, staring now at God and eternity.

***

I don't know how long I lay there, gazing down at what had once been the Big Hole, but the storm seemed to be moving away when I finally came to my senses and realized I needed to leave. I arose slowly, wincing as I straightened up, and stood there for several long seconds with my face turned to the sky, letting the rain wash the muck from my body. I took one last look at what had once been the coolest place a kid could ever play, then turned and hurried through the trees, coming out just across from the Magic Oak Tree. The rain was still coming down in buckets, and it was hard to see more than a few feet in front of me, but I moved as quickly as I could. Still, it took longer than usual to reach Whitfield Avenue. I didn't bother to look both ways before I crossed; I couldn't have seen a car coming until it was too late anyway. I breathed a little easier when the pavement ended and I felt the grass of the school-yard squelching beneath my feet. A minute or so later, the grass turned to mud and I knew I'd reached Old Montgomery Road. I angled to my right and sighed with relief when I found our driveway. I passed our car (What was my father doing home so early?) and hurried up the steps to the porch, where I stopped just long enough to kick off my sneakers and strip down to my tee shirt and panties. I was still angry at my mother, but I knew she would kill me if I tracked mud in on her clean floor.

I tossed my wet, muddy clothes onto the porch swing and stepped into the house.

241

For the second time in two days, my father reached me before my mother could. He grabbed me and held me to him, and I experienced a flash of déjà vu.

"Oh, thank God you girls are alright! Everyone's been worried sick!" My father stopped and looked behind me. "Rachel, where's Della?" He looked confused. "Isn't she with you?"

"No, Daddy," I answered truthfully. "She was for awhile. We walked out to the end of Morgan's dock so she could see how much different the river looks when it rains. But then the storm blew in, so we went into the fishing shack to wait it out. We walked home just as soon as we were able. I haven't seen Della since we reached the end of Beckman Avenue. When we got to Whitfield, she turned right toward her house and I crossed over and came here. I offered to walk her all the way home, but she said she'd be fine, that it was just a few more steps." I paused and looked from my father to my mother. "Why are you asking me that?" I looked back at my father. "Della should be home by now."

My father released me and looked over at my mother. She wrapped her arms around herself. "Oh no, not again," she moaned.

"I'd better call the Rooneys." My father turned and quickly headed for the kitchen.

My mother just stood there in the middle of the living room, hugging herself and looking worried. I still didn't want to talk to her so, wet and shivering, I turned and headed down the hall to grab a hot shower and change into dry clothes.

I didn't want to catch my death.

CHAPTER 46

When Bo disappeared, the police hadn't responded. When his father had called, they'd told him Bo had to be missing for twenty-four hours before a report could be filed.

When the police were called this time, in light of what had happened to my cousin, they arrived within minutes.

The first thing they wanted to do, of course, was speak with me. I was sitting at the kitchen table sipping hot tea and eating a bowl of tomato soup with saltines broken into it when a police car, blue lights flashing, pulled into the driveway. The officer who came to take my statement pulled a small pad and a pencil out of his breast pocket and asked me to tell him what had happened. Hands in my lap, I stared into my bowl of soup and told him the same story I'd told my parents: Della had been fine the last time I'd seen her, soaked from the rain but fine, and we had gone our separate ways at the end of Beckman Avenue. She had turned right toward her house, and I had crossed Whitfield Avenue to get to mine. That was the last time I'd seen her. The officer thanked me, tipped his hat to my parents, and headed for his car. We had followed him as far as the living room and watched through the windows as he drove away.

"Well," my father said, shaking his head, "I'd better get a move on. The men who went out looking for Bo last night are meeting at the church again tonight. We're going to go out looking for Della. I pray we find her; I don't know what the Rooneys will do if something has happened to that child." He rubbed his temples and pulled on his jacket, but then just stood there, staring at the floor. "Sweet Jesus!" He seemed to be praying. "What is going on around here?" He pushed open the screen door, crossed the porch, and disappeared into the dark.

After several seconds of silence, I looked up at my mother.

"Mama?" She turned to me, shocked that I'd spoken to her, and so sweetly to boot! "Mama, I want to see Bo."

It took her a second to respond, but then she smiled widely, relieved that I had apparently forgiven her.

"Why, of course, honey," she gushed. "Of course you can go see Bo." Her smile grew larger. "Oh, and I have the most wonderful news for you: They've taken him off the respirator and he's breathing on his own! Isn't that wonderful?" I nodded, and she rushed on, "Now, he's still in a coma, so he's not out of the woods yet—and any number of things could still go wrong—but breathing on his own is a big step. If nothing bad happens, he may just pull through. Now, hurry, get your jacket on and let's go."

I did as I was told.

***

The hospital was just as cold and quiet when we arrived as it had been the night before, and I disliked it just as much, but it would be worth the discomfort if I got to spend some time with my cousin.

I had to sit in the waiting room while my mother went to tell Bo's folks I was there. It took her a little longer to return than I would've expected, so I assumed she was catching them up on the news about Della. When she returned, they came with her and both gave me big hugs, saying they were so sorry to hear about Della but were sure she'd turn up soon. I nodded silently, then stood staring at the floor. I had decided that the less I said on the subject, the better.

I heard my mother whisper over my head that I hadn't been acting right since I'd found Bo and she thought that maybe, between Bo getting hurt and Della going missing, well, I just had to be in shock or something. I stifled a smile as I continued to stare at the floor. She was acting like I was two years old and couldn't hear or understand anything she said when she whispered over the top of me like that. I shook my head. Any minute she'd probably start talking to me in baby talk and spelling out words when she didn't want me to understand what she was saying.

I let her go on for a few more seconds before I interrupted, "I want to see Bo."

"Well, now," my uncle said, "you know, he doesn't really look like himself. He's pretty bruised and swollen, and he's covered head to toe in bandages. Do you really think you want to see that? It's pretty scary."

"He can't look any scarier than he did when I found him hanging upside-down in that tree." There! Let him argue with *that*.

My uncle seemed taken aback by my words; he looked to the two women for guidance. My aunt shrugged and my mother lifted her hands in a "there ya go" gesture. My uncle ran his hand through his hair and smiled wanly. "There's certainly truth in that," he said. "Let's go talk to the doctor and see what we can do."

The doctor we spoke with was the same one who had found me in Bo's room the night before. At first, he seemed reluctant to allow me in with Bo, but the adults took him to one side and spoke quietly with him. I overheard Della's name and the words "in shock" (this from my mother), and I could tell he was starting to come around. He finally told them that he wanted to speak with me first, to gauge for himself whether I'd be able to handle seeing my cousin in the condition he was in. It may be something he could allow, he said, for just a little while.

The adults waited in the hall while the doctor led me back to the waiting room and sat me in one of the chairs. He took a seat next to me and looked into my eyes. I looked back, unblinking, and his eyes were just as kind as I remembered.

"So, I hear you've had a rough couple of days," he began.

"Not as rough as Bo." He wasn't the only one who could state the obvious.

He chuckled and shook his head. "No, not as rough as Bo," he agreed. "I understand you had another bad experience today. One of your best friends went missing during the storm? That's got to be pretty hard on you."

I shrugged. "I don't know. I guess it hasn't really sunk in yet that she's gone." Be careful, I told myself. Less is more. I looked back up into the doctor's kind eyes and sighed. "I just want to be with my cousin. We've never gone this long without seeing each other. I just know I'll feel better if I could see him and, who knows, maybe he'll know I'm there and it'll help him feel better, too." I paused, then rushed on, "I promise I won't be scared by how he looks. I already saw him last night, remember? It didn't upset me at all. He doesn't look nearly as bad as he did when he was hanging in that tree. I just really need to see him, and I know he needs me. We need each other! Please, Doctor! Oh, please let me sit with him for awhile. I promise I'll be okay. I just want my cousin. I just want my Bo!" I put as much longing and pleading into my eyes as I could.

The doctor looked back at me for several seconds, weighing my response to the situation and trying to make the right decision. Finally, he smiled and said, "I suppose it wouldn't hurt to let you sit with

Robert—I mean, Bo—for a little while. You're right; I'm sure he'll be happy to know you're there."

I let out the breath I hadn't known I was holding and laughed. "Oh, thank you, Doctor! Thank you so much!" I held out my hand but winced when he shook it. I saw his face grow serious as he looked down and saw the lacerations on my right palm and fingers. I ducked my head slightly, wincing again as he turned my hand over and examined the gouges on the back. His gaze wandered up to the pricks and scratches on my arm. He frowned as he lifted my other hand and found the same injuries there.

"Some of these are pretty deep," he said. "Has your mother seen them?"

I decided honesty, whenever possible, would be the best thing. "I don't think so," I said. "I mean, I didn't show them to her. So much has happened in the last two days, I guess a few cuts and scratches just didn't seem all that important. I think my mama knows about the cuts on my hand. I accidentally broke a glass I was holding when I was upset about Bo, but I wouldn't let her see it. She must've figured it wasn't that bad if I didn't need her help." I knew my mother would tell the same story if asked.

"As for the scratches, I hadn't even noticed them until now. I got stuck out in the storm with Della. It was really windy and there were all sorts of things blowing around and bouncing off of us. She's really tiny and the wind was blowing her all over the place. At one point, it nearly blew us apart from each other. But I grabbed her by the hands and pulled her back. I told her to hold on to me, to hold on and not let go and I'd get her home safe." I let the volume of my voice rise. "I tried to shield her from the storm as much as I could. Maybe that's when I got scratched up. I really don't remember." I stopped and swallowed hard. "I told her I'd get her home safe, but I didn't." I worked up some tears. "She's alright, don't you think? She's got to be. I promised!" I looked bleakly up at him. "May I please see Bo now? I really need to be with him."

The doctor looked back at me for a few seconds, then put his hands on his knees and stood up. "I'll tell you what," he said. "Why don't you come with me and let me tend to your cuts and scratches, and then we'll get you in to see your cousin? How does that sound?"

I wanted to hug the man! "Oh, that sounds wonderful," I gushed. "Thank you! Thank you so much!" I stood and followed the doctor down the hall to let my mother know what was happening.

A short time later, I was seated in a chair next to Bo's bed, watching him breathe and willing him to wake up. No one else was there; I had asked for some alone time with him. I was gently holding his hand in mine and was comforted by the fact that the tubes that had been down his throat the night before had been removed and the big, noisy respirator was switched off and sitting quietly in the corner of his room. The only sound now was the less offensive beeping that came from his heart monitor and the reassuring sound of Bo drawing breath without any assistance. He was still wrapped up like a mummy, and the small area of skin I could see around his one good eye was still swollen and purple, but this was my Bo and he was alive. Nothing else mattered at that moment. Nothing existed for me outside of that room, and I was sure Bo would be his old self in no time at all, so I was content to just sit there and wait for him to wake up.

The sound of footsteps entering his room interrupted my thoughts. I turned in my seat and was surprised to see a rather large, imposing man in a suit and tie standing behind me. Unsure of who he was or what he wanted, I leaped out of the chair and turned to face him.

"I'm sorry if I startled you, Rachel," he said. "My name is Mitchell Ferguson and I'm a detective with the Savannah Police Department. I talked to your mother, and she's given me permission to speak with you."

I just stood there and stared back at him. I saw him glance down at the bandages on my hands and wrists. Oh, I thought, this one is perceptive. I will definitely need to exercise some caution when I talk to him. Short and sweet, I reminded myself. Short and sweet.

I waited until his eyes returned to mine, then worked up some tears.

"Is this about Della?" I let my eyes overflow and saw his expression soften. "She's still missing, isn't she?" I sobbed softly.

Detective Ferguson walked over and put an arm around me. I pulled a tissue out of the box that was sitting on the table next to Bo's bed and wiped my eyes. I blew my nose and looked up at the detective miserably.

"Do you think you're up to answering a few questions, Rachel?" His eyes were gentle, but I reminded myself that he could probably be just as cagey as me. I would need to be very careful right now.

"Yes," I answered. "I can if it will help find Della. She needs to come home!" I let my lips quiver as more crocodile tears slid down my cheeks.

"Okay, sweetie. We'll try to do this as quickly and painlessly as we can." Detective Ferguson pulled a pad of paper and a pen from his inside suit pocket. "Now, you told the police officer you spoke with earlier that you and Della had walked out on someone's dock earlier this afternoon. Is that correct?"

"Yes, sir." Couldn't get more short and sweet than that, I thought.

"And is that something you do often, go out on someone else's dock?"

"Yes, sir," I answered. "A couple of people in the neighborhood let us use their docks whenever we want so we have a place to swim and to tie up to when one of our friends comes over in his boat. We've been doing it all summer, almost every day." I watched as Detective Ferguson wrote my answer on his notepad. Ooh! I'd have to be careful AND remember everything I said.

"And did you make it a habit of going to the river when it stormed?" He cocked an eyebrow as he looked at me.

"Oh, no, sir," I answered. "We've only gone down there when it was sunny."

He wrote that down and asked, "What made you go there this time?"

I paused and wiped my eyes again before I answered. "The river is very special to me and my friends, but Della had never experienced being on a river before this summer," I explained. "Us kids promised to show her everything. We took her tubing and swimming and skiing. We even went on a campout this past weekend. She's been having the time of her life." I paused again and took a deep breath. "Whenever I feel bad, I go to the river. It makes me feel better to sit there and look at the water. Today I was really upset about what happened to my cousin last night, so I decided to walk down there for awhile. I started across the schoolyard, but for some reason I ended up in the dugout at the kickball field. I think I wanted to be somewhere that was special to Bo.

"Della saw me out there through her living room window and came out to check on me. We talked for a few minutes; then I decided to go on to the river. It was only raining a little, and I thought it would be okay. Della decided to come with me. It occurred to me that she'd never been down there in the rain. I told her how different it looked, almost like a whole nother river. She was a little nervous, but she still wanted to come. We sat down on the end of the dock and chatted and looked at the water. It started to rain harder, and she started to get a little frightened, so we decided to come home. But the storm blew in so fast, we were afraid to walk on the dock. Della's so little that the wind really blows her around, and we were afraid the wind would blow her right off into the water! Anyway, there's a fishing shack built onto the end of the dock, so we went in there to wait out the storm. It swayed really badly in the wind, and the thunder and lightning seemed to be striking all around us, but there was nothing we could do. Della was pretty scared by then and concerned that her mama would be worried about her. We hadn't told anyone where we were going because we thought we'd be right back.

"Anyway, as soon as the storm let up enough, we headed for home. We probably should've waited longer because it was still raining pretty hard and I had to hold on to Della to keep the wind from blowing her away, but she just wanted her mama so much. It was hard going and took forever, but we finally made it to the end of Beckman Avenue. By then, I knew my mother would be worried, too, and I wanted to get home as much as Della did, but I offered to walk her home first. She told me she'd be fine, that it was just a few steps to her front yard. I still had to cross two roads and a schoolyard. . . ." I swallowed hard and took two quick, breaths. "I should've gone with her anyway! I should've made sure she got home! I don't know what I was thinking. Why didn't I walk her home? I always walked her home. Oh, this is all my fault!" I cried like my heart was breaking, so it was no surprise when I felt Detective Ferguson move up next to me and put an arm around me. "You have to find her," I sobbed into his chest. "You have to bring her home. Please! Her mama's going to be so worried!" I cried harder as the detective patted my back, then pulled fresh tissues out of the box for me. I pulled myself together and blew my nose.

Detective Ferguson stepped back and looked at me closely. I assumed he was trying to decide if I was alright or if maybe he needed to go get my mother. I sniffed and stared at the floor.

When he spoke again, his voice was soft. "I know you're upset," he said. "I just have a couple more questions I need answered. Do you think you can do that?"

I sniffed again and nodded.

"Okay, I want you to think very carefully, Rachel." He looked me right in the eye, and I could tell these were the real questions he wanted answers to. "Do you remember at any point today seeing anyone, and I mean anyone, while you and Della were out walking around?"

Oh, this could be dangerous! Careful, I thought to myself. Be ever so careful.

"No, sir, not that I recall," I answered.

"Okay," the detective went on. "And how about the past few days? Do you remember anyone hanging around or watching you, maybe even stopping to talk with you?"

A *huge* lightbulb went on over my head.

"Foxy Sikes!" I almost shouted it. "Our church's youth director and her sister took us camping on Bird Island this past weekend. On Saturday afternoon, when we were on our way to her truck to go home, this really scary man that lives near the water yelled at us. Della accidentally ran into him on the footpath and he pushed her down. She dropped her camping gear and everything. Then he started screaming at her. Bo got so mad he stepped right up to the man and was just about nose to nose with him. It looked like it was about to get ugly, but Foxy Sikes backed off and started to walk away. Then Bo hollered out something about Sikes being short for 'psycho.' You could tell Foxy heard him, and I was scared he might come back, but he just kept walking."

Detective Ferguson was scribbling madly in his notebook. He stopped and looked at me. "And where exactly did this happen?" he asked.

I let my eyes widen as I paused to get the full effect before I answered. "It happened exactly underneath the tree branch Bo was hanging from when we found him!"

Detective Ferguson's face grew grim. He stuffed the notebook and pen back into his pocket and placed a hand on my shoulder.

"Thank you, Rachel," he said. "You've been more than helpful." He turned and strode from the room.

"And I'm more than happy to see you go," I said out loud.

"Rachel." No more than a whisper, it came from behind me.

I spun around and saw a single, sea-green eye staring up at me.

"Bo! Oh, Bo, you woke up! I knew you would. I knew if they let me see you, you would just have to wake up!" I started toward the bed, but something in his eye stopped me.

"Rachel." His voice, muffled by the bandages, was raspy and weak. "What did you do?" His one eye looked accusingly up at me and I thought, Cousins: nobody knew you better.

I swallowed hard and took another hesitant step toward the bed as Bo sucked in a deep breath.

"WHAT DID YOU DO?"

I gasped and staggered backward at the same time the screen on his heart monitor flatlined and all the bells and whistles went off. Behind me, I heard the sound of many soft-soled shoes running into the room; then someone unceremoniously shoved me out of the way. It looked like every doctor and nurse in the hospital was there working on my cousin, including the tall doctor with the kind eyes who had bandaged my hands and let me visit. All I could do was watch in horror as nothing they did seemed to help.

"Bo?" I whimpered. Then realization hit and I screamed his name, long and loud:

"BO!"

CHAPTER 47

Bo had been attacked on Monday, and Della had disappeared on Tuesday. The next night, instead of our regular Wednesday night service, Brother Arms decided to hold a candlelight prayer vigil. Dry-eyed, I stood between my parents in the darkened sanctuary, the light from my candle joining the hundreds of others being held by the grief-stricken congregation and other members of the community as they prayed together and listened to music.

I hadn't spoken a word since Bo had flatlined the night before, but when I'd come out of my room dressed and ready for church Wednesday night, my parents quickly got ready and walked over with me. My mother was still convinced I was in shock, and I'd heard my father mention that maybe I needed to go to a "special" doctor, but my mother was having none of it. She insisted I would be fine if they simply left me alone to grieve. I had gone through so much in the past two days! They were still discussing it, so I just left them to it. At that point, I didn't care what they decided.

It was a beautiful service, and at the end, the Rooneys, barely able to contain their tears, stood up and thanked everyone for their continued prayers and support. The men were planning to go out every day to search for Della, and the ladies had filled the Rooneys' freezer with enough covered dishes to keep them fed for a month of Sundays. No one wanted to give up. No one was ready to admit that little Della Rooney might never come home.

After the service, Scott approached me and asked if we could talk. I hadn't seen him since the night we found Bo in the tree. I shrugged, and he led me out of the sanctuary and down the back hall, stopping in a quiet corner next to Brother Arms's office.

"Listen, Rae." I'd never seen Scott Bashlor so uncomfortable, nor had he ever before had to struggle for words. "I don't know, maybe this isn't the right time for this, considering . . . everything that's happened . . . but I don't know if I'll see you again before Saturday." He held out a small, gift-wrapped box. "Remember the dinner and dance at the Yacht Club I was taking Della to Saturday night?" I tasted bile in the back of my throat. "Well," Scott continued, "it was actually going to be a party for you." I frowned in confusion and looked up at him as he continued. "See, we knew it was your birthday, so we were going to surprise you by taking you with us. That's why your mother made you buy a ball gown." He smiled sadly. "We were all in on it. Della was so excited and couldn't wait to surprise you, and Bo was supposed to go, too. He was going to hang out with Della so I could sort of be with you." Scott paused, closed his eyes, and pinched the bridge of his nose. I, meanwhile, was reeling from shock.

"Anyway," Scott went on, "I don't know if it's appropriate, but I wanted to give you your present. You don't have to open it now; I just wanted to make sure you got it before your birthday." He placed the box in my hand, then just stood there looking uncomfortable. He seemed to be trying to make up his mind about something. Finally, he reached into his pocket and pulled out a second box, identical to the one he'd just given me. "I bought Della the same thing I bought you. I figured, well, you two being so close, it would be neat if you matched." He cleared his throat. "I want you to hang on to it for now. You can give it to her when she comes home." He placed the second box in my hand.

I just stood there staring at it, not saying a word.

Scott cleared his throat. "Well, okay then. I guess I'll see you later, Rae. Take care and feel better soon." He stood there for a second or two longer, then bent down and gently kissed me on the cheek. I couldn't move as he turned and walked away.

After a few more seconds, I reached up and touched the place on my cheek where his lips had been and thought about what he'd just said: I was going to the ball and there was going to be a surprise party for me. Bo was going to go as Della's escort for the evening, which meant Scott was going to be mine. He was going to be mine the whole time and I never knew it. The little hallway where I stood began to spin, and I put my back against the wall and slid down to the floor. I looked down at the beautiful, matching gift-wrapped boxes still clutched in my hands. Scott Bashlor was going to take *me* to the ball. Not someone else—ME!

That's when the walls closed in and something inside of me shattered into a million jagged little pieces.

"Well, who'd-a-thought?" I whispered as darkness overtook me.

PRESENT DAY

I shook my head to clear the cobwebs. I hadn't penciled in a trip down memory lane in my day planner for today, and if I had, these were certainly not the memories I would have chosen to revisit.

Behind me, the bulldozer sat idling while, beyond it, a dump truck waited with another load of fill-dirt to deposit on top of the one it had already delivered. The only thing stopping them was me, standing in their way. Let them wait, I thought. I'm not quite done remembering.

I looked down at what lay at my feet and took a long, deep breath. This was the first time I'd been here since the night of the storm, four decades ago. The depression in the ground that stretched out before me gave no indication that it had once been the most infamous landmark in the neighborhood. There certainly was nothing "Big" about it now. It wasn't even deep enough to ride a bike down into, evidenced by the lack of trails running through it. It was just a low spot in the middle of the woods, a sad reminder of a past long dead, and I knew the time had come to lay it to rest.

I sighed, then smiled as I felt my husband's strong arms slip around my waist. His breath tickled my ear when he leaned in to nuzzle my neck. I turned, wrapped my arms around him, and looked up into his laughing, glacier-blue eyes.

"Are you sure you want to build our house here, Rae?" He gently kissed my lips. "There are so many other places you might like better." He kissed me again.

"No," I answered. "This is the place. It was always special to me when we were kids, and it feels like I'm supposed to be here now. This is where I want to live and, someday, this is where I want to die. I feel like that's how it was always meant to be."

I watched as a small frown furrowed his brow and he took a step back. "That's all well and good, but I'd really rather not talk about you dying right now. This is a happy day, and I don't want to even think about something so morbid."

I laughed and he pulled me into his arms again for another long kiss. We broke apart when a voice floated down to us from atop the bulldozer:

"Hey, GODfrey! How's about you an' your ol' lady find somewhere else to make out? Some've us got work to do! Jesus Christ!"

That broke the spell, and Scott and I turned and smiled up at the muscular, green-eyed man sitting atop the dozer. He spit into the dirt and grinned back. In the dump truck behind him, a large man with graying strawberry-blond hair and a bad sunburn was frowning and tapping his watch.

Still smiling, Scott shook his head and started to walk away. I didn't move, and he turned back to check on me.

"It's alright, dear," I assured him. "I'm fine. I just need a moment alone." I gave him another smile, and he headed off toward where we were parked.

When he was gone, I stood toying with the small gold cross hanging around my neck. My husband had given it to me for my twelfth birthday, and I never took it off. After a moment, I reached into my pocket and pulled out another one just like it. I squeezed it ("Squozen!") in my fist and felt it dig into the old scars that were still there. Then I held it out and let it dangle from the chain. I watched the sunlight bounce off of it as it spun in little circles, then I let go and watched it fall into what was left of the coolest place a kid could ever play.

I turned to leave but stopped short when I realized the man atop the bulldozer was still staring down at me. He looked confused for a moment as he looked back and forth between me and the place I'd dropped the necklace. Then I saw the lightbulb go on over his head as realization set in. A thought came to me then, and not for the first time. Cousins: nobody knew you better.

I held my breath, waiting to see what he would do. Our eyes remained locked for a moment more; then he put the dozer in gear, scooped up a load of dirt, and dropped it on top of the tiny gold cross. I sighed with relief. Good ol' Bo, I thought as he continued to drop dirt into the sunken place behind me.

I sighed as I walked toward my husband, then frowned to myself as it occurred to me that the Big Hole wasn't some redneck Disneyland from my childhood, it wasn't a shelter from a storm, and it certainly wasn't a graveyard. In fact, this wasn't really the Big Hole at all; it never had been. I realized the real Big Hole was much more sinister than that. In fact, the real Big Hole still existed and, if not carefully controlled and kept hidden, it could become a place where insanity gave birth to ruthlessness and death. The real Big Hole was a place that hid horrible secrets, a dark place capable of devouring small, frightened children while wreaking havoc on everyone they love; and it was a place that craved eyes—lifeless, soulless eyes. Empty eyes. Doll's eyes. Yes, the Big Hole was real, and it was alive and well, I thought as I smiled up at Scott and stepped into his arms.

The Big Hole was the abyss deep inside where my soul should have been.

9 781944 313265